Soul Mates Forever

Layton Richards

PublishAmerica
Baltimore

First printing

ISBN: 1-4137-4596-2
PUBLISHED BY PUBLISHAMERICA, LLLP
www.publishamerica.com
Baltimore

Printed in the United States of America

Dedicated to

Mandy, David, Anthony,
and
Thelma

Special thanks to:

Barb Jollymore & Janice Gallant
Dawn, Heather, Jane, Kathy, Tommy
R. A. Murtha & Associates Barristers and Solicitors, Inc.
&
Mom

Preface

My brother Brad and I had just finished opening a small print shop and were finally getting a few small orders for the presses. We had talked about wanting our own business for years, and finally, the opportunity came. I was away at college, taking aircraft engineering, and I knew it wasn't going to be my life's ambition. My brother had started working for various printers around the city straight from high school. Shortly after that, he got married, bought a house, and was kind of stuck working at various places where he really wasn't happy but had bills to pay. His wife, Liane, had a great job working for a supermarket chain where she had been working for years. She had started with them while she was still in high school. Recently promoted, Liane was making a good wage, and Brad figured it was now or never if he was ever going to have his own print shop. The company he had been working for went bust, and the opportunity was there to purchase the printing presses and other equipment cheap. I, on the other hand, just came along for the ride. I wasn't sure what I wanted to do in life, but I knew it wasn't building and repairing aircraft. I was seven months into the course that I had only taken because I was laid off from Eastern Provincial Airways, where I had been working in the maintenance parts department. I loved the travel benefits that came with the job and felt that was my true calling: travelling.

I had moved from Calgary to Halifax about two years earlier after being laid off from Dover Elevators. Dover had a lot of work happening in Halifax at the time, so it was a win/win situation. I got to move away from home and was hoping to be able to continue doing a job that I really liked, and it didn't hurt that I was moving back east. I had always missed it since our family had moved to Calgary from New Brunswick when I was six. However, the elevator union basically kept me from pursuing my career with them. It was true that things were getting busy, but I had no seniority and was considered a real outsider coming from out west. As luck would have it, I met one of the vice presidents from Eastern Provincial Airways who had rented a cabin next to mine on Lake Fletcher. The company had just moved their maintenance operations from Newfoundland to Halifax. He offered me a temporary position with the airlines while they settled into Halifax. That lasted ten months, and then, at the company's urging, I took the course in Aircraft Engineering. Now, here I was, back in Calgary, almost exactly two years from the day I left, going into business with my brother. I had taken Graphic Arts in high school and had a knack for it, so who knows? Maybe this might be my forte. I had always been good at sales and administration and crunching numbers.

I left the shop and was on my way to get a quote and set up an account at T & B Graphics. My brother had dealt with the owner, Tina, in the past, and he was happy with the prices and service that she provided, so he told me to get a quote from her and see how things went.

When I walked into the typography shop with the work to be typeset, Julie, a young girl of about 20 who was training to be a typographer, met me.

"I'm looking for Tina. I'm David Beals from B&D Printing, and I need to get some quotes on some typesetting."

Julie told me to take a seat as Tina was on the phone but would be with me momentarily. As I sat there, I gazed around the office and began daydreaming of how quick I had gone from being in college one week to being in business with my brother the next, with a little financial help from our dad.

I was stirred from my daydream by a sweet soft voice telling me to come into her office. As I entered the office filled with the bright spring sunshine, I looked across the mahogany desk at the most beautiful woman I had ever seen. She was a fine-looking mulatto lady of Jamaican and American decent with the most beautiful bronze skin and the kindest face I had ever looked into.

"Hi, I'm David Beals, Brad's brother. He sent me here with some work to get quotes on. He used to be with Malibu Printing, but since they closed, we opened a print shop of our own a couple of weeks ago, and we need to find a typographer who is close and reasonable and quick." I reached down and pulled the files out of my briefcase to show her the work I needed to have quoted. I set it down on her desk, and she motioned for me to come around to her side of the desk so we could both look at the work from the same angle.

I moved around the desk and stood next to her, half mesmerized by her beauty, and leaned over to explain what we needed done.

I was captivated by the incredibly sexy sensual scent that was emanating from her. "Your perfume is intoxicating," I told her as I stood next to her, being more forward than I would normally be, but there was something about Tina that intrigued me and sent shivers through my whole body.

"It's Shalimar," she replied.

"It is very nice," I commented, then stood there, dumbfounded as to what the heck I should say to her next.

She quoted me a price that seemed fairly reasonable and told me if I left it with her she could have it all ready for me by the next morning.

"Great," I replied, and I turned and exited her office quickly to avoid another awkward moment.

I returned to B&D and told my brother the work was quoted within the guideline he had given me and would be ready in the morning for pickup.

"Great," he replied. "By the way, what did you think of Julie? She's pretty," he said.

"Oh, yes, I guess so," I replied. "But what can you tell me about Tina?"

He looked at me and laughed. "I didn't know you liked the exotic, little brother, but I think she's already married with a couple of kids."

That evening, as I lay in bed, I couldn't stop thinking about her and could hardly wait for morning to come so I could see her again.

The next day I eagerly left the office and went to T&B Graphics to pick up our typesetting. When I entered the shop, Tina's door was closed, but I could hear a man and a woman arguing in there. Julie quickly came to the door and passed me the work I was there to pickup.

"Thank you," I said and turned and left, disappointed that I didn't get to see my Jamaican beauty again.

Over the next few weeks, I would drop off and pickup work at the typesetters, sometimes to Julie and other times to Tina. I noticed sadness was developing in Tina. She didn't have the same sweet, carefree smile and the joy in her voice as she had when I first met her, but I just put it down to the pressures of having your own business and having deadlines to keep.

Our own business was slowly getting busier. When we first started, we spent a lot of time just sitting in the office playing cards to fill our day, now those days of getting to play cards were getting harder and harder to come by. I had quoted a rather large job, and Brad and I were both hoping to get it. It was to do a community news booklet. Finally, something a little more interesting than just our usual flyers, letterheads, envelopes, and business cards. I got the job, but in my haste, I had promised a near-impossible delivery date.

I dropped the job off to Tina to be typeset and explained to her the urgency and that we needed to get it back as quick as possible. She said she would stay late and get as much of it done for us as possible, if not all of it. The next day, I picked up what was done, and she said she would drop the rest off on her way home. I noticed she kept on her sunglasses when I was there, and although her office was quite bright, I found it a bit odd to be wearing sunglasses inside.

Back at our office, we worked our butts off all day. My mom had come in and helped us all day. Aside from my trip to the typesetters, I stayed in the shop and worked on the production of the news booklet instead of making my usual sales calls. My dad brought our supper for us on his way home and pitched in to give us a hand. We were taking a break, having a quick game of cards in the office, waiting for Tina to drop off the rest of the typesetting when I heard the front door buzzer. It was Tina.

"Hi," I said. "Come on in. I'll show you around." I took the work from her and put it on counter. I showed Tina around the shop and the equipment and some samples of the type of work we do.

She said that, on occasion, she farms out some printing and would keep us in mind to quote on it in the future. The final stop of the tour was our office where I introduced her to my mom and dad. She already knew my brother. She noticed the deck of cards on the table and asked what we were playing.

"Two hundred," I replied.

She sat down and watched while we finished the game we had in progress, asking a couple questions about the game while we played. She had an immediate in with my family, as she liked cards as much as we did, but she didn't get the opportunity to play much anymore. We started another game and dealt Tina in. We talked and played cards for almost two hours, and then, Tina realized how late it was getting and said she must be getting home. We all said goodbye, and I thanked her again for the prompt service and for delivering the last of the job to us. I felt sad after Tina had left but didn't know why, I just did. I had enjoyed her company and the conversation.

Over the next several weeks, I would drop jobs off at her office, and we would chat. She then started offering to drop the work off to our office on her way home rather than have me pick it up the next morning, as was the usual practice. My brother preferred this service, and so did I. The only catch was we always ended up playing a game or two of cards with Tina before she went home.

One morning when I was dropping off some work for Tina and we were having our usual chitchat, I asked her if I could take her to lunch as a thank you for some of the rush orders she had recently done for us.

To my delight she said, "Sure, I would love to go to lunch with you."

"Fine. I'll pick you up at 12:30, if that's okay."

"That's fine."

I could hardly wait for lunch that day. I knew she was married, but from our chats, I knew she wasn't happy, and I didn't really care. I just loved to talk with her. We had so much in common: the same dreams and desires and ambitions. Finally, it was time for lunch. The anticipation was driving me crazy. I arrived at Tina's office, and she was patiently waiting.

"Where are we going?" she asked.

I thought we would go to the Castle Restaurant, as it was close and quiet and somewhat intimate. I thought it would be a great place to take her for a quiet chat, and I'd heard the food was pretty good as well. I learned a lot about her.

Tina was indeed married, not happily, to an African man from Guyana. They had three children: a girl, Odelia, her oldest, who was eight, and two boys, Ekow, who was six, and Kofi, who was only four.

Tina had grown up in a little place called Jericho, not far from the town of Lucia in Jamaica and had been raised by her Great Aunt Eula and her Grandmother Etta Mae. Her mom had emigrated to the United States years earlier with her new husband, an African American who worked for the railroad and provided a comfortable living for Tina's mom and her four children, who had remained in Jamaica with various family members. It was a time when people did what they did to survive. They had not grown up poor. Tina's mom was a nurse, and her grandmother was the kitchen manager for one of the most posh resorts in the area. That came with a lot of benefits for the kids, including use of the swimming pool and the recreational facilities when times were slow.

Over the years, Hyacinth, Tina's mother, brought three of her children to Rochester, New York, to live. Tina was 17 and the third and last to come to Rochester. Her oldest sister, Claudette, had remained in Jamaica. Tina had so much to adjust to: the snow and cold, and her stepfather, Jesse, was a stern disciplinarian, and her mother was quick to follow. The sudden tightening of the reins was especially hard on Tina. Unlike her sisters, she was the only one who had remained in the country growing up. Her other two sisters had grown up in larger towns close to Montego Bay and were more adapted to city life and thus more worldly and less gullible. Tina was quick to make friends in Rochester and quickly advanced her education by taking a business course. She landed a fantastic job working at Eastman Kodak as a typographer. Tina had accomplished a lot in the two years that she had lived in Rochester, but she was 19 and wanted some freedom, and she felt uneasy living under Jesse and her mother's roof and all their rules.

Her opportunity came when she travelled with a girlfriend to Toronto one weekend. Her girlfriend had met a Canadian guy at a bar a few weeks previously in Rochester, and after seeing him a couple of times, he invited her to Toronto, and she had the good sense not to go alone. Her friend's boyfriend introduced Tina to his friend Frank, and although she wasn't attracted to him physically, she liked how he bought her nice things and took her for dinners. It wasn't long, and Frank was travelling to Rochester with his buddy so they could both be with their girlfriends. Within a very short time, Frank popped the question. Although Tina wasn't madly in love with him, she was desperate to get out from under her stepfather and mother's oppression and agreed to marry him. What a mistake that turned out to be.

Lunch was going great. We talked about so much, and Tina had given me a run down of her life and history of how she ended up with Frank. We were so at ease with one another, and I opened up to her as much as she did to me. She continued talking to me about her husband and family and the problems her husband and her were having. I disliked him immediately when Tina revealed to me how abusive he was to her, hitting her and yelling at her and constantly tearing her down. He had difficulty dealing with her success in business, and when she had meetings with clients, he would accuse her of screwing around on him. This all stemmed from his own philandering ways.

Tina told me how she had tried to leave him in the past, just after her second child was born. Her best friend, Sue, was at her house helping her out when Tina's husband Frank offered to give Sue a ride home. Tina thought it was odd for Frank to offer to do anything nice like this, but she thought maybe with the new baby and the fact she had produced a son for him that maybe he was trying to change his ways and be more caring and supportive. Tina went on to tell me that shortly after her son Ekow was born, she took him and her daughter Odelia to Rochester, New York, to visit with her mom and stepfather and let them see the new baby. Upon returning home from Rochester, her neighbour informed her that, while she was away, Frank and her friend Sue were together a lot and that she had stayed the night on at least one occasion. Tina told me how she confronted Sue, and she confessed that, yes, her and Frank had been having an affair. With the affair confirmed, Tina packed the kids up and returned to her mom's in Rochester. Her mom was less than supportive and encouraged Tina to take the kids and go home and give Frank another chance. She finally gave in to the pressure from her family and returned to Frank. By the time she was pregnant and had her third child two years later, she said her marriage was pretty much over. Frank continued with his women on the side, and Tina said she immersed herself into the typesetting business she had recently acquired from her former employers.

"Well," I said as I looked at my watch. "We sure talked about a lot, but it's time for us both to get back to work."

Our lunch had already consumed three and a half hours of the day, so I paid the bill and dropped Tina back at her office. She thanked me for lunch and for listening, as it had been a long time since she felt safe and comfortable enough with someone to be able to empty all that off her chest. I told her that it was no problem, as I thoroughly enjoyed lunch, and told her to feel free to talk to me anytime she needed to unload on someone. During that three and a half hour lunch, we had cemented a real connection and a deep trust and bond, nothing sexual, just two good friends who were both able to relay their troubles to each other.

Things were not going well in the Cooke household. Frank was still being both physically and verbally abusive, but Tina was excited when she told me her Aunt Eula was coming over from Jamaica to see her, and she could hardly wait. Aunt Eula was as close to Tina, if not closer than her real mother. Tina lived with and was raised by her Aunt Eula in Jamaica. Aunt Eula was very strict with Tina, but Tina realized it was for the best. She ensured that Tina received an education and didn't end up pregnant like a lot of young girls in Jamaica.

Even with the arrival of Aunt Eula, things didn't change. Frank was as rude and mean as ever. Eula told Tina that she could do better than this and encouraged her to leave Frank and take the children and get away. Tina thought about her Aunt's advice but was desperate to have her kids grow up in a family unit that included both a mother and father together. It was something she had wanted her whole life for herself.

Tina returned home after work one evening and that was the final straw. Frank erupted in a rage again and became very violent with her in front of the children and her aunt. He slapped her, kicked her, and threw her down the stairs. Tina ran to the bedroom and locked the door. Frank kicked the door open and demanded sex. Tina said no and told him to leave, but he refused and forced her onto the bed and proceeded to rape her. Tina's daughter Odelia came to the bedroom door, and unbeknownst to both of them, watched her father rape her mother, an incident that would scar her young mind for life.

The next day, when Tina returned home from work, emotionally battered, her daughter Odelia greeted her at the door and told her, "Mommy, I know what daddy did, and I fixed it so he can't do it again."

"What do you mean, Odelia?" Tina asked.

Odelia took her mother upstairs to her parent's bedroom where she saw the carpet was soaked. Odelia had sliced the waterbed to shreds with a knife. "Now Daddy can't do that to you again."

Tina hugged Odelia, fearful of what Frank would do to her, but determined more than ever to get her kids away from this situation. Over the next few days, Tina took refuge in her aunt's bedroom so Frank wouldn't hurt her. That lasted for three nights before Frank barged in and dragged her out of the room, slapping her. Odelia overheard the commotion and called the police. The police arrived but did little to help the situation. They took Frank away for the night and advised Tina that she would have to leave the house as they could legally only keep him away from the house for 24 hours. Domestic violence laws were not very helpful in the early eighties.

The next day, I went with Tina and helped her locate a four-bedroom townhouse that she rented for herself and her three children and Aunt Eula. She arranged for a mover to come in and take her belongings immediately. She thought she would be safe from Frank because she had acted quickly to find a new place to live and moved out while she thought Frank was still in police custody. He wasn't, as the police only held him overnight and ordered him to stay away from the house for 24 hours. Unbeknownst to Tina, he had followed her all day and knew where she had moved with the children and her aunt.

Frank sat outside her new home and made threat after threat. Tina called the police, who said there was nothing they could do until she got a restraining order. She immediately contacted her lawyer and had a restraining order placed on the townhouse and one on her business. That didn't stop Frank. He continued to harass her by looking in the windows and banging on the doors. By the time the police arrived, he would be gone from the area. Tina was terrified of Frank; he was driving her crazy following her, threatening her and her family in Rochester. He told her he would leave her alone if she would give Ekow, their oldest son, to him.

"No way," she told him. "Just leave me alone."

She returned home from work one day to find out that Kofi, her youngest son, had let his dad in the townhouse through the back door, and after he searched through the place, he had left with Ekow, pushing Tina's Aunt Eula aside as she tried to stop him. Tina called me and was hysterical and asked me what she could do. I told her I would go with her, and we would get him back. When we arrived at her old house, Tina and Frank argued. He insisted that Ekow wished to stay with him and that he wasn't going to be going home with her. She begged Frank to let her talk to Ekow, and when she did, Ekow told her that he wanted to stay with his father but that he would come and stay with her and his brother and sister on weekends. That absolutely crushed Tina, and we left with Tina sobbing.

Tina could hardly wait for the weekend to see Ekow, but for the remainder of the week, she went to the school at lunch hour and watched him play in the schoolyard. Finally, the weekend arrived, and Ekow joined his brother and sister at the townhouse. Tina talked with Ekow, heartbroken that he didn't want to stay with her.

He told her, "Mommy, I love you. I only want to live with Daddy so when I get bigger, I can beat him up for you."

As time went by, the children would visit their father every other weekend, and Tina tried to get on with running her business and her life, never knowing when Frank would erupt again, but for now there was calm in her life.

I had begun seeing Tina on a regular basis, and her Aunt Eula had gone to Rochester to visit with Tina's grandmother and mother and then back to Jamaica. As Tina and I started to date, Odelia didn't warm up to me very much. She seemed to be jealous of the relationship that her mother and I had and the bond I had formed with her brothers, especially Kofi.

Over the course of that first year, I had done a lot with the kids. The biggest thrill for me was teaching the boys to swim and just going to a field to fly a kite or kick around a soccer ball. It was such a different way of life for them. They never had playtime with their dad, and it just wasn't part of his custom. It was always Tina who would play games with the kids and wrap birthday and Christmas gifts for them.

The more time we spent as a family unit, the more incensed Frank became. He couldn't stand the fact that his wife had left him for, in his mind, was such a young white kid, and the fact that his children had anything to do with me only enraged him more.

The stress that Frank was putting on our blossoming relationship, at times, was too much for me, a young man of 22, to deal with. Tina sensed this and suggested maybe we needed a vacation away, just the two of us. I was on a business course and met a schoolteacher who spent his summers doing sail and learn trips out of Sooke in British Columbia. We made a deal: I provided the printing and typesetting that he needed, and we got a free, one week cruise-and-learn in exchange. Tina was thrilled about the trip. We both love the sea, but she wasn't too sure how she would like the boat. It was summer now and things were looking up. Frank was eager to have the kids stay with him while we were away on our trip, so our plans were set.

Time to Go Sailing

The week had gone pretty well, aside from Frank showing up at Tina's office trying to make demands that she was his woman, and it was time for her to come home to him. Being the proud African man that he was, he just couldn't accept the fact that his wife was in love with me, a young white man nine years Tina's junior, and there was nothing for him to do but accept it. I walked into the middle of the argument and told him to get out and leave us alone. He was noncompliant, and a scuffle ensued between Frank and me. I was trying to throw him out of the office when punches were thrown. I hit him hard above the eye, and my ring cut his eye open. He began to bleed. Although he was older and bigger than me, I had enough of his bullshit, and the adrenaline was surging through me enough to find the strength to beat him. We saw, through the office window, a police cruiser pull up. Apparently, someone at a neighbouring business had called them when they heard the commotion coming from Tina's office. Frank fled through the backdoor, and Tina and I told the police what had happened and that he was in violation of a restraining order again.

We thought no more of it. We were leaving the next day, Saturday, to drive to Sooke, where we would board the boat Sunday evening for our week of sailing in the San Juan Islands and British Columbia Inlets. Saturday morning arrived. Tina said how she kind of thought it was amusing that I had hurt Frank's African pride and how ashamed he would feel in front of his friends that the little white boy, as he called me, had stolen his woman, beaten him up, and left him scarred.

We got to Horseshoe Bay early in the afternoon to catch the ferry to Vancouver Island. Then we had a few hours drive to Sooke where we were to meet the boat on Sunday.

We arrived at the marina and pitched a tent for the night in the marina campground. After we were settled in, we took a drive into the town of Sooke and had dinner at a pub that looked like it was right out of jolly old England. It felt so good to get away from all our troubles and just enjoy each other's company. After dinner and a couple of drinks, we were tired and decided to head back to the marina and go to sleep. When we went outside, it had started to rain, and by the time we reached the marina, it was a real downpour. It just seemed to add to the romance as we huddled together in our little pup tent and made love to each other for hours, pausing in between to listen to the rain beat down on the tent. We finally collapsed in exhaustion and fell asleep, entwined in each other's arms.

We awoke the next morning to everything feeling wet. The rain had not let up all night, and it was still misting. We grabbed our towels and bathroom kits and ran over to the shower house. The rain was keeping almost everyone inside their campers or tents, so we showered together in the ladies' shower room and made love again. The danger of being caught together only added to the passion we both were feeling.

After we cleaned up and got dressed, we grabbed an umbrella and went down to the dock to see if Allan, our skipper, was there yet. His boat, *Midnight Sun*, was just docking when we walked up. As we helped him to tie up the boat, he asked where we were staying.

"We camped out," I told him.

He said we could pack up our gear and come aboard the boat, as it would be dryer than staying in the tent. We packed up our gear and headed to the boat. We got familiar with the boat, and Allan said he had to go to the marina office, as he was expecting one more passenger who was taking the cruise to get his navigation papers. When he returned, he had a guy named Conrad with him. He had arrived the night before as well but had stayed in a cabin.

We all got acquainted with each other and packed away the rest of the gear. They gave Tina and me the V-Berth, up front. Conrad took the aft cabin, as it had a single bunk, and Allan took the table bunk overhead. I was eager to go, even though we weren't slated to leave until morning. Allan checked the weather and high winds were supposed to hit by midnight, so the decision was made to stay put for the night and leave in the morning when the storm had past. We sat around, listening to golden oldies music, drinking wine, and talking about ourselves, and what we hoped to get out of the trip.

Allan, our skipper, was in his late thirties or early forties. He was average height and build, with a salt and pepper beard and thinning hair on top. This was the first year, and he was actually leasing a sailboat and doing charters all summer. In previous summers, he and his wife had chartered the *Midnight Sun*, a 40-foot ketch, for only two to three weeks at a time. Then they would return home to Calgary, wishing they could sail all summer long. He finally did something about it and discovered that by doing cruise-and-learn cruises; they could afford to lease the boat for the whole summer. It was the last week of June. His wife had to finish up some business in Calgary and was going to meet him at the end of our cruise.

Conrad was a single accountant who met Allan during an accounting course and had made an arrangement similar to mine. In exchange for teaching Allan about setting up books for a small business, he, too, was getting a free week of sailing. He had quite a bit of previous sailing experience and was more interested in getting some experience navigating so he could get his own captain's papers and be able to do his own bareboat chartering in the Caribbean. Before a person can bareboat charter, which, he explained, is to rent a boat without crew, he has to be a certified captain. This means he must be able to navigate and sail a boat unassisted. So, that was his goal on this trip. At the end of the trip, Allan would administer the test for Conrad to get his certification.

The trip should be perfect, I thought. Tina and I were more interested in learning the basics of sailing; Conrad had his own agenda to get his certification, so he was more into the navigating; and Allan was just happy to have some familiar people on board to help him on his shakeout cruise to get the boat ready for the next week when his paying passengers and wife would be arriving.

It was getting late and still raining and blowing hard, so Allan suggested that maybe we should all try to get a little sleep and get an early start in the morning. He had checked on the weather, and the storm was supposed to be out of the area sometime between 4:00 and 5:00 a.m. We all agreed and headed off to bed.

Tina and I snuggled together in our v-berth, looking up and watching the rain beat down on the windowed hatch over our heads as the wind gently rocked the boat and us to one of the best sleeps either of us had in weeks.

When I awoke, the sun was shining through the hatch onto my face. I looked at my watch: it was about twenty minutes after six. I looked over at Tina, sleeping like a little angel, and my heart skipped a beat. Every time I looked at her, I got such a warm, peaceful feeling all over. I pulled the sheet up over her head to keep the sun out of her eyes and lay there, just mesmerized how my life had changed in the last four months since I met her.

I felt like I had been to hell and back with all the trouble with her estranged husband and the turmoil he kept dishing at us. I knew one thing for sure: at times, I had thought, *What the hell am I doing in the middle of this mess?* But now, I knew I was in love with this woman lying so serenely next to me. I was so tired of going to bars and picking up strange women to have sex with that meant nothing to me. It had taken me four years to learn that there was more to life. Having sex, I realized, doesn't mean shit if I don't care about who I am having it with. And now, not only did I care about whom it was that I was with, but I also loved Tina more than I knew any one person could ever love another.

I heard movement outside our cabin door and decided it was time to get up. I got dressed and slipped into the head to use the bathroom. We had a connecting door from our cabin into the head, which was nice because we wouldn't have to disturb anyone if we needed to use the washroom in the middle of the night. Tina liked it as well; it gave her a little more privacy. I washed up and exited the head through the main door into the dining room of the boat. Allan was standing in the galley, drinking coffee and looking over some charts.

"Good morning, Captain," I said.

Allan replied, "Good morning, David. How did you sleep?"

"Great!" I said.

"Would you like a coffee?" he asked.

"Sure," I replied. "I'd love one."

He told me that Conrad was on deck, taking the covers off the sails, and he was hoping we would be underway within a half hour. He said he thought we would sail out of the harbour before the entranceway got too busy. He wanted to sail to a little island about two hours away where we could drop anchor and have breakfast.

"Sounds like a great plan to me," I replied.

I especially liked the idea of breakfast…I was famished. I went up top and greeted Conrad and asked him how I could help. There were a couple of sail covers that still needed to be removed, so I gave him a hand with those and then stored them in the sail locker topside. He then put me to work coiling up the sail lines. Allan joined us and told us the game plan. We would motor out of the marina, and once we cleared the mouth of the harbour, he wanted to hoist some sail right away and take advantage of the strong winds we were having that morning.

Allan stayed topside to check on a couple of things, and I went down below to check on Tina. I opened the cabin door as gently as I could so as not to disturb her, but she was already slightly awake. She was looking as sexy as ever. I think she looked her most beautiful first thing in the morning and just before bed, when she was a little sleepy and her eyes were so sultry.

"Good morning, hon," she said. "What's happening?"

"We are just about to cast off and head to a little island about two hours away where Allan said we would drop anchor and have breakfast. Are you getting up, babe?" I asked.

"Ah, I was having such a good sleep," Tina replied. "Just let me have about 20 more minutes, and then I'll get up. Is that okay with you?"

"Hey babe," I said. "It's our vacation. You do what you want, when you want. We have no schedules to follow and no deadlines to meet. So, you just relax and enjoy yourself." With that, I gave her a quick kiss on the cheek and told her I was going topside to help, and I would see her in a little bit.

When I went back up topside, Allan inquired about Tina. I told him that she was still sleeping, as she hadn't gotten much rest the night before when we had slept in the tent, and I wanted to let her sleep a while longer. He said that it was no problem. He was ready to cast off the lines and get underway. Before Allan started the small inboard engine to let it warm up, he showed me how to turn on the blower first, which, he said, was very important. The blower exhausts any fumes that may have built up in the hold and helps eliminate the chance of causing a fire in the hold. The little inboard engine chugged away, and the lines were cast. We were finally underway. I was so happy to be heading out of the harbour and getting this long needed and anticipated vacation underway. It took about fifteen minutes to motor out of the harbour and into the open sea. Allan had me take the wheel and turn the boat into the wind while he and Conrad winched up the sails. Then Allan gave me a tree in the distance to watch and told me to keep the bow aimed for that tree and to cut the engine.

When the sails filled with wind, I was expecting a big surge in speed, but I was wrong. We were on a heavy, ocean-crossing, steel-hulled ketch with a nine-ton keel. While it was a very safe and stable sailboat, it was not very fast.

I hadn't really thought about the actual boat all that much in preparing for the trip. I had just imagined how nice it would be to get away with my sweetheart and enjoy a little sun and sea and fun. It felt like we were barely moving towards the tree that I was supposed to steer towards, but when I looked at my watch, it had been about an hour since we had left the port. Just then, Tina popped her head up through the main hatchway and asked Conrad to give her a hand. While we were getting underway, she had prepared breakfast for us. *What a sweetheart she is,* I thought to myself. There were bagels with cream cheese and jam and some orange wedges.

"Wow, honey, thanks," I said.

Allan and Conrad chimed in with their thanks. Conrad took the tray from Tina and placed it on a small table in the cockpit of the boat, a small sitting area located behind the wheel used for steering the boat. Tina came on deck and sat on the windward side of the cockpit and held the rail with one hand. I could tell she was a little timid at being out on the open sea with the boat heeled over to one side. She was staying on the windward side, as far from the water as possible.

I scooted over beside her and gave her a hug and a reassuring kiss. "Don't worry, babe. We are pretty safe on this old steel-hulled boat" I said. "We've got a nine ton keel below us that will keep us upright, no matter how hard the wind blows."

My comments didn't seem to reassure her very much. She was still looking a little bit frightened as we sat there, side by side, eating our bagels and orange slices. After we had all finished eating, Allan asked Tina if she would like to take the wheel, but she declined. She stated that she was happy right where she was for the moment. He then asked me to take the wheel so that he and Conrad could go below and look at the charts. He thought that since we had just eaten, we could just keep going and try to make it to Friday Harbour. I told him no problem, and I would yell if I needed his help.

Allan and Conrad went below and I took the wheel, keeping it aimed at the same tree as before, off the point of a small island ahead. Tina and I chatted about how quiet and peaceful it was at sea and how relaxing it was.

"Is it hard to drive the boat?" she asked me.

"No," I replied. "Come here, and I'll show you."

She inched her way down to the centre of the cockpit and then stood up behind the wheel.

"Just grab hold of the wheel," I told her. "And I'll stand right here with you."

She took the wheel, and I stood behind her and put my arms around her. She was enjoying the feel of the boat, and I was enjoying the feel of her body in front of mine. I found that the motion of the boat was rubbing me against Tina and I was getting extremely aroused. I reached around and began caressing her breasts. She quietly told me to stop, but I continued to nuzzle the back of her neck and caress her breasts. I pushed my hard member against her butt. She moaned softly and pushed back against me. All I wanted to do was take her there and then. I was having a hard time controlling myself. When Allan and Conrad came back on deck, I stopped what I was doing immediately, but they had already realized what was happening between us.

"Honeymooners," Conrad said.

We all had a little chuckle.

"Tina, how do you like steering the boat?" Allan asked.

"It's fun," she said. "I'm not nearly as scared anymore."

With that, I said I was feeling a little tired and was going below for a nap. Tina stayed at the wheel, and I went below to our cabin. The sun had gotten hotter, and I found it quite warm down below now, so I changed into some shorts and a t-shirt. I lay down on our bunk and stared out the ceiling hatch just watching the clouds and birds float by until I drifted off to sleep.

When I woke, Tina was stroking her hand through my hair. I gazed up into her eyes.

"Oh, hi. I guess I drifted off," I said. "How long did I sleep?"

"Not long," she replied, as she continued stroking my hair. She had a sheepish grin on her face, and I could see through the tight t-shirt she had changed into that her nipples were as hard and as big as a couple of ripe cherries.

"Care to join me for a nap?" I inquired.

"Sure," she said, as she slipped underneath the covers beside me.

I gently caressed her budding nipples with my hand and rubbed her sweet spot with my other hand. Her red cotton shorts were so tight that I could feel her lips pulsating through the cloth. I continued to rub her through the shorts while she helped me remove her little white t-shirt.

"Oh, baby," I moaned in her ear. "I want you so bad."

"Me too," she whispered back. "I'm so wet. I want you to take me now, my big, white stud boy."

"Not yet, baby," I panted, as I put my lips on her nipples and began to lick them ever so gently while still rubbing her hot fire through her shorts.

I could feel her moisture penetrating through the cotton and the scent of sex filled our little cabin. The next thing, I knew I was laying on top of her, grinding my hard rod against her warm burning fire as I continued to caress her breasts with my mouth. I felt that I was ready to blow at any time.

"Take me," she begged. "Take me now!"

"Oh, yes, baby, I'll do you all right," I responded as I reached down and unzipped my shorts.

She reached down, grabbed my hot pulsing rod, and began stroking it. I reached down and moved her shorts to the side to expose her quivering lips. She then guided me into her burning fire. I thrust myself deep inside of her. We clung to one other as I pumped deeply, but briefly, into her. The anticipation of the lovemaking had been too much for me, I couldn't hold back any longer. I released myself deep inside of her. Our bodies quivered simultaneously. I thought I had disappointed her by coming so fast, but she too had been ready, and we had both came at the same time. We lay there exhausted, our sweaty bodies strewn together, as we drifted off to a blissful and peaceful sleep, both of us grinning from ear to ear.

We were awakened by the sound of footsteps overhead. I peered out of our porthole and could see that we were approaching a marina. I turned to Tina and told her that I thought we might be at Friday Harbour and that we had better get up and go topside. Tina slipped into the bathroom, and I popped open our roof hatch and hoisted myself up onto the deck. Up on deck, Allan was at the wheel, and Conrad was busy dropping the sails and lashing them to the masts and booms. I went over and gave him a hand putting the sail covers back on.

"Good nap?" he asked as he looked at me with a stupid grin on his face.

"Yes, it was," I replied. "Must be all this fresh air. It made me more tired than I thought."

Allan was motoring us in to tie up at the dock. He told us that we should all take advantage of being at the marina tonight and use the facilities while we were there. He said that it might be a couple of days before we docked at another marina and have the chance to shower again. We got the *Midnight Sun* docked and securely tied up, and then we all went down below to get clean clothes and our shaving kits. Tina was lounging on the couch, reading a book. I told her what was happening and where we were. She got up and grabbed some clean clothes and her bathroom kit bag. I grabbed mine, and we all walked down to the shower house to shower and change. I told Tina that I would wait outside for her, figuring that I would finish before her. When

Allan and Conrad were done showering, they said they would meet us back at the boat. I sat outside the shower house, just taking in the sights and waiting for Tina to finish up. When she emerged, she was wearing a little, one-piece red cotton jumpsuit. I thought it was a very sexy outfit with shorts and top joined together. I had told her that I thought red was her most flattering colour, so I guess she had packed a lot of red. We kissed and walked back to the boat.

Allan and Conrad were waiting for us to return. Allan informed us that they had been told to move the boat. Apparently, we were not allowed to remain at the dock overnight. We had to anchor the boat to one of the buoys in the harbour. Allan suggested that we move the boat, then we could bring the dingy in to shore and see the sights. He thought that maybe we could have a bite to eat in one of the local pubs. Everyone agreed that it sounded like a great idea.

By the time we moved the boat and were securely tied up to one of the docking buoys, it was getting dark. Allan lit a hurricane lamp and hung it off one of the mast guy wires. Then, we all climbed down into the dinghy and went ashore. We laughed and joked about the day's events as we walked up the cobbled street from the marina to downtown Friday Harbour. It wasn't a large town, but it was clean and quaint with a lot of history. We all strolled around together like we were all long-lost buddies. It was nice that we were all getting along so well. We did a bit of window-shopping, then came across a nice little tavern called Seahorse. Allan said he had been there before and that the food was pretty good, so we all agreed to go in and have supper.

After feasting on fish and chips and drinking a few beers, we all had a pretty good buzz going. We started playing some good old Golden Oldies on the jukebox. Before long, we were having a few more beers and all singing along to "The Duke of Earl." This song had kind of become our theme song on the boat. Then we moved on to "The Twist and Shout." Conrad asked Tina to dance, and they got up and twisted away. It was really entertaining to watch them. It didn't look to me like Conrad got out much, and I could tell that he sure didn't dance much, but that didn't matter as we were all having a great time.

Before we knew it, it was close to midnight and time to go. We all staggered back to the marina, breaking out in a choruses of "Duke, Duke, Duke, Duke of Earl" every few minutes or so. I soon understood why Allan had lit the hurricane lamp before we left the boat. It was pitch black out on the harbour. Cloud cover hid the moon, and we never would have found our way back to the boat if not for the lamp. We made it back to the boat safe and sound, and everyone was ready for sleep.

"Good night all," Tina and I said in unison and off we went to our cabin to crash. We were both exhausted; it had been a great day. Tina and I got ready for bed, chatted for a few minutes, then kissed and went to sleep.

In the morning, I looked up at the hatch overhead, and it was covered with droplets of water. *Oh, shit,* I thought, *It's raining. Just what we need.* I thought we had left the rain behind. I looked over at my sweetheart. She was still sleeping like a little angel. Every time I looked at her, I got that warm fuzzy feeling all over. I couldn't believe how lucky I was to have found the love of my life. I knew it came with complications, but I didn't care. She was worth every ounce of trouble that came with her. I got up and pulled on my clothes and bent over to kiss her on the cheek. I just couldn't help myself. One look at her, and I had to touch her or kiss her. She mumbled a good morning as I turned away to go out of our cabin.

"Good morning, babe," I said as I looked back. "How did you sleep?"

"Great," she replied, "And you?"

"Like a baby," I answered, "I think it's raining out there though, honey."

"Oh," she said, "That doesn't matter, as long as we are together everyday feels like a sunny day."

I turned back and kissed her again. Then I told her to stay in bed and have a lie in. I was going to put the coffee on.

"Would you like a coffee, babe?" I asked her.

"Sure," she said, "That would be wonderful."

I entered the galley through the dining room. Allan was still sleeping in his drop down bunk over the table, so I tried to be quiet while I made the coffee.

"That coffee smells good," he said from his bunk.

"Oh, good morning. I hope I didn't wake you," I said.

"No, that's okay," he replied. "It was time for me to get up anyway."

I told him that I thought it was raining out. I pulled the hatch back that led up on deck to let the steam escape that was building up in the galley from the coffee. I poked my head out and discovered that it wasn't raining after all. There was just a lot of moisture on the deck from the dew, I guessed. It was actually looking like it would be a nice day once the sun came out and dried everything up. I poured myself a coffee and took one to the cabin for Tina, but when I opened the door, she wasn't there. She had already gotten up and was in the bathroom, freshening up. I knocked on the door and told her that her coffee was in the galley on the counter, then I took my coffee, grabbed a rag, and went topside to give Allan some privacy when he got up. I took the rag and wiped the seats dry, then sat down to drink my coffee. After a couple of minutes had passed, Tina came up with her coffee.

"Hey, babe, look at the red sky. Isn't it gorgeous?" I looked toward her.

"Yes," she replied, "Isn't there some old nautical saying about red sky at night sailors' delight, and red sky at dawn sailors be warned?"

"Yea, I think so, but I'm not sure how it goes," I replied.

We sat across from one another, drinking our coffee in silence. We were enjoying the quiet and the fresh sea air. Some time passed before Allan appeared on deck with his coffee. He asked if we both liked salmon. Tina said yes, and I lied and said yes, too, even though I wasn't crazy about it. He said he was going to go ashore after his coffee and get some fresh salmon at the fish market. He said that we would be anchoring that night at a little inlet halfway to our next port of Rosario, and he thought we could barbeque the salmon on the fantail of the boat for dinner later that evening. Allan finished his coffee and was getting ready to go ashore when Conrad popped up on deck and offered to go with him. Tina and I told them both that we would have breakfast ready when they returned. Away they went, and we finished our coffee and went down below to start the bacon. I turned to Tina and asked her if she wanted to go for a quick tussle in the cabin while we had the boat to ourselves.

She looked at me and said, "Don't you think of anything else?"

"No," I replied, "How could I think of anything else with such a beautiful woman around?"

She laughed and said, "Okay, just a quick one. The guys will be back in no time, and we don't want them to catch us in bed again."

We ran to the cabin and removed our clothes in seconds.

Then Tina looked at me and said, "This one is for you, so just be quick and don't worry about the foreplay. We don't have time."

I looked at her and said, "Honey, for you, I will always make the time."

I pushed her back on the bed and buried my mouth deep between her thighs licking and biting at her honey pot like a man possessed. My burst of passion was interrupted by the smell of burnt coffee wafting into our cabin.

"Oh shit!" I lifted my head. "Nobody thought to turn the coffee pot off and it is boiling over! Don't move. I'll be right back."

I pulled on my underwear and went out to the galley to turn the coffee off. The mess wasn't too bad, as the stove had a ridge around it to contain any spills if cooking while under sail. I turned the burner off and put the coffee pot in the sink. As I turned to go back to the cabin, Tina was standing there in the doorway. She had gotten dressed.

"The boat has sailed. Get dressed, and let's get breakfast ready," she said with a grin. "The others will be back soon."

Damn, I thought, but she was right: the moment had passed. I went to the cabin and got dressed and came back out to help her with breakfast. The bacon was almost done, and we had the coffee mess cleaned up when we heard the guys coming back aboard.

I looked out the hatch and told Allan, "That was quick."

"We caught a break," he said. "As soon as we got ashore, there was a fisherman who had been out early, and so we bought a whole salmon from him."

"Great," I said. "Breakfast is almost ready. We just need to make the eggs."

Tina set the table and put out some croissants and cream cheese while I fried the eggs. I dished the food onto the plates and passed them to Tina, who put them on the table and told Allan and Conrad to come and get it. We all sat down and ate breakfast. It was nothing special, but it seems like on the water, everything tastes better than it does at home. After breakfast, Conrad offered to do the washing up, and Tina and I helped Allan tie the dingy back onto the fantail and got the boat ready to sail. Allan asked me to start the engine while he untied us from the anchoring buoys. I turned on the blower, waited a couple minutes, and started the engine. He gave me directions to motor out of the harbour and had Tina give him a hand untying the sails and getting them ready to winch them up. It was a cruise-and-learn trip after all.

Once we were clear of the harbour, Allan had me turn the boat into the wind, and he and Tina winched the sails up and tied them off. Then I turned the boat out of the wind and the sails flapped a few times before the wind billowed the sails out, and I shut off the engine.

With the engine off, I could hear the faint sound of "The Duke of Earl" playing below. Conrad had popped the cassette in the stereo down below. From then on, every time we came into or left a harbour, we played our song.

Tina was getting to be an old salt by this point in time. She was no longer scared to be on the windward or leeward side of the boat and was happy to take the wheel anytime it was offered. Now that everyone was feeling comfortable aboard the boat, Allan asked if anyone was interested in taking a ride in the Captain's Chair. I asked what he meant. Allan explained that it was a little canvas chair that hooks onto the main mast line. Somebody sits in it and get winched to the top of the main mast. I was willing to try anything, even though I have a fear of heights. Allan hooked the chair up and said this was a perfect time to give it a try as we were passing between two islands and the water was very calm. I got strapped in and up the mast I started.

"Hold on a minute," Tina yelled. "Are you sure you really want to do this? It looks pretty high up there."

"Yes," I replied, "It will be fun, but, quick! Pass me the camera so that I can take some aerial pictures while I'm up there."

Once at the top, I looked around. What a view! I snapped a few shots of the boat and surrounding islands. From my vantage point, I could see a car ferry coming from behind one of the islands. *Cool*, I thought, but boy, was I wrong. The ferry passed well ahead of us with no problem until we crossed the ferry's wake. Our boat rolled from side to side with me feeling as though I was going to be tossed into the ocean at any time.

Tina was screaming from below, "Oh my God! Hang on, David! Hang on!"

I finally managed to grab hold of the mast and clung to it for dear life. The boat finally settled calmly back in the water. All I wanted now was to get my feet planted firmly back on the deck. When they lowered me back down, Tina flung her arms around me.

"Don't you ever do that again, you crazy fool!" Tina screamed at me.

"No problem," I reassured her. Then, I turned to Allan and Conrad. "Ah, the price we men pay to try to impress our women."

Tina and I grabbed a couple of books and laid out on the front deck, sunning ourselves. I asked Tina to put some sun screen on me. She began rubbing it on my back, then my stomach, then my legs. *She seemed to be spending a lot of time on my legs,* I thought as her fingers slipped inside my shorts every time she was in an upward motion. *Man, is she doing this on purpose or what?* Just her touch alone turned me on, let alone her fingers slipping up inside my shorts and tapping against my hot nuts.

I turned to her and said, "If you keep that up, I'll need another nap."

She grinned at me, and then replied, "Now that you mention it, I'm kind of tired myself."

With that she got up and announced that she was going to the bathroom. I like a dog in heat never wanting to miss an opportunity, popped the hatch to our cabin and slipped down into our cabin, unnoticed by Allan and Conrad. I tapped lightly at the bathroom door.

Tina whispered, "Who is it?"

"Me," I replied.

She unlatched the door, and I squeezed in. I dropped my shorts, and my hot, swollen member sprang out. She was still sitting on the little porcelain throne, and my shaft was right in her face. She grabbed it before I could say a word and put it into her hot, wet mouth. She licked and caressed my shaft with her piercing tongue. I reached up and grabbed the bar overhead and hung on. As she sucked my hot shaft in and out of her sweet little mouth, I tried to be quiet, but couldn't help but moan with pleasure. She had to stop momentarily to tell me to be quiet.

"Sh! They are going to hear us," she said as she resumed working me over.

"I'm trying to be as quiet as I can," I said. My body was weak and trembling. I could barely remain standing. Finally, I released myself inside her mouth. I wanted to scream out for the pleasure she had just given me but knew that I had to control myself. She pulled up my shorts, and with that, I slipped out the door and back into our cabin then through the hatch and back onto the deck. Allan and Conrad were still at the back of the boat looking at some charts and talking away. They were none the wiser to what had just transpired deep in the hold of the *Midnight Sun*. I laid back down and picked up my book and went back to reading.

I was entranced into my book when I heard Tina call from the back of the boat that lunch was ready. I folded over the page I was on and hopped up and walked to the stern of the boat. There, on the table, was a plate of sandwiches, a basket of fruit, and some ice tea. Allan and Tina had made lunch together while Conrad steered the boat. I guess I had been so engrossed in my book that I hadn't realized an hour and half to two hours had passed since our little rendezvous below deck. We ate and looked at the charts. Allan pointed out the little inlet that we were heading to in order to anchor for the night. He indicated that it would take us about two to three hours to get there. We ate our sandwiches and peeled some oranges. Allan told us to save the orange peels, and he would teach us how to calculate the speed of the boat after lunch.

Allan explained that the ketch was 40 feet long and what we had to do was drop the orange peel into the water from the bow spirit, at the front of the boat, and time how long it took for the peel to reach the stern, at the back of the boat. He explained that there were 6,000 feet in a nautical mile, and by doing a series of mathematical calculations, we could calculate how many knots per hour we were going. We did it a couple of times and calculated that we were going between three and four knots per hour. *Not very fast,* I thought, but we were in no hurry to go anywhere. At first, I had a hard time getting used to the slow travel because I was so used to the city life—always being in a rush to get somewhere—but now time and speed didn't really matter. All I new now was that I didn't want our trip to ever end. I felt like I was in paradise.

We played with the sails a little and put up the spinnaker at the front of the boat so we could run with the wind as it was now blowing directly behind us. With the spinnaker deployed we were really moving along.

"Gee," I joked, "We are really zipping along now. I bet we might get a speeding ticket. We must be doing five knots now!"

It only took us two and quarter hours to reach the inlet where we were going to anchor for the night. We dropped anchor off a little stretch of sandy beach and dropped the dingy back into the water. I thought we were close enough to shore that I could swim but, I was wrong. The water was much too cold, even though it was the end of June. So, we rowed ashore and did a little exploring of the beach and the island we were on. There really wasn't much to see. Allan suggested that we collect some firewood while it was still light so that we could have a bonfire on the beach later that evening after supper. With the wood piled on the beach ready for a fire, we headed back to the boat to make supper. Everyone was feeling hungry.

Back on the boat, we opened some wine and put on some music and everyone pitched in to get supper ready. Allan had a small barbeque lashed to the fantail railing at the back of the boat, so we barbequed the salmon, roasted some potatoes, and toasted some garlic bread. It was a very pleasant meal with everyone chatting and sipping wine.

After we finished dinner we cleaned up the dishes, grabbed a couple bottles of wine, a game of Trivial Pursuit, a couple of beach blankets, and got into the dinghy and went ashore to light the bonfire. It was quite cool now that the sun was down, so we were eager to get the fire started. It took no time to get it roaring. We spread out the blankets and opened a bottle of wine. We chatted about tomorrow's agenda to sail into Rosario. It was a posh yachting destination, an upper-crust resort with a great spa and fine dining, Allan told us. We never did play Trivial Pursuit; we just sat there and talked about ourselves and what we all dreamed of doing with our lives. When the fire had burned down and we were out of wood, we decided to pack up and call it a night.

Back aboard the boat, we stowed away everything we had taken ashore. Tina said good night to us and headed off to bed to read for a while. I told her I would be there soon. Allan asked Conrad and me if we wanted a nightcap.

We both said yes, so he made three rum and cokes, and we sat at the table and had a game of cribbage and drank our drinks. After two nightcaps and a game of crib, I called it a night and went to bed. Tina was still awake reading her book. I undressed and crawled in beside her.

She reached over and squeezed me, then kissed me on the cheek and said, "Thanks, honey."

When I asked her for what, she said just for being myself. I just smiled and turned over to go to sleep.

When I awoke the next morning, Tina wasn't in bed. She had woken up before me and was already topside as was Allan and Conrad. I guess those nightcaps really put me out. Either that or the couple of bottles of wine we drank ashore. Anyway, I got up and got dressed and cleaned up. When I went topside, everyone had already eaten a light breakfast and was busy getting ready to set sail, so I grabbed a muffin and glass of juice and then lent a hand hoisting the anchor. It was another beautiful day. The sun was out, the birds were singing and the air was crisp and fresh. *This was the life*, I thought.

We weren't long sailing, it seemed, when we arrived at Rosario. We pulled in to the harbour master's office to register our arrival in U.S. waters and were assigned a berth where we could dock. This was luxury! We had water and electric hook-up and could get on and off the boat at our leisure. As nice as it was at sea, it still felt good now and then to feel solid ground under foot. The trouble is that even when ashore, we still walked as though we were at sea with the constant swaying under our feet.

Tina and I went ashore to shower and cleanup then went into the resort to look around. It was beautiful. The rich cherry and mahogany wood trims and mouldings were impressive. Allan and Conrad had bought a day pass to the spa and were swimming in the indoor pool. As we passed a payphone, Tina decided to phone the kids and see how things were going back at home. The phone rang, but there was no answer. She decided to try again later. I hadn't had much breakfast and was hungry, so we went into the café and had a bite of lunch. We chatted to each other about how nice it would be to retire and just sail through the Caribbean. *Dreamers*, I thought, *we were both dreamers.*

After lunch, we walked around the resort a bit and then walked around the marina, checking out how the other half lived. There were some pretty fancy, posh yachts in the harbour. We ran into Allan and Conrad again. They were doing the same thing—seeing how the rich and famous lived. Allan asked if we had looked at the restaurant when we were touring the resort. I told him that yes, we had, and that it looked very nice. He then suggested that we have dinner there that evening. We all agreed that it was an excellent idea, so he and Conrad set off to make reservations. Tina and I headed back to the boat to do a little sunbathing and reading. I couldn't believe how much reading I was doing on this trip. I was never really a big reader, but I couldn't seem to get enough of it on this trip. Tina was always reading and encouraging me to read. She had bought me three Louis L'Amour western novels to read. She had a hunch that since I liked western movies, I might enjoy these books. It was a good hunch; I loved them. We laid out on deck and read for a few hours.

Allan and Conrad came back and said they had made reservations for seven o'clock. I looked at my watch; it was just ten minutes past five. We decided to get ready for dinner, and by the time we walked up to the restaurant, we should have enough time to go into the lounge and have a couple drinks beforehand. I hadn't packed anything too fancy, so I put on a pair of Dockers and a golf shirt and my brown leather deck shoes. Tina put on a khaki skirt and jacket and a cream blouse and a pair of tan, flat shoes. All I could notice was her long sexy legs. Allan and Conrad were dressed similar to me, so I figured I was dressed up enough for the restaurant. I guess in yachting circles people dress for casual elegance.

By the time we got to the lounge, it was 20 minutes after six. *Perfect,* I thought, *enough time for a couple drinks and then dinner. I am starving.* Tina was as hungry as I was, so we ordered a couple of Caesars so that we would have the celery to nibble on until dinner. We sat and chatted until the hostess arrived to bring us to our table. We followed her and the bartender brought our unfinished drinks to our table on a glistening silver tray.

Our table was located in front of the windows overlooking the marina. The view was breathtaking. The reflection of the resort lights shimmered in the water. The warmth and crackle of the large stone fireplace not far away only added to the romantic ambience of this truly remarkable resort and the spectacular lady that I had the pleasure of dining with. I still couldn't believe my good fortune to have met such a wonderful person and to have become so intimate with her in such a short time. All the troubles of the past months seemed like a distant memory. This trip had rejuvenated me and only strengthened my resolve to make Tina as happy as I could. It was just dawning on me that we only had two more days of paradise and then it was back to Calgary to deal with Frank and all of his bullshit. But that didn't matter. I still had two more glorious days to spend with the true love of my life. *Who knows,* I thought, *maybe while we were away, Frank might have mellowed out a bit.*

Maybe he would let us live our lives in peace, and we could all actually get along. After all, he did offer to take the kids so we could go away.

My thoughts were broken by the sound of Tina asking me what I was going to order for dinner.

"Oh, I don't know. I haven't even looked at the menu yet," I replied. "I guess I was daydreaming, babe. Sorry, I didn't mean to hold you guys up. I know you are all starving." I picked up the menu and took a quick look at it. "What are you going to have, babe?"

Tina replied that she was having a house salad and the grilled snapper.

I looked to Allan and Conrad, "What about you guys, what are you having?"

Allan replied that he was having the filet mignon with mushrooms and baked potato, and Conrad said he was having the seafood pasta.

I took another quick look at the menu and decided on the filet, as well, with a double stuffed baked potato and stuffed mushroom caps for an appetizer.

I turned to Tina. "Would you like wine, honey?" I inquired.

"Sure," she replied. "I'll have wine if anyone else is going to have some. Should we order red or white?"

The overall consensus was white, so I ordered a bottle of Black Tower since I knew that was one of Tina's favourites. With dinner ordered, we sipped on our cocktails, and I asked Allan what our schedule would be for the next day. He said that we weren't far from Victoria, and it should be an easy day of sailing. He thought that in the morning we could go to breakfast at a café close to the marina that he and Conrad had found when they were out walking. As he talked, I reached down and caressed Tina's leg under the table. She smiled at me. I knew we were thinking the same thing— I wanted her, and she wanted me.

Our wine arrived and I smelled the cork and swished the sample around in my glass then held it up to the light to check the body of the wine, then passed the glass under my nose and allowed the aroma of the wine to waft into my nostrils. I then took a small sip and told the wine steward that it was fine. I was trying to impress Tina with my knowledge of wines, which in reality was very little. I was only doing what I had just observed the gentleman doing at the next table to ours. The steward filled Tina's glass first then everyone else's. Our salad and appetizers arrived shortly after the wine and we all began to eat like we hadn't eaten in days. It all tasted great. I could hardly wait for my steak.

When the main course arrived, it looked and smelled great. I cut a small bite of my steak and offered it to Tina. She opened her mouth, and I gently place my fork into her mouth.

"Mmm," she moaned. "That is delicious. Here, try a bite of my snapper."

I declined, telling her that I wasn't a big fish eater. As we ate, Conrad inquired if anyone was interested in going into the resort's disco after dinner. Allan piped up that he was game for a little excitement. I was thinking, *Great! Tina and I can go back to the boat and have some time to ourselves*. I was getting aroused just looking at her across the table, but Tina had other ideas. She said that she would love to go dancing after dinner.

With dinner finished and the wine polished off, our waitress returned to inquire if anyone wanted coffee or desert. I looked to Tina as I knew how much she liked a bit of something sweet and had noticed earlier that they had strawberry cheesecake on the menu, one of Tina's favourite desserts. Allan ordered coffee and piece of pie, and Conrad had tea and slice of carrot cake. I ordered two Spanish coffees and a slice of strawberry cheesecake with two forks. I knew Tina wanted desert but would decline, as she was always trying to maintain her fantastic figure. When the bill arrived, we split it four ways and left the dining room to go to the disco. At the top of the stairs, Tina stopped to gaze out through the restaurant's window at the reflection of the moonlight shimmering on the water. I put my arm around her and kissed her gently on the lips. I thanked her for being the best thing that had ever happened to me. She placed her hand on my face and drew me nearer to her, then she gave me the most sensual and passionate kiss I had ever experienced in my life.

"Are you sure you want to go dancing?" I inquired.

"No, not really," she replied with a chuckle.

We caught up to Allan and Conrad just outside the entrance of the restaurant. We let them know that we had decided to take a walk instead of going to the disco.

We parted company at that point, and Tina and I made our way outside and walked hand in hand along the waterfront towards the marina. We gazed up at the stars and walked in silence both dreaming and recalling what a fantastic trip we were having. When we reached a bench along the waters edge, close to the entrance to the marina, we sat and held each other. We kissed and snuggled, telling each other how much we loved one another and how lucky we were to have each other. I think it was at this moment that I realized this was my soul mate. I didn't want this day to ever end, let alone the most romantic trip I had ever been on in my life.

I don't know how long we snuggled on that bench before Tina told me she was getting cold and wanted to go to the boat. We walked over to the marina entrance and made our way back to our home away from home, the *Midnight Sun*. Once on board, Tina went to change into her warm snugly sweat suit and reappeared in the dining area where I was lounging on the sofa playing a game of solitaire. She asked if I wanted to play a game of cards, but I said I would prefer a game of backgammon instead.

"Shall we play for our usual stakes?" I inquired with a devilish smile on my face.

"Okay," she replied.

Our usual stakes involved playing for time: five minutes of personal service from the loser of the game and ten minutes for a gammon. I usually won, which is why I suggested backgammon. Tina was a good sport though and always paid off on her losses. I, on the other hand, was a poor loser and would reluctantly pay up. We were almost done the game, and I was losing, when Allan and Conrad returned and came below.

"You guys are back early. How was the disco?" I asked.

"It was pretty quiet," Conrad replied, "Not very many people there, but I guess we shouldn't have expected too much since it is early on, and the yachting season hasn't really started yet."

They sat at the table and watched us finish our game.

"Damn, I lost," I said sulkily to Tina. "That's five I owe you."

Allan asked if we were playing for five dollars a game, and I told him it was something like that.

Allan said he was sorry to be a party pooper, but he was tired and was ready for bed. This meant we had to move, as his bunk dropped down directly over top of the table. We were ready for bed by this point anyway, so we all said goodnight, and Tina and I headed into our cabin. We both got undressed and slipped beneath the covers of our berth. I was in my underwear, and Tina was wearing panties and an oversized cotton t-shirt.

"Well," she said as she turned to face me. "Are you going to pay up?"

"Yes," I said, hopeful that she would ask me to go ahead and do what I wanted to her. But then she instructed me that she wanted a back massage, which was not what I had in mind at all.

She rolled over onto her stomach, and I placed my hands under her t-shirt and began to rub her around her neck and at the top of her shoulders.

"This t-shirt is too tight, "I told her. I can't do a good job with it on. I really think you should take it off."

"Nice try," she replied. "The shirt stays on. You'll just have to work around it."

"I'll try," I replied. "But it would be so much easier if you took it off."

But she would not comply. I continued to massage her back, working my way down. Then I lifted her shirt a little bit to expose the small of her back and gently caressed that area with my tongue. Slowly, I worked my way up her back, carefully lifting her shirt towards her neck, my tongue finally reaching her neck. I bit her ever so gently on the neck and worked my tongue around to her left ear lobe. As soon as my tongue touched her ear lobe, she flipped over onto her back, turned to me and said thanks.

"I think my five minutes are up now," she said. "Good night."

"Oh, you nasty tease you," I replied. "What am I suppose to do now?"

"That's your problem," she indicated, pointing towards the bathroom door. "You could take it into the bathroom right over there."

"Thanks, but no thanks," I replied.

I rose up onto my elbows, leaned down, and gave her a tender kiss goodnight. Then I flipped over onto my stomach and felt my hardness pressed against the mattress. I lay there, waiting for the passion to dissipate, then drifted off to sleep beside my soul mate.

I had a great sleep. When I woke, I looked over at Tina. She was just starting to wake up as well. I reached over and brushed her hair out of her face so that I could see all of her beauty. She opened her eyes and smiled at me. *That smile of hers that could melt butter on the coldest of days,* I thought to myself.

"Good morning," she said.

"Good morning, baby," I replied. "How'd you sleep?"

"Like a log," she replied with a sigh. "What time is it?"

"I'm not sure," I said as I grabbed my watch to check the time. "It's almost six thirty."

I looked up at the hatch and noticed that it wasn't as bright out as normal. It was misty. A little rain was falling, and it seemed quite windy judging by the rocking of the boat against the bumpers that were cushioning our boat against the dock.

"Hmm..." I said. "Looks like a nice day to stay in bed."

"Yes, I wish we could," Tina laughed as she grabbed her clothes and slipped into the bathroom to get dressed and cleaned up.

I lay in bed, nuzzled deep down inside the covers. I really didn't want to get up. When Tina emerged from the bathroom, I reluctantly got out of bed and grabbed my clothes and went into the head and got dressed and cleaned up. When I was finished, I entered our cabin, and Tina was lounging on our berth, reading a book. I lay down beside her and snuggled up to her and read my book as well. She said she didn't want to leave the cabin yet, as Allan and Conrad weren't up yet, and she didn't want to wake them. We both lay on our berth, side by side, and read for about an hour before we heard any movement outside the cabin. I quietly told Tina that someone was up and that we should give them about 15 minutes then go out. In the past, we always managed to pop out of the hatch and go topside without disturbing anyone, but today the rain trapped us below.

When we left the cabin and entered the dining room, Allan's bunk was up, and he had started coffee in the galley.

"Good morning," we said.

"Good morning," he replied. "Nice weather, eh?"

We nodded as Tina took a seat at the table, and I got us some coffee. Allan joined us at the table with his coffee. He said we had to make a small change in plans. It seemed that our easy sail to Victoria was not going to be so easy after all. He explained that with the rain and the change in wind it would take us the best part of the day to get there. Because of the wind, we would not be able to sail straight and direct to Victoria, but instead we would have to tack side to side into the wind, which would make it a very slow trip. He suggested that we skip going ashore for breakfast and get underway right soon. We agreed. As we were talking, the hatch opened from above, and Conrad came down the stairs with an umbrella. He had gotten up before everyone else and had gone ashore to use the shower and get cleaned up.

"How bad is it out there?" we asked.

"Not too much rain," he replied. "But it's very windy."

Allan got out rain gear from the storage locker for all of us to put on. We had to laugh as we looked at one another. We looked like four big, yellow rubber ducks. Then we went topside and started the engine to let it warm up while we uncovered the sails, released the lines, and pushed off. Tina took the helm and motored us out of the harbour while we got the sails ready to hoist. Once we cleared the harbour, we hoisted the sails and cut the motor. Allan got out a blue windscreen and snapped it around the cockpit area. It gave us a little shelter from the wind and rain. We slowly made our way towards Victoria with Tina at the helm. She was quite comfortable driving and moving about on the boat now. We stayed quite tight into the wind, which heeled the boat over a lot. It felt like the leeward side was going to go right under the water, but it didn't.

My stomach started to growl. I was hungry. Tina said she was hungry also, so Conrad and I went below to cook breakfast while Allan remained topside with Tina. I now knew why the stove had a railing around the edge; to keep the pots and pans from sliding off when the boat was so far heeled over. We cooked some bacon and fried some eggs and made sandwiches out of them. We figured that would be a lot easier to eat, given the weather we were sailing in. Allan came below to see how we were making out. About two minutes later, the boat shifted and heeled over the other way and the water looked like it was going to come over the galley portholes. We grabbed the sandwiches, now wrapped in tinfoil, and scurried back topside. Tina was smiling; she had tacked the boat all by herself and was very proud of her accomplishment.

"We'll make a sailor out of you yet!" Allan exclaimed.

We ate our sandwiches, and then Allan and Conrad went below to look at the charts to see how we were progressing. They reappeared a few minutes later and said we weren't making great progress and that we were going to motor, as well as sail, until we cleared the point off in the distance. Then, they explained, we would be in a position to run with the wind and make better time. The rain stopped and eventually the sun came out, but the wind remained strong and steady. Once we rounded the point, we cut the engine and were back under sail only. *Great,* I thought, *I hate motoring. It was too noisy and spoiled the tranquillity we had been enjoying most days of sailing.*

We took turns at the helm and remained quite busy tending to the sails. For lunch, we just snacked on cheese and crackers and fruit. It was about three thirty when Victoria came into sight. Allan said we should be dockside in about half an hour—not bad timing considering the weather we had. As we got nearer, Allan went to start the engine so we could drop the sails and motor in, but the engine wouldn't start. We looked to Allan.

"Now what?" we asked.

"No problem," he said. "We will just have to come in and dock under the power of sail. It's not a big deal, just a little trickier, that's all."

He took over the helm, while we dropped most of the sails and secured them. We left the main sail up, and then we grabbed the fending poles that were lashed to the forward deck. They were long wooden poles about ten feet in length and quite springy. We put them over the side rail to slow our approach to the dock. Conrad was at the bow of the boat and was the first to use his pole. I was about mid-ship with mine, and Tina was towards the stern closer to Allan, so that he could instruct her what to do. I watched Conrad to see exactly what to do.

"Place the pole against the dock and hold on with all your might," he instructed.

The pole bent to absorb the impact and slow our ascent into the dock. Then, I heard a cracking noise. *What the hell was that?* I wondered, but was too busy to look around to see. Then we hit the dock with a thud. The bumpers hanging over the side helped to cushion us in addition to the fending poles. I put my pole on the deck and hopped onto the dock and ran to the stern to take the line that Allan threw to tie off with. Conrad was tying off the bow. Allan and Tina stepped onto the dock, and Allan walked from the stern of the boat to the bow checking the side of the hull for damages. As we got to the bow of the boat, Conrad was holding his fending pole, a piece in each hand; it had snapped in half. Allan commended us for a job well done and was happy the only damage suffered was one fending pole.

Allan went to the marina office to see if we could stay docked where we were. He also had to call the charter company to inquire about getting the engine repaired. Conrad, Tina, and I tidied up the boat and stowed everything away then changed into some cooler clothes and went topside to tan. Allan returned from the marina office. They told him to go ahead and have the engine repaired locally. He said he had gotten hold of a mechanic but that he wouldn't be able to look at the engine until later the next afternoon. He explained that we had two options. Option number one was to spend the night in Victoria, then sail to our next stop, which had no amenities, and then back to Sooke, as previously planned. The only problem with this option was that we wouldn't have an engine and would have to conserve the batteries for emergency lighting only. Option number two was to spend two days in Victoria and then sail directly into Sooke. After some discussion, we decided to spend two days in Victoria, do some sight seeing, and then sail into Sooke on Saturday.

Tina and I spent those two days in Victoria mostly by ourselves. We went to the aquarium, visited some museums, and did a lot of walking around taking in the different sights. On Friday, I arranged for a horse-drawn carriage to take us for a tour of the historic properties and through the Victoria Public Gardens. Tina was so impressed by this thoughtful, romantic gesture that she rewarded me when we returned to the *Midnight Sun* that evening with a complete body massage.

Everyone was up fairly early Saturday morning and had breakfast, and with our engine repaired, we readied the boat to set sail for Sooke. I was feeling saddened by the thought that our little escape to paradise was almost over, but Tina said that, although she had a great time, she was missing her kids and was anxious to see them. We had a full day's sail to Sooke and didn't arrive at the marina until late Saturday evening. It was decided that we would spend the night on the boat and drive back to Calgary early the next morning. The four of us drove to the little English pub where Tina and I had gone when we first got to Sooke.

We ate and then returned to the marina to go to bed for the night. Allan and Conrad went directly to the boat when we got back, but Tina wanted to stop at the pay phone and try to call the kids again. There was still no answer, and this time a message indicated that the phone had been disconnected. She told me she hoped everything was all right. I reassured her that I was sure things were fine. Tina said that she assumed the phone was probably disconnected because Frank hadn't been too diligent in keeping the bills paid after she had left him. She said that she had a couple of calls at her office over the last couple of months from utility companies and the bank. They had told her that the bills hadn't been paid and the mortgage on the house was in arrears. She had explained to the creditors that her and Frank had been separated for over a year and that the bills had nothing to do with her. She had instructed them to contact Frank about them, still angry at how he had screwed her out of her house.

We returned to the boat after a short stroll around the marina. Tina told me what a wonderful time she had and that it would be tough to go home and have to go back to work. I told her that I agreed that it would be strange not waking up beside her every morning.

When we went below, Allan and Conrad were having a game of crib. We spoke with them briefly, and then turned in for the night, telling them that we wanted to get an early start in the morning.

It was about five in the morning when I woke up. I nudged Tina awake, and we got dressed and packed up. I threw our bags up on deck, through the hatch of our cabin, carried them to the car, and placed them in the trunk. I had to deal with a wet, foul smelling tent and sleeping bags that we had hastily thrown in the car a week ago. When I returned to the boat, Tina was having a glass of juice on deck with Conrad and Allan was down below getting dressed. I said goodbye to Conrad and told him how much we had enjoyed meeting him and what a great time we had. Allan popped up on deck and passed me my "Golden Oldies" cassette. I told him to keep it for the rest of his charters. With that, we all said our good-byes and vowed to keep in touch. Tina and I walked over to the car for our long drive home to Calgary.

Our Homecoming

As we crested the hill on the Trans Canada Highway, we could see how the lights of the city of Calgary illuminated the sky.

We were only about 30 minutes from home. Our journey home had been a pleasant one. We had talked and talked the whole way about how we wouldn't let Frank disrupt our lives the way he had in the past months. We both felt renewed and rejuvenated from our holiday on the sea. We were more committed to each other than we knew could be possible. We both felt that it was going to be hard to be apart. I had stayed overnight at Tina's townhouse a couple of night's per week over the last year, but to be totally devoted to one another for a whole week had just proved to us that we were meant to be. As we entered the city, sadness came over me. I knew it wouldn't be long, and I would drop Tina off at her home and then drive to my parent's home where I had been living since returning home from college. I helped Tina take her bags into her home, and we embraced and kissed. I told her have a goodnight and that I would see her the next day at her workplace, and I turned and left to go home.

I arrived home and talked to my family about my trip and inquired about how the business was doing. It was about eleven o'clock. I was tired and headed off to bed. It had been about three hours since I had dropped Tina off when the phone rang. When I lifted the receiver, it was Tina sobbing on the other end of the phone.

"Baby, calm down. Tell me what's wrong," I said.

She told me that when she had gone by Frank's house in Riverbend to check on the kids, the house was deserted.

"What do you mean?" I asked. "The house is empty?"

"Frank's gone," she said. "He packed up the furniture and the kids and moved while we were away sailing."

"Moved where?" I asked.

"Toronto," she sobbed. "He left me a note saying that he and the kids had moved to Toronto and that, if I ever wanted to see them again, I would have to dump you and follow them there."

"What are you going to do?" I asked her, my mind reeling from the news. "Are you planning on going to Toronto?"

She replied, "No, I don't want to be with him. I love you, David, but I need my kids."

"Call the police!" I yelled into the phone. "You have custody. He's kidnapped them! He can't get away with that!"

Her reply was that it wasn't that simple. I asked her to please explain, as I didn't understand. I wanted to go over and see her, but she said she wanted time to herself to think besides I had work in the morning and she said I needed to get a good night's sleep.

"I'll see you tomorrow and we can discuss things then—just let me sleep on it?" she asked.

I couldn't get any sleep after the call, so I jumped out of bed, got dressed and drove over to Tina's townhouse. I rang the doorbell and when she opened it, I could see that her eyes were swollen and puffy from crying. She threw her arms around me and hugged me ever so tightly.

"I'm so glad you're here," she said. "I just don't know what to do first."

"Ok, let's be calm about this. First of all, did you call the police?" I asked.

"No," she replied. "I didn't call them, because in the note, Frank says that if I don't go back to him then I had better not try to take the kids. He threatens that he will send the kids to Africa and that I will never have any hope of seeing them again. He also reminded me that he knows where my family lives in Rochester and says that he would hate to see them get hurt."

"You don't really think he'd hurt your family or send the kids away?" I asked her.

"Yes," she replied. "He's crazy! You don't know the hell he put me through when I left him one time before and started divorce proceedings after Ekow was born."

"Well, what do you want to do?" I asked, putting my arms around her.

"I don't know," she replied, the tears starting to fall again. "I just don't know."

"Come on now. You don't even know for sure if he really did move to Toronto," I reassured her, although in my own mind I really didn't know what he was capable of doing. "He could be bluffing just to get you going."

"You could be right," she replied hopefully. "Maybe they're still here in Calgary. I should make some calls."

Although it was quite late now she called Dacosta, a friend of Frank's, with whom she had remained on good terms after their separation. He told her that yes, they had moved. Apparently, Frank had planned the whole thing before she had even left to go on her trip. Dacosta told her that Frank had been embarrassed about the teasing he was getting from his friends. They had been talking about how this young white boy had come along, stolen his woman, and beat him up. Frank felt that if he moved away with the kids, Tina would have no choice but to leave her new man and follow him to Toronto where they could make a fresh start. Tina asked Dacosta if he knew how to reach Frank in Toronto, but he replied no. He told her to try Frank's brother, Charles, in New York City.

After Tina had filled me in on what had been said, I told her there wasn't much she could do right now. I reassured her that the kids were safe for now with their father and, that despite everything he had done, he wouldn't hurt them. I told her that it was late, and she should go to bed, and things would look better in the morning. She turned to me and asked if I would stay. I told her that I wasn't going anywhere. She thanked me for coming over even though she had told me to stay away.

I laid awake for hours next to Tina, worrying that maybe she would leave and go to Toronto and our relationship would be finished. I couldn't help but feel ashamed that all I was thinking about was how this would affect me and what would I do if Tina left. I hated Frank now more than ever. *Why couldn't he just accept the fact that he messed up his marriage to Tina and move on without trying to destroy her life,* I thought. I thought about what had transpired over the last year, and I couldn't believe how much had happened. I remembered teaching the kids to swim and how hard little Kofi, the youngest boy, had tried to make me proud of him. Of the three kids, he was the one I was closest to. He had just accepted me right away, without much thought. Ekow, however, was very independent. He hadn't wanted my help very much. He had just wanted to show me what a big boy he was and how he could do things on his own. I remembered how he had wanted to assemble his bed by himself when they had first moved into the townhouse. Here was a little six-year-old, showing so much resolve and independence that it was hard for me to realise he was only six; he seemed so mature and grown up. Then there was Odelia. We never really hit it off. She had made me feel like she resented my presence from the first day that I met her. She seemed to feel that if it hadn't been for me, her mom and dad would be together still. I did keep my distance from her after she made up a story that I asked her to shower with me. I had drawn a bath for the boys and, after I bathed them and got them out, I told her to go take a bath. I guess she was jealous that I didn't offer to bathe her, but I didn't feel it was appropriate, as she was a girl, and she was older than the boys. Anyway, by the time the story was told to her father, it had been twisted around to make me sound like a paedophile or child molester. Frank had complained to Tina, but she had stopped him dead in his tracks. She had told him that he could think what he wanted, but that she had been at home when this event took place, and she knew exactly what had happened.

I had good memories and bad memories of the time I spent with the kids, but now I was being selfish, thinking that, without the kids around, things would be a lot easier for me and Tina. The more I thought about it, the more I realized that I had to think about how Tina would be affected if she didn't get her kids back, not my own feelings. *Still, it was a lot of stress for a 22-year-old to deal with,* I thought. What was I getting myself into?

The alarm went off at 7:00 a.m. I awoke, tired. I don't know how long I laid there, thinking about things before I finally fell asleep. I turned to Tina and told her that I was sorry, but that I had to get up and go to work. I was already getting grief from my brother and family about my lack of attention to the business since I had met Tina. There had been a lot of long lunches and late arrivals in the mornings. In all fairness, I really hadn't been pulling my weight, but Tina was the most important thing in the world to me, and that was all I could manage to handle at the time. Tina had been getting grief from her work, as well. Her employee, Julie, felt that the bulk of the work was now being dumped on her, and she was the one having to deal with customer complaints of missed deadlines and errors in the work.

When I arrived at the shop, my brother, Brad, was already there.

"So, he asked. "How was your vacation?"

"Oh, the vacation was great," I replied. "It was the coming home that was the trouble."

I told him the whole story of what had transpired once we got back to Calgary. He inquired as to how Tina was doing and what she was planning to do about the situation. I told him that I didn't know; things were in such a mess at the moment. I went on to say that every time things started to go our way, something bad seemed to happen to screw things up. I went into my office to call Tina. Julie answered the phone and said that Tina had called and said that she wouldn't be in the office until after lunch. I told her that I would call later and hung up the phone.

"Here," Brad said as he came into my office and laid a stack of paperwork on my desk. "You better get busy. These are the quotes that I need you to do up and then ring the customers back."

"Okay," I said. "I'll get right on it."

Brad left the office, and I heard the printing press start up. I leafed through the paperwork he gave and got out my paper price guide and started to do up the quotes. I had a hard time concentrating but muddled through my work. After I finished the quotes and contacted the customers, Brad asked me to go and deliver a couple of jobs that were completed and asked if I would pick up lunch at the same time. I was glad to get out of the office, so I jumped at the chance. When I arrived back with our lunch, Brad informed me that Tina had called and that I could call her at her office. I took my lunch into the office and called Tina back right away.

"Hi, how are you doing?" I inquired.

"Oh," she replied. "I'm coping, I guess. I have some things to take care of this afternoon, so I'll talk to you later this evening."

After that brief conversation, I felt a little uneasy. *What things did she have to take care of?* I wondered. I helped out in the shop for the afternoon, as I didn't feel much like making sales calls the rest of the day. Just before the day was over, we had a customer walk in who needed five hundred flyers printed up for a mail drop he was doing in a couple of days. I told him that it was no problem, and then I let Brad know that I would take the information over to Tina to get it typeset and that I would see him in the morning. I was glad to have a viable excuse to go see her.

When I arrived at Tina's shop, I could see her sitting in her office at her desk. I tried the front door; it was locked, so I knocked. Tina came and opened the door for me. I gave her a hug and kiss and told her I had a little job for her. She thanked me. I indicated that I thought she had been a little vague earlier, and I wanted her to explain what was going on. She told me that she had called her mom earlier that day and that she had heard from Frank. He had called to tell her that he had moved to Toronto with the kids. He had told her that Tina had run off with her "fancy man" and that she didn't give a damn about what happened to her kids. Tina said that she had tried to set her mother straight, but her mom didn't really want to hear about it. She wasn't happy about Tina leaving Frank to begin with. She thought that, for the sake of the kids, she should've tried to make a go of it.

Hearing this made me so angry with her mother. *Maybe if she had been more supportive of her daughter in the past, she wouldn't have gone back to him so many times,* I thought to myself. I told Tina that I couldn't believe that her mother would stick up for Frank, especially after Aunt Eula had told her what had taken place when she was visiting. Tina said her mom was more interested in getting paid back the thousand dollars she had borrowed from her when they bought the house and had some unexpected expenses.

"Speaking of the house," I inquired. "Can you sell it now that he's gone or move back in at least?"

"No," she said. "I found out from the bank that Frank stopped making the mortgage payments over ten months ago, and when he left, he turned the keys over to the bank since they were on the verge of foreclosing on it."

"Great," I replied, my temper was rising. "All your hard work to buy that house, and he ruins your credit and screws you out of all the money you put into it to begin with!"

"It's my own fault," she said. "I should have dealt with the house and property when I left, but I just wanted to avoid any unnecessary confrontations with Frank at that time. The less we had to talk about and deal with, the better."

I told her I understood and not to worry. "Some day, I'll build you your dream house."

I asked her if she found out anything about the kids. She said that she had called his brother, Charles, and that he said he hadn't heard from Frank, but that if he did he would call her.

"Now what?" I asked.

"I don't know. I can't think beyond the here and now at the moment," she replied. "I'm meeting with my lawyer tomorrow afternoon. Hopefully, she will have some answers for me."

I asked her if she wanted to go home, but she stated that she had too much work to catch up on. I offered to stay and keep her company, which she gladly accepted and sat back down at her desk. I made my way around behind her and massaged her shoulders while she worked away. After a little while, I told Tina that I had something that I had to do and that I would be back shortly.

I returned about an hour later with a big bottle of Black Tower wine and two small lasagnes with garlic bread.

"Oh, I'm so glad your back," she said as I entered her office. "And you brought food! Great, I'm starving!"

As I uncorked the wine, Tina closed the blinds to her office. Almost everyone else in the building had left for the day, but she didn't want anyone driving by to be able to see in. We ate the lasagne and drank most of the wine, then I excused myself and went into the other room to turn on Julie's radio. Tina entered through her side office door. We were both feeling a little tipsy from the wine. When Whitney Houston's song "Hold Me" came on, I grabbed her, and we began to slow dance. I immediately began nuzzling at her neck and was soon aroused. She reached down and felt my hardness through my dress pants and asked me if I ever had enough. I replied that I could never have enough of her. The song ended, but we continued to slow dance. I moved down her body, caressing her legs as we danced, then slid back up and ran my hands over her back to the button on her black skirt. I undid it, then lowered myself to my knees and removed her skirt and tossed it aside. I pressed my mouth against her hot white cotton panties, gently biting and licking at her warm mound. I wanted her so badly now. She reached down and drew me up to my feet, and we resumed our slow grind while she undid my shirt buttons. She then reached down and unbuckled my belt and opened my pants. They dropped to my knees, and my soldier sprang to attention, forcing my cotton shorts to stretch outwards. I awkwardly managed to kick off my shoes, then kicked my trousers off into the corner. I started to remove my shirt, but Tina told me to leave it on; she said I looked sexy standing there in my underwear and unbuttoned dress shirt. She knelt down before me and put her mouth on my underwear and blew her hot breath through my shorts. The sensation was driving me wild with anticipation. She was tormenting me with her hot breath. I began to unbutton her blouse but could only reach the top two buttons, so I pulled her to her feet and continued until I could pull it back to reveal the sexy white satin bra with a little pink rose embroidered at the centre where the two cups met. I slowly moved my hand up the curvature of her spine until my fingers reached the tiny bra clasp that was containing those beautiful breasts and with a quick flip of the fingers they were released from their satin home. Next, I slipped the straps of the bra off her shoulders and tossed it off to the side.

Using my hot tongue, I caressed her neck and shoulders, working my way slowly to her warm, full breasts. When my tongue reached her nipples, they were hard and erect, eagerly anticipating the caress of my warm mouth. I worked over one nipple with my mouth until Tina playfully exclaimed that the other was getting jealous. Then I moved from one to the other caressing each equally until Tina could stand it no more and begged me to take her.

I was ready, too. We sank to the floor, as I reached down and ripped her panties off her sweet little bottom. Tina lay back on the office rug, her blouse hanging open, leaving her breasts and stomach exposed. I left my shorts on and laid on top of her using my arms to support my body, arching my back as I rubbed my burning member against her hot wet quivering lips. The head of my member was now sticking out above the elastic waistband of my underwear, begging to be released. Tina begged me to enter her. I reached down, slid my shorts down to my knees and continued rubbing against her wetness. Then, without warning, I slid into her all the way. She let out a scream.

"Did I hurt you?" I asked, starting to withdraw.

"Oh God, no," she replied in a trembling voice, pulling me closer and begging me to continue.

Without any more hesitation, I moved deeper and deeper into her warm tunnel. I grabbed her legs and lifted them up. Tina quickly wrapped them around me like a vice and used them to pull me even deeper inside of her. Finally, after what seemed like an eternity, I felt her body start to shiver as she was wracked by an orgasm. I released myself deep inside of her. My salty sweat burned my eyes as it dripped from my brow. I was too weak to hold my weight any longer and collapsed on top of Tina. She wrapped her arms around me and held me tight to her still shaking body. After several minutes of clutching one another, Tina released her grip, and I rolled over onto my back, totally exhausted. We lay there in silence. I could hear nothing but the sound of both of our hearts beating loudly and rapidly in our chests.

We got dressed and returned to Tina's office, she seemed distracted.

"Hey, baby, what is it?" I asked.

"Well," she said. "I was wondering...Why don't you grab some clothes from your parents' house and bring them over to the townhouse. I was hoping you would stay with me 'til I get things sorted out with the kids. I really don't want to be alone."

"No problem," I said. "Let's just go to your place now. I will pick up some stuff tomorrow. I'll follow you in my car."

I pulled up outside Tina's townhouse within minutes of her and went inside. The place seemed so empty without the kids. It was a big townhouse: four bedrooms on four levels, plus the basement. We walked up the stairs to Tina's bedroom, which was on the top floor by itself. She paused on the third floor where the kids' rooms were and peered in through the open door to Kofi's room.

"I wonder how little Kofi is doing," she said.

He was her baby; such a cute little kid, real bubbly and full of personality. I found myself starting to well up with tears. I turned away from Tina and wiped my eyes. I had to be strong for Tina.

"I'm sure the kids are fine, honey," I reassured her. "They are with their dad, and I'm sure they will be okay."

We continued up the stairs, but when we went into Tina's room, she took off her blazer, dropped it onto a chair in the corner, then she lay on the bed and began to cry. I didn't know what to do or say. My heart was weeping for her. I tried to console her, but she was too upset.

"Just wait and see what your lawyer tells you tomorrow," I said. "I'm sure that she will have some good news for you."

"I'm so scared," she responded. "I don't know what to do. What if I never see my kids again? I don't think I could bear it."

"Don't worry," I told her. "That will never happen. We won't let that happen."

"David, you have no idea what Frank is capable of," she said. "He just wants to hurt me and will stop at nothing to do it. What if he sends the kids to Africa? I'll never find them then."

I told her that he would need some kind of paperwork to take them out of the country, so she shouldn't worry about that. We lay on the bed, side by side, talking about the kids. Tina recalled things she had done with them in the past and told me story after story until we both drifted off to sleep.

The alarm went off at 7:00 a.m., and we both woke up. I turned to Tina, kissed her and told her I had to go to my parents' house and get dressed for work. I said that I would pack some clothes and my shaving kit so I wouldn't have to leave so early every morning. I wished her the best of luck with the lawyer and promised to call her later.

I had a busy day at work, lots of deliveries and a couple of quotes to do. I went by Tina's office around one o'clock to pick up the job I had dropped off the night before. Julie had it ready, but Tina was nowhere in sight. When I inquired as to her whereabouts, Julie informed me that she was meeting with her lawyer. Julie then filled me in on what was happening at the office. She told me that Tina was getting behind in her bills and that I should try to get her to focus on her business. Julie said that since Tina and I had met, and she had separated from Frank, she hadn't been staying on top of things. The work wasn't getting done on time, and the customers were starting to go elsewhere. Julie attributed this to the fact that since Tina had separated from Frank, she wasn't able to work as late as she had before. She had to be home to look after the kids in the evenings. She said that Tina would bring them to the office some nights when she had a lot of work to do, but they would get bored after a couple hours and want to go home, so she would have to leave.

I told Julie that I would talk to her about it, but for her to cut her some slack because she was going through a tough time. Julie said she understood but that she was only an employee and couldn't handle dealing with everything plus try to get her work done. I told her not to worry, and I would talk to her.

Tina called me at my office a little before four o'clock.

"How did things go at the lawyers?" I asked.

"Good and bad," she replied. "I'll tell you all about it tonight. Are you staying over with me tonight?"

"Yes," I replied. "Unless you don't want me to."

"Why would you say that?" she asked.

"I don't know," I responded. "I just thought that maybe you asked me to stay with you in haste and maybe had changed your mind."

"David, honey," she said. "You're the only thing keeping me sane right now. You know I'd be lost without you. I need you and love you."

"I love you, too, babe. I just didn't want to crowd you," I explained. "I know that you have a lot on your plate right now, and I don't want to add to that."

Tina then told me to stop by her office when I was finished for the day. I agreed and hung up the phone. I leaned back in my chair with my hands clasped behind my head. I was overwhelmed with how complicated things had become. The past year of dealing with Frank had been bad, but I had convinced myself that the sex made it all worthwhile. I realized how deeply in love I was, and there was no turning back. I wished Tina didn't have so many complications in her life, but I knew that when a person truly loved someone, he had to take the good with the bad. I just had to hope that there would be more good than bad. I liked Tina's kids, especially the boys. I couldn't help but think that with Frank and the kid's, gone life would be less stressful on Tina and me. I felt ashamed of myself for being so selfish. I was so confused, and I didn't know what to do.

Brad came into my office and said he was going home. I heard the front door buzzer ring when he left. I got up and went to the front door and locked it then checked the back door. It was already locked. I went back to the office and grabbed the newspaper. I thought that maybe if I read the paper, it would take my mind off things. I was tired of thinking about everything. I went over to the fridge and grabbed a can of Coke. Then, I took out the bottle of rum and made myself a drink. I sat back down at my desk and started to read the paper. I finished the first drink and made another, then another. I was starting to feel better and continued to read the paper. When I finished the paper, it was almost six thirty. I picked up the phone and called Tina.

"Hi," I said. "I'm just on my way. Do you need anything?"

"Well," she responded. "I have a lot of work to do, but I am hungry. Would you mind stopping to get me a hamburger and fries on the way?"

I told her that it was no problem, and I would be there in about twenty minutes. When I walked into Tina's office, she was busy working at the typesetter. I could see that she had a lot of work in front of her. She said "thank you" as I passed her the bag with her fries and burger. She got up from the typesetter and went into her office. When she returned she had her purse. She opened it up and took out a key.

"Here," she said. "I had this made for you today . I think it will make life a lot easier. Did you pick up your stuff from your parents' house yet?"

"Yes," I replied. "I got enough clothes to last me the rest of the week."

"Good," she said. "Why don't you go home and make yourself comfortable? I have a lot of work to do, and you know that if you stay, I'll never get it done."

"Yeah, yeah." I laughed. "I know. See you later."

We kissed, and I left.

When I got to the townhouse, I took my stuff in and put it away in the closet, then went down to the kitchen to make myself something to eat. There wasn't much there. I realized that with so much happening these days, Tina had probably never even thought about getting groceries. I grabbed my coat and went to the supermarket and picked up a few things. As I went down the aisles, I was thinking about how good it felt to be gaining some independence. Living at my parents' house for the past year since coming back from college was okay, but I had missed living on my own.

With the groceries put away, I went upstairs and took off my suit and put on some comfy clothes, then went down to the kitchen to make myself a sandwich to eat. I looked at the clock; it was almost nine o'clock. I took my sandwich up to the living room and turned on the television. After a little channel surfing, I found that there wasn't much on except reruns, so I ate my sandwich and watched some Much Music videos. I was surprised that Tina still wasn't home yet. I went down to the kitchen to put my plate and glass in the dishwasher, then decided to go up to bed and read while I waited for her to get home.

I had been reading for a couple hours, when I heard Tina come in.

"Hi," I said. "Kind of late, isn't it?"

"Yes, I know," she said. "I'm still trying to get caught up on things."

"Hey," I said as I remembered something. "You didn't tell me how things went at the lawyers."

"Oh. So, so," she offered. "She's looking into things, and I'll know more next week."

"What about the kids?" I inquired. "You mean, she expects you to wait until next week to find out about your own children? Did the lawyer say you should go to the police and have him charged with kidnapping?"

"Apparently, I have to wait and see what his next move will be," she replied calmly. "It's really complicated, and I just don't want to talk about it right now. Is that okay?"

"Sure," I replied curtly, rolling over and closing my eyes. "Whatever. Good night."

"Are you upset with me or something?" Tina asked.

"No," I responded. "I'm just tired, and I can't think about this every second of the day. I just wish things didn't have to be so complicated."

"Do you think I'm happy that Frank ran off with my kids and don't know where the hell they are or if they're even okay?" she yelled.

"Listen, I'm sorry," I apologized. "Please don't yell at me. We are both just stressed out by the whole situation. Why don't you come to bed, and we will worry about things tomorrow. Remember what we said on the way home from sailing? We said that no matter what Frank did, we wouldn't let him control our lives and come between us. Don't let him win, baby. You have a right to have some happiness in life, too, you know. Who says that when a couple separates, the mother should have the children? Let him see how it feels to look after them twenty-four seven. I give it a couple of weeks, and those kids will be back with you. Please try not to worry."

"Do you really think so?" Tina said hopefully.

"Yes," I added encouragingly. "Odelia has probably already driven him half way up the wall. You know that he can't handle her any better than you can."

"Maybe you're right," she said, slipping out of her clothes and into bed. "Let's get some sleep."

I woke up before the alarm went off. Tina was not in the bed beside me, so I got up, slipped on a t-shirt and shorts, and went downstairs to find her. She was startled when I walked into the kitchen.

"Oh, shoot," she said disappointedly. "You spoiled my surprise! I was going to serve you breakfast in bed."

"Oh, I can go back to bed if you want," I responded.

"No, that's okay. The coffee is over there. Why don't you pour us each a cup. Breakfast will be ready in a couple more minutes."

"Gee, honey," I cooed in her ear. "You didn't have to do that."

"I know," she said. "I wanted our first morning of living together to be a little special."

I told her that any morning I woke up with her at my side was going to be special. With that, she put down the spatula and gave me a big hug and kiss. She then dished up the bacon and eggs onto our plates and pulled a plate of toast out of the oven and placed it on the table. Over breakfast, she told me that I had been right about what I said the night before. There was nothing wrong with the kids being with their father for now. She also agreed that Frank wouldn't be able to handle them for long on his own and that then she would have them back.

We didn't know it at this time, but we soon found out that when Frank went to Toronto, he was not alone: he was with another woman and her daughter. It turned out that this girl, who was not only the same age as Tina's oldest son, but had been born in the same hospital as Ekow, on the same day. In fact, as it turned out, Frank was her father as well.

After eating our breakfast we went upstairs and showered together to save time. I was done before Tina and got out and dressed for work. Tina came into the bedroom as I was ready to leave, and I gave her a big hug and kiss and told her I couldn't be late, and that I had been getting enough grief from my family lately and didn't need anymore.

"Get going, then," she said. "Call me later."

"Okay, I will" I thanked her again for the special breakfast.

When I got to work, my brother and mom were sitting, drinking coffee and reading the morning paper.

Brad looked up at me and in a sarcastic tone said, " Oh, if it isn't Don Juan."

"What is that supposed to mean?" I demanded angrily.

"Well, are you here to work, or are you going to take the first opportunity to go off and meet your sugar momma?" He glared at me.

"What the hell do you mean by that?" I asked.

My mom spoke first. "David, do you really know what you have gotten yourself into? This woman is nine years older than you and has three children. Have you thought about this? And now, her ex-husband has run off with her kids. What are you going to do now? Don't get me wrong. We think Tina is a lovely girl, and your dad thinks the world of her, too, but come on. How long will it last? Look at the mess she has gotten you into."

"It is none of your business," I responded heatedly. "No one got me into any mess, and besides, I thought you told me you were proud of how I got involved and tried to help Tina when I discovered she was being abused by Frank last year. You even got involved yourself, Mom."

"Yes," she continued. "But that was before you two shacked up together! Now, the kids are paying the price for your little love affair. I don't think it is fair to them."

"Mom," I said trying to maintain some composure. "You have no idea what Tina has been through. If you only knew half the things she's been through with him, you'd sing a different tune." I turned and stormed out of the office. My blood was boiling over. I had to go see Tina.

As I drove to her office, the conversation replayed in my mind. The anger had not subsided by the time I entered the front door of Tina's office. She took one look at me and asked what was wrong. I explained that I had just had a row with my mother and brother. It didn't take her any time to guess that it was about my relationship with her. I tried to deny it, not wanting her to feel responsible. I told her that it was about the business. When Brad and I had first opened it, I had worked long hours doing up quotes and making sales calls. Now that we were getting a lot of repeat business, they expected me to do more of the grunt work in the office. I wasn't entirely lying to Tina; this particular fight had occurred a couple of days before the sailing trip. Since I had not told her about it before, I thought it would make a plausible story now.

Tina accepted it. She came around from her desk and gently massaged my shoulders. She told me that she knew how hard I had worked to build up the clientele that we had at B&D Printing over the last year. She also said that she understood the pressures of running a business and that she had experienced a similar scenario with her old bosses. She was doing all the work building up a rapport with the clientele and when things got good, they took all the glory and profits for themselves. She said that it had left her feeling so unappreciated. She suggested that I sit down and talk with my family about how I felt. She then went on to say how, in the last year, she felt that she had become very close with my parents. She even remarked on how supportive and understanding my mother had been. *She really didn't know the other side of my mother,* I thought to myself. *Yes, she could be very compassionate and understanding, but she could turn on you in a second. I know she tried to be there for me, but every time I let my guard down and thought that things were going to be different, she let me down and hurt me worse than before. I couldn't understand how a parent could hurt her own child the way she had hurt me over the years.* (It would be another 14 years of hell with this woman, my mother, before my family finally discovered that she was bipolar. With this diagnosis, and the proper medication, I was able to communicate and bond with her like a mother and son should. The trust that she had lost, so many years before, was slowly regained. It felt so nice to have her in my life again.)

I hadn't told Tina much about how abusive my mother had been and what a traumatic childhood I had. The truth was that my brother and I could hardly wait to get away from home and be out on our own. Here I was, stuck in business with my brother and my mother. Originally, it was supposed to be just Brad and myself, with our father as a silent partner. Then, at the last minute, my mother got involved. She threw a monkey wrench into our plans by refusing to allow my dad to lend us money unless she was involved. Since my father couldn't stand up to her, and Brad and I felt we had gone too far to just walk away; we both agreed to their terms. My brother said, at the time, that as long as we had a united front against her, we would be able to handle whatever came up. Here I was, battling against both of them. *So much for the united front,* I thought to myself. *I should have known better. My mother always easily manipulated Brad, and this time was proving to be no different.*

Tina suggested that I go for a drive. She knew that driving helped me to think about things that were troubling me. I took her advice and left for a long drive towards the mountains. As I travelled closer and closer towards the majestic peaks of the Rockies, things became clearer to me. *I wouldn't let them drive me out of the business and rob me of all the hard work that I put into it until I was good and ready,* I thought. *I could play their little mind games.*

I turned around and headed back to Calgary. I was still too pissed off to go back to the office, so I drove to the liquor store near the townhouse and bought a bottle of rum. Back at Tina's, I cracked open the rum and proceeded to get a pretty good buzz going. The phone rang a couple of times, but I ignored it and continued to gorge myself on my old buddy, Ron Bacardi. By the time

Tina got home, I had almost finished off the bottle of rum and was pretty well trashed. She wasn't too pleased with me. She said it wasn't because I was drunk as a skunk, but because I hadn't called her to let her know how I was. She said that she knew I was upset when I left the office, which had been hours earlier. She was mad that she hadn't heard from me. I told her I was sorry for making her worry, but that I would be happy to make it up to her if she would like to go upstairs.

Smiling, she remarked, "I doubt that you would be of any use to me in your present state. Just go to bed, you crazy fool, and sleep it off."

The next morning, I awoke with a terrible headache. After downing some Tylenol, I noted that I was feeling a little fuzzy and couldn't remember how I had gotten to bed the night before. I hoped that I hadn't made a fool of myself in front of Tina. I decided to make her some breakfast and take it up to her, just in case. With a toasted bagel with cream cheese, a glass of juice, and a quartered orange on a breakfast tray, I made my way back up to the bedroom. When I opened the bedroom door, Tina was sitting up in bed.

"Well, good morning," she said coyly. "How do you feel today?"

"Oh, a little bit rough," I replied, bringing the breakfast tray over to her on the bed.

I got myself ready for work while she ate. She inquired as to whether I could help her get some things sorted out at work. She explained that her cash flow wasn't very good, and she was hoping that I could stop by after work and have a look through her books to see what she could do to improve things. I told her that I would be happy to have a look and would see her later.

When I got to work, nothing was said about what had happened the previous day, but there was a definite chill in the air. I prepared the quotes that were left on my desk and called the clients back, then I noticed that there were a couple of deliveries at the back door. I loaded them into my car and, with a brief good-bye, headed out to deliver them to the clients. This became my routine for the rest of the summer. I was starting to feel like a real outcast, but I didn't really care. I was in love, and that was all that really mattered to me.

Every day after work, I would go over to Tina's business and work on her books. One of her biggest problems was outstanding receivables, so I would prepare a list for her each evening and during the next day she would call the clients on the list. She would explain to them that their accounts were way overdue and try to collect from them. The next thing I looked at was to address her high overhead costs. Her rent was very high, but she had way more office space than she needed. Since her lease was up at the end of the month and she had so much free space in the townhouse, I suggested that she move her business there. Tina, however, did not think that it would be a good idea. She felt that it was too much of a residential area and too far away from her clients. She thought that she would lose a lot of "walk-in" business. What she really wanted to do, she told me, was buy some new typesetting equipment so that she could handle the larger, more lucrative jobs. Unfortunately, she was in no position to finance such a large venture at the time.

Then, there was the issue of her children. Many weeks had past, but there was still no word from the kids or Frank. She finally confessed to me that she was afraid to move her business as she thought the kids would be able to find her there. I told her that, while I understood her reasoning, she had to do something soon or there would be no business left for them to find.

After a few weeks of me being consistently at her, Tina conceded to look for new premises, and we went out looking on the last Saturday in August. We had an appointment to look at a small office space in the Mayfair, a combination of retail and professional offices and also residential . The main floor was retail, and the next two floors were professional offices, and the rest of the building was high-rise residential. The building wasn't located very far from her current premises. After finding a small, suitable office space, out of curiosity, we had the leasing agent show us a couple of apartments and the amenities of the building: indoor swimming pool, sauna, weight room. It had it all, and the apartments were very large and nice as well. We left the leasing agent in the lobby office and told her we were going to discuss things over lunch and would be back within an hour. Over lunch, I laid out a few different business options to Tina, and we finally both agreed that it was in her best interest to rent one of the larger apartments and move both the business and ourselves into it. With the long, late hours, she was working it would cut down on the travel, and we both didn't like her working so late in an industrial park by herself.

Her next issue was to deal with was Julie. She had been a well-trusted employee, but as she was planning to leave work in January to have a baby, I thought that now might be a good time to start cutting back on her hours and, therefore, cut back on some more overhead expenses. Tina thought about it and realised that she would be better off. Instead of working 60 and 70 hour weeks to make payroll, she would be able to work less hours and have more money in her own pocket. She decided she would have a talk with Julie on

Monday. It turned out that Julie was very happy with the idea. They easily reached an agreement.

October first came fast, and Tina was excited to move. She felt like it was a new beginning for her. Meanwhile, things for me had not improved much with my family, and I had been helping Tina more and more with her business, doing the books and collecting outstanding debts. With her excess equipment sold and the lower overhead, Tina was caught up on her overdue bills and found that working from home was working out great. Fax machines saved a lot of time and allowed Tina to concentrate more on production and less on running all over town. While doing my job for B&D Printing, I was also able to do deliveries and pick up supplies for Tina, freeing up even more of her time to work on production. Her customers were impressed with the quicker improved service. I was able to pick up a few jobs from some of Tina's non-print shop customers, which appeased my family a little bit.

The problems with my family dissipated over the months, and we began going over to my brother's and his wife's house for dinner and cards occasionally. We also visited my parents. My mom and I would continue to knock heads over different issues, while Tina and my dad just seemed to get closer and closer, becoming really good friends. As December approached, Tina's mood darkened. November had been hard on her: both the boys' birthdays had passed without any word. With Christmas fast approaching, I couldn't begin to imagine how the holidays would affect her.

I was at the mall, doing some early Christmas shopping and walked by a travel agency. There was a trip to Hawaii on sale for the week of December 10-1. I had been to Hawaii when I was 13 with my family and had really enjoyed it. In fact, it was one of my few good childhood memories. Without giving it too much thought, I decided to surprise Tina and booked the trip. Traditionally, Christmas was a slow time in the printing business, so I was confident that Julie could handle the office for Tina. I didn't tell Tina about the trip until the week before we were scheduled to leave. She was thrilled but had a million questions about how she would be able to leave the business. I told her about the arrangements I had made with Julie, and she was satisfied. She would inform her customers that she would be away but that the office would be open.

Hawaiian Vacation

The week of anticipation was finally over. It was a cool, crisp Thursday morning, and we would soon be flying over the Pacific Ocean on our way to Hawaii. We had set the alarm for 4:30 a.m.; my dad was coming to pick us up on his way to work at around six to drive us to the airport. It was about a twenty-minute trip to the airport, and our flight was due to leave at 7:10. Tina thought we should leave earlier, but I hated waiting around airports for hours and hours. We both got showered and then dressed and did our final packing. Neither of us could eat any breakfast…we were both too excited. I paced around the apartment, eagerly waiting for my dad, and kept looking down the street from our bedroom window to see if he was coming.

Finally, I said to Tina, "Let's take our bags down and wait in the lobby. This waiting is driving me crazy!"

Just then the door buzzer sounded. It was Dad. "Your limousine is here," he said into the intercom.

"Great," I replied. "We will be right down."

We carried our bags to the elevator and pushed the button. I went back to double check that I had locked the door. We exited the elevator, and my dad was waiting inside the lobby. He greeted Tina and took her bag. Once the bags were loaded into the trunk, I got into the backseat with Tina.

"The airport please driver," I said jokingly to my father.

I was glad the car was warmed up, as we both had on summer clothes, and our winter coats weren't doing much to fend off the cold. We arrived at the airport in good time. My dad came into the departure area with us and took our winter coats from us. He gave Tina a big hug and told us to make sure we had fun and relaxed. As we proceeded through security and made our way to the gate, we were both starting to feel tired. We hadn't slept long the night before, and I hadn't been sleeping well all week long. I guess I was just too excited. We weren't at the gate very long when they boarded our flight.

"See, baby," I said. "Isn't it nice? No long wait at the gate."

"Yes," she replied. "I guess you timed it perfectly. How long did you say the flight is going to be?"

"It should be about eight hours," I responded. "Depends on the wind. It's a long bloody flight, in any case."

We were on an Air Canada L10-11: a very large and comfortable aircraft. We were seated about midway on the plane, just over the wings in the centre row, with an empty seat beside us. *Great,* I thought, *a little more room for us to stretch out and maybe even get a little sleep en route.* After take off, we lifted the armrests that were between us and made ourselves cozy with the pillows and blankets provided by the airline. Before long, we had fallen asleep leaning against one another. After about an hour, we woke up just long enough to eat breakfast and then drifted right back to sleep. It didn't seem like we were asleep very long when we were awoken again for lunch. After lunch, the pilot announced that we were due to arrive at Honolulu International Airport at about 10:30 a.m., local time. I figured that, with the four-hour time difference, we had been in the air for about four and a half hours already. I calculated that our total flight time would be about seven and a half hours.

Tina asked me all kinds of questions about Hawaii. She wondered if it would be like Jamaica. I told her that I didn't know how it would compare to Jamaica, as I had never been there before, and I had been very young when I had last visited Hawaii. We talked and played cards, which made the last three hours passed fairly quickly. When the captain made the announcement that we were starting our descent into Honolulu, Tina looked past me straining to see out of the window. The aircraft banked to the left, giving us a beautiful view of the island.

"Oh," Tina exclaimed. "Look how blue the water is! The island looks so lush!"

The plane touched down smoothly, and we gathered up our things and grabbed our carry on bag from the overhead bin. As we exited the plane and walked down the stairway to the tarmac, we felt the hot, humid air engulf us as the sweet smell of tropical flowers filled our nostrils. I had forgotten what a tropical paradise even the airport was here in Honolulu, so different from any airport I had ever been to before. Tina was overwhelmed by the scents and beauty that filled her senses; it took her back to her native Jamaica. As we walked through the garden pathways towards the terminal, she excitedly pointed to the vegetation and flowers and trees and told me what each one was. Seeing the happiness on her face made me smile. I was so glad I had booked this trip.

We made our way to the luggage carousel, then found our tour representative and boarded the bus that was to take us to our hotel. The Waikiki Surf was located directly across from the beach. It was close to Fort Needham and the famous Hilton Hawaiian Village. When we arrived at the hotel, we checked in and toured around the grounds and lobby, checking out the swimming pool first. We then took an elevator up to our room. It was a lovely hotel. Our room was comfortable. It was equipped with a little kitchenette area. Tina wondered why the bed was sitting on what appeared to be wax discs. I told her that I had no idea. The room, however, was very hot and musty smelling; it appeared to have been vacant for a while, so we turned on the air conditioning. When the bellman arrived with our bags, he suggested that we open the patio door to allow some fresh air to flow through. He explained that, during the slow season, some floors were closed off. Tina then asked about the wax at the base of the bed legs. He told us that it was paraffin wax, which deterred any crawling insects from climbing up onto the bed. I was not impressed by that bit of information but wasn't too worried. What I could remember about being in Hawaii before; there had been very few insects anyway. I tipped the bellman and thanked him for his help.

Before we left to go for a swim, I checked the mini-fridge to ensure that it was on. I wanted to get some snacks, beer, and bottled water to put in it for later. When I opened the fridge door, I was horrified at what I saw: huge bugs were coming out of the cooling vent in the back. Tina laughed at my reaction and told me that they were just cockroaches. I had never seen a cockroach before in my life. I told her that I wasn't staying there with the cockroaches. I called down to the front desk and explained what I had found. I was informed that they wouldn't be able to move us for a couple days, not until they reopened some more floors, but they did say that they would send up a maintenance man to spray the room. We were told that we should take what we needed from the room and stay out for about three hours. I was so disgusted that I told Tina I wanted to find another hotel and call our travel agent and let her deal with the problem. Tina tried to calm me down and said just let them come and spray for the bugs and it would probably be okay.

"No way," I replied. "At least, let's see what other accommodations we can find while they spray." Then I remembered the name of the hotel I had stayed at as a kid with my parents, Aloha Surf. It wasn't close to the beach, but what I could remember of it was that it was next to the canal and from there we would walk to Woolworth's for the best coconut cream pie I ever had in my life.

"Okay," Tina conceded. "Let's forget about the swim and go for a walk and see if we can find you your pie and that hotel."

I was amazed how much I remembered about Waikiki, as we walked down Ala Moana Boulevard towards the centre of the Waikiki Beach and hotel district. I knew we were heading in the right direction as I was using Diamond Head, a famous Volcano, as my landmark. As we strolled around, I recanted the things I remembered from my trip there as a child. I recalled that there was, next to the hotel, a miniature golf course and an arcade. My brother and I had spent a lot of time there. Also, across from that was an ABC store, Hawaii's answer to 7-11. Just at that moment, Tina interrupted me and pointed across the street: it was the Woolworth's store. We crossed the street and entered the store. We went over and sat at the lunch counter. The pies and cakes were displayed exactly the way I remembered, under large glass domes in a refrigerated display case. As we sat, staring at the pies, waiting to be served, a cockroach appeared from behind the pie plate and crawled up onto the pie. We stood up simultaneously, without saying a word to each other, walked outside, and burst out laughing.

I was so disappointed with what I had seen of Hawaii on this trip. It seemed to have grown so much in the last ten years and gotten so dirty! There was garbage piled up beside the hotels and stores, and there were dogs, cats, and rodents rummaging through it. Tina, however, seemed to be having a great time. None of this seemed to be affecting her, but I was the one with the bug phobia. We continued walking until we saw a sign with "Canal" written on it and an arrow pointing down the street. As we got closer to the canal, we could hear what sounded like screeching monkeys. On the right side of the street was the ABC store, to our left, there was a huge Banyan tree full of birds all cawing and screeching. The noise they made was deafening. I felt sorry for the poor vendors who were selling their goods out of a small craft market beneath the tree, a few steps away was the Aloha Surf Hotel. I stopped and looked around. I couldn't believe all the changes; the arcade and mini-golf course had been located where the Banyan tree and small craft market now stood.

We entered the hotel through the open-air lobby and inquired about a room. They were in the same price range as the hotel where we were already booked, so we got a couple of keys from the desk clerk and went to look at the rooms. They weren't near as nice as the room we had at the Waikiki Surf, but there did not appear to be any cockroaches. The only problem here was that, even with the windows closed, you could still hear the screeching of the birds next door.

"It's up to you," Tina said. "But I prefer the other hotel. The room is nicer, and we were so much closer to the beach."

"Well, I don't know what to do," I answered. "I can't stand bugs, but the noise here is too much, and you're right about the beach."

"Well," Tina said. "Why don't we walk back along the beach, and by the time we get back, maybe the problem will have been fixed. I want you to do whatever will make you happy."

I explained our predicament to the woman at the front desk. She said that she would hold a room for us until six o'clock and passed me a business card with her name and the hotel phone number on it. As we walked back towards the beach, I told Tina that I wasn't trying to be difficult but that I just wanted things to be perfect. She responded that we were in a tropical paradise together; how much more perfect could things be? I stopped and gave her a long, passionate kiss. She was so right. I had to stop letting little mishaps bring me down.

We reached Ala Moana Boulevard and crossed the street. Tina's expression was pure delight as we removed our sandals and stepped onto the warm sand of Waikiki beach. Now, I knew why we were here. *Why was I wasting so much time fretting about a few bugs,* I thought. *Here I was, in a tropical paradise, with the most beautiful, intelligent, witty, charming, intuitive woman I had ever met it my life. What more could a man ask for?* I mean, sure the sex with Tina was great, but I was more impressed with the fact we could talk for hours, and I found our conversations were always so intriguing.

We walked to the water's edge, and the waves lapped at our feet. The water was so warm and soothing. Tina turned to me and said that she had to go swimming right away. She removed her swimsuit cover-up and handed it to me as she walked toward the warm, inviting water. She submerged herself below the frothy, swirling waves. When she surfaced, she motioned for me to join her. I took off my t-shirt and the fanny pack, that contained my wallet and our room keys, and placed them on the beach along with the clothing, and then I swam out to meet her. We swam and played together in the ocean for hours, embracing and kissing and hugging. I was so turned on by my

Jamaican beauty that I wanted to take her right there in the beautiful Pacific, but with a few thousand people laying on the beach, and another few hundred others in the water around us, it just wasn't going to happen. Finally, when I could stand it no longer, I begged Tina to return to our hotel room with me. We walked out of the ocean, picked up our belongings and continued our walk along the beach towards our hotel. It took us about a half-hour to reach the hotel. The desk clerk noticed us enter the lobby and relayed to us that our room had indeed been fumigated but that we would have to wait about half an hour while they aired out the room before we could go in it. We exited the lobby and headed for the pool.

The pool was empty. *Perfect,* I thought. We placed our things on one of the lounge chairs and dove into the pool together. We swam around, checking out the pool. It was surprisingly deep in the centre, so we swam to the far end where there was some type of ledge about four and a half feet below the water and about four inches wide that we were able to stand on. I still wanted her since our time on the beach and as we stood there on the ledge, fooling around with each other, I was quickly aroused again. As I nibbled on her ear, I whispered that I wanted her right now.

"What? Right here in the pool?" she questioned.

"Yea," I responded with urgency. "Come on. There is nobody around. We can stay right here in the pool and do it. I need it, baby."

Tina reached down and felt how swollen and hard I had become.

"Oh, baby, you do need it," she said as she reached up the leg of my swimming shorts and stroked me a few times.

I caressed her body and teased her with my fingers. She pulled her bathing suit over to one side and guided me into her. We took turns holding on to the edge of the pool while the other set the pace. The excitement of getting caught by someone added to our pleasure. We both still had our bathing suits on, so if anyone walked out into the pool area, it would just look like we were cuddling. I was just getting close to reaching a climax when tragedy struck: three couples noisily entered the pool area. That ended our private party. Tina was off me like a shot. She said she felt so embarrassed she thought she would die. I reassured her that they had no idea what we were doing. Still unsure, she did not want to face the strangers. I released her and swam from one end to the other, encouraging her to do the same.

When we returned to our room, I checked the fridge. Thankfully, there was no sign of our unwanted friends, the cockroaches. I called the front desk clerk at the Aloha Surf Hotel and cancelled the room we had tentatively booked. When I hung up the phone, Tina was laying naked on the bed.

She smiled at me and said, "I believe we have some unfinished business to take care of."

"Why yes we do," I replied in an excited tone.

After we made love, I showered and dressed first, and then Tina suggested that I could go downstairs to the bar and have a drink while she got ready. I told her that was a great idea and headed down to the lounge. The lounge seemed dark, after having just been outside in the bright daylight. My eyes took a few moments to adjust before I could locate the bar. About twenty feet ahead of me, there was a huge aquarium providing backlighting behind the bar. I sat at a stool and ordered a spicy Caesar. Unfortunately, the bartender did not have the makings for that cocktail, so I ordered a White Russian instead. My eyes had now fully adjusted to the dim lighting, and I could get a better look around the lounge now. It appeared to be very clean and quaint; the small round tables each held a candle. The bartender, whose name tag read Andy, brought my drink and asked me where I was from. I told him Calgary, Alberta. From the strange expression on his face, I could tell that he didn't know where Calgary was, so I added Canada. He knew of Canada and inquired as to how cold it was this time of year. We continued to make small talk and, as we chatted, I watched the aquarium behind him. I hadn't seen any fish swimming in it since I had arrived. When I asked him about it, he looked at me with a puzzled look on his face. Two men sitting at the bar chuckled. He glanced over at them and then replied that they get some very special fish, which sometimes put on quite a show for the tourists.

I turned as I heard Tina call my name. She came over and sat down beside me.

"What are you having to drink?" she asked.

"A White Russian," I replied. "Would you like one?"

"Ooh, sounds good," she responded.

I ordered two more drinks, as Tina glanced around the bar.

She said that it had a nice warm, comfortable feeling to it, and then asked if I'd thought about where we should go for dinner. She indicated that she was starving.

Andy didn't miss a trick and brought over a bowl of peanuts with our drinks. Tina was looking straight ahead with a horrified look on her face.

"What is it?" I asked, "What's the matter?"

"Oh my god," she said as she pointed towards the aquarium. "Look for yourself."

I turned around and there, in what I thought was an aquarium, and we could see a couple swimming. It dawned on me. It wasn't an aquarium after all, but a large window that looked into the swimming pool.

"Quick," she said. "Let's get out of here now. I am so embarrassed."

As I slugged back my drink, I watched as the couple in the pool were now standing directly in front of the window; he had his hands all over her.

Andy walked by and said, "See. I told you the fish could put on quite a show. It happens all the time."

We quickly downed our drinks, paid our tab, and left. Once outside, Tina said she couldn't show her face in the lounge again. But then we started to laugh as we tried to recall exactly what we had done in front of that window. I tried to reassure her that no one would have seen our faces, but she responded by asking me how many racially mixed couples I thought were staying there at the time. I agreed that I hadn't thought about that, maybe we were a little more identifiable after all.

We strolled along the main strip towards the centre of Waikiki, stopping to check out some restaurant menus that were posted on the sidewalk. We finally came to a sign with an arrow pointing towards the beach. The sign read The Wave Bar and Grill. We decided to give it a try. It was done in true native Hawaiian motif with thatched grass and tikis and small fake coconut trees everywhere. It was lively, and it was on the beach side, so it seemed perfect. We sat at a table and perused the menu. Our waitress came over and asked if we would like a beverage. She indicated that banana daiquiris were the special of the hour, so we ordered one each. Tina put down her menu and told me that she would really like to have some authentic Hawaiian food. I told her that all I could remember about the local food was a dish called poi. It was, as I recalled, very bland and tasted like wallpaper paste. She didn't think that it sounded very appetizing, so we decided to order the mixed appetizer platter, which had a variety of North American and Hawaiian foods on it.

As the lounge was lively, we were both enjoying the eye candy buffet all around us when the MC announced that the evening's entertainment was about to begin. It was a "Bikini Babes "and "Buff Boys" contest. The house band began playing some upbeat, Hawaiian music, as the first two contestants were announced. The format was that they paired up a guy and girl and the guy stood on the dance floor, posing to show off his muscles, while the girl danced around him, appealing to the crowd for applause. The longest and/or loudest applause determined the winner. We were both enjoying the floorshow equally, picking apart the contestants flaws in fun when our dinner arrived. I sampled the poi, but it was just as I had remembered. Tina wasn't impressed with it either, but everything else was pretty good. We drank and ate and watched the entertainment. I was especially impressed with the bikinis that were painted on, but Tina couldn't believe that some of the girls wore only body paint as bikini tops.

We decided to walk along the beach to go back to our hotel after the show ended.

It was quite dark, low cloud cover hid the moon, so the only lighting was that which managed to make it from the beach hotels past the coconut and palm trees. It was so romantic, the light crash of the ocean against the beach, the aromatic scent of exotic flowers, and the distant sound of Hawaiian music filling the warm night air. We were feeling a little tipsy from our drinks, so when Tina suggested that we go for a swim, I was apprehensive at first and reminded her that we didn't have our swimwear with us.

"What do we need swimwear for," she said as she began removing her clothing and started heading for the waters edge.

In a hushed tone, I reminded her that we were on a public beach.

"I know," she giggled as she dropped the last of her clothing on the beach and began wading out into the warm ocean. I knew it had to be the drinks because Tina had never been so open about public nudity, and she really surprised me now after what had happened earlier in the pool. *Ah, what the hell,* I thought and took a quick look around and couldn't see anyone close by. The feel of the warm ocean water caressing our naked bodies was exhilarating and stimulating. We played in the water, floating and swimming. We took turns diving below the surface, brushing against each other's sex organ as we swam between one another's legs. I had never in my 23 years been so in love and so attracted to another person. The connection I felt with Tina was overwhelming. I was really experiencing what love was all about for the first time in my life. At that moment, I felt like we were the only two people that existed in the world. We started kissing so passionately that we lost track of where we were. The next thing I knew, we were laying down at the water's edge with the waves gently washing over our intertwined bodies. I entered Tina and began thrusting myself into her wildly as she grabbed my buttocks and pulled me deeper into her. We continued our savage lust for each other, totally oblivious to our surroundings. We realized that our area of the beach had become quite a bit brighter now, but that didn't deter our passion as we continued our lovemaking until we both reached our breaking point and released all of our sexual energy into one another. We lay slumped together, a mass of exotic rapture trying to regain enough strength to move. After a few minutes, we returned to the sanctity of the ocean and allowed it to cleanse our bodies before slowly making our way to shore, reclaiming our scattered belongings.

Tina looked at me with a sheepish grin and exclaimed, "I can't believe we did that."

"Me either," I replied, then added, "but I'm glad we did."

We walked back to our hotel barely speaking a word to each other, just enjoying the solitude and beauty of this tropical paradise that surrounded us.

We were both exhausted. When we entered our room, Tina undressed and immediately climbed into bed. She was asleep immediately. I undressed and climbed into bed. Leaned over and kissed her on the cheek, then laid back and drifted off to sleep as well.

I awoke to the sound of knocking at our door. I looked over, but Tina was not there. Then, I heard the shower running. *Well, I thought to myself, who could possibly be at the door?* I slipped on a pair of shorts and t-shirt and went to the door.

"Who is it?" I inquired.

"Room service," came the reply.

I unlocked the door, and the waiter rolled in a breakfast cart.

"Where do you want it?" he asked.

"Over there, by the table, please," I responded, pointing to the other side of the room.

He passed me the bill to sign, and I grabbed a couple of dollar bills off of the dresser and tipped him. After he exited our room, I knocked on the bathroom door.

Tina replied, "It's open, come in."

I entered the bathroom and watched momentarily while Tina was towelling herself dry. "Breakfast was just delivered," I told her.

"Oh, shoot, I didn't think they would be so fast. I wanted to surprise you," she said.

"What did you order?" I asked.

"You will just have to wait and see," she replied.

I had already noticed coffee and orange juice on the tray but hadn't looked under the silver plate covers. Tina brushed past me, and I told her I would be out momentarily. When I emerged from the bathroom, Tina was sitting at the small room service table with a towel still wrapped around her hair and another around her body. The bright morning sunlight was filtered threw a slit in the still drawn curtains, illuminating her like a spot light on a work of art hanging in a museum.

Tina poured me a coffee, then, "Ta da!" she exclaimed, as she lifted the silver lids that covered the food.

I could hardly believe my eyes! There before me were two huge pieces of coconut cream pie. *What more could a man want?* I asked myself. *Here was this beautiful, intelligent woman who was so thoughtful that she ordered my favourite pie for breakfast.*

"You blow me away, baby," I said. "I just never know what you are going to do next."

"Why, thank you, honey," she replied.

The pie and coffee were delicious, the orange juice we had to cover and put in the fridge for later as it was just too sour after eating the sweet pie.

"Well, honey, what would you like to do today?" I asked

Tina replied that she thought we could do a little shopping and sightseeing in the morning and spend the afternoon at the beach.

"Hey that sounds great to me. Just let me take a quick shower, and I'll be ready to go in about twenty minutes."

I shaved and showered and was dressed in a golf shirt and pair of shorts in less than twenty minutes. Tina had quickly gotten herself dressed and ready to go and had popped down to the lobby to pick up some tour brochures .

"Do you see anything in the brochures that interests you?" I inquired.

She replied, "Yes. Pearl Harbour, Kodak Hula Show, a Luau, Sealife Park, Waiimea Botanical Gardens, Fort Needham, Hannumah Bay, the Circle Island Tour..." The list went on and on.

"Well, don't forget we have six more days. We don't have to see it all today."

It turned out that there was a bus tour of Pearl Harbour leaving from the hotel lobby in 40 minutes, so we decided to catch that first.

We went to the lobby and booked ourselves on the tour bus, then browsed through a few stores and sidewalk vendors close to the hotel entrance. Tina fell in love with a huge hanging plant holder made of shells. We haggled with the vendor and finally bought it for $25. I purchased a conch horn for myself and took our purchases back to our room. Tina continued to browse, and by the time I returned, she had two shopping bags full of assorted shell jewellery boxes, shell necklaces, and woven baskets and other knickknacks. By my watch, we had just enough time to hustle back to our hotel, drop off the purchases, and catch the bus tour.

When we arrived at the front door, the bus still hadn't arrived, so we went into the hotel lounge and had a cold beverage while we waited. We both noticed the swimmers in the pool through the lounge window and laughed. The horn sounded, and we boarded the bus for Pearl Harbour. It was an interesting trip. I appreciated it much more as an adult. When I went with my family, I was 13 years old, and at that time, I found it boring. Tina was saddened by what she saw, thinking about the thousands of people who had been killed.

By the time we got back to the hotel, it was just after two o'clock, and we were both starving. We decided to skip the beach, opting instead to go down to the pool for a swim and order something to eat from the poolside grill. We staked out a spot at the pool and placed our towels on a couple of lounge chairs. We ordered some drinks and a couple of orders of burgers and fries from the waitress. The pool area was pretty busy compared to the previous day, but we found out that a lot more people came into the hotel from the mainland on Fridays for weekend stays. After we ate, we played a few games of backgammon before heading into the pool. While Tina swam some laps, I set off to explore the window that looked into the bar. When I located it, I tried to look through into the bar, but I couldn't see a thing. It turned out that the window was mirrored on the poolside.

We swam and lounged for a couple of hours until the hotel blocked the sun, then it was up to our room to clean up and get dressed for dinner. By the time, Tina had shown me all the things she had bought earlier in the day; it was getting to be dusk. We went downstairs and saw a couple of bicycle rickshaws parked outside. We hired one to show us a few of the local sights and then take us up to a restaurant in Diamondhead that he recommended. Tina ran out of film on the drive, so the driver took us to a store to buy some more. When we arrived at the store, he said that he had to make a purchase for himself, so he would pick up the film for us. While he was gone, I climbed up onto the seat to massage Tina's shoulders, when all of a sudden *whomp*! We rolled out of the back of the rickshaw onto the sidewalk. The driver, Kenny, came out of the store and helped Tina up. He asked us if we were hurt and then he asked us what had happened. I told him that we were just sitting there, when the rickshaw tipped over backwards. He checked his rickshaw for damages. The battery for the running lights had fallen out of its holder, but that was all. With that replaced, we got back in and continued our journey.

Kenny headed into a remote residential area. Tina and I were starting to get concerned when he stopped and told us to get out and follow him. We apprehensively followed him down a narrow path, with six-foot concrete walls on either side that led towards the water. We emerged at a small clearing where there was barely enough room for the three of us to stand in. It was the most beautiful scenery, he said, in the area. He told us that he brought all of his customers to this spot to take pictures. We looked out and the moon was shining past Diamond Head Mountain, reflecting into the water before us. It was like a post card. Tina snapped a couple of beautiful shots, and we made our way back to the rickshaw and continued on to the restaurant. We thanked Kenny for the trip and paid him. He offered to come back for us in a couple of hours, and we accepted.

The restaurant was small and cozy. We enjoyed a leisurely meal with a bottle of wine. We chatted about our day and made plans for the next day. Before we knew it, two hours had passed. Kenny was already waiting for us out front when we emerged. As we climbed into the rickshaw, he asked us what kind of entertainment we had in mind for the evening. Tina and I looked at each other. We knew each other well enough by now to know that we just wanted to go back to the hotel and chill. We were about a block away from our hotel when suddenly we heard a loud bang, almost like a gunshot. Our rickshaw slowed to a stop. Kenny explained the rickshaw had blown a tire. Tina erupted into an uncontrollable fit of laughter. I was embarrassed so I quickly passed Kenny some money and told him that we would walk the rest of the way.

At the hotel, we headed into the lounge for a nightcap. I turned to Tina and asked her what was so funny.

"Just think about it," she giggled. "In the two short days that we've been here, we have sure had our share of situations. First the bugs, then the roach pies, then the pool incident, and now the rickshaw! It just makes me wonder what's coming next."

Little did I know how those words would haunt us by the end of the trip.

After a couple of drinks, we decided to call it a night. Over dinner earlier, we had decided on taking the Islander the next day. Part of the transit service, it was a public bus that circled the island, and passengers could get off and on where they liked. It stopped at all the major attractions.

After a good night's sleep, we packed a few things into a beach bag and went down to the hotel coffee shop for a quick breakfast. Then we made our way to the bus stop. We had decided to use the public transit, instead of a guided tour to see the island so that we could take our time. Our first stop was Sunset Beach and the Waiimea Falls and Botanical Gardens. Tina was very excited by the plants and trees. She ran from one to the other, naming them off for me, until she finally realized that I was less than thrilled. She apologized, but explained that it had been over fifteen years since she was last in Jamaica, and she had grown up with all the plants and trees that were in this garden. The more she talked, the more interested I became until I found myself envisioning Tina as a young girl in Jamaica. We wove our way through countless plants and trees, and I listened intently to everything Tina was telling me. We emerged through a grove of banana trees, and before us was a magnificent waterfall carved out of this jungle paradise: Waiimea Falls. We followed a path to a small clearing overlooking the falls. A couple of locals were there, cliff diving into a pool of water at the bottom of the falls. Tina commented to me about their striking physiques and a quick pang of jealousy hit me. I hid it long enough to take a picture of Tina standing between a couple of these Hawaiian gods.

We then made our way back down the path, through the park and crossed the highway to Sunset Beach. Huge sand dunes and the largest waves I'd ever seen greeted us there. Tina was again in awe with what she saw...surfers everywhere. The surf seemed a little too rough for swimming, so we spread out our beach towels and watched the surfers while we enjoyed the heat of the sun on our bodies. We grabbed a piece of pizza at the surfing hut before the next bus was due to arrive.

Back on the bus, we continued our island tour. Our next stop was the Polynesian Cultural Centre, an exploration of the many cultures that make up Polynesia. This wasn't one of my favourite stops, and Tina wasn't all that taken with it, either. So, after a quick look around, we caught the next bus and headed for one of my favourite places that I could remember from my last trip: Sea Life Park.

Upon arrival, we immediately made our way to the dolphin show. I was sure that Tina would enjoy the show that they put on in the lagoon. An old ship is set up in the middle of the lagoon, and there are a few actors that put on a bit of a comedy performance involving the dolphins. Tina enjoyed it thoroughly, and from there, we toured the rest of the water park.

I told Tina that I had hoped that we would get to Hannumah Bay that day as well, but we were already running out of daylight. The park wasn't far outside of Honolulu and has an incredible underwater park and reef located in the bay, where the snorkelling was amazing. Tina suggested we stop and take a quick look around so that we could determine if we thought it was worth another trip later in the week. I agreed. When we arrived at Hannumah Bay, the bus driver told us that there was a bus stop in the park but that the last bus stopped there at 3:30. He told us that the gates were locked, but that we could still hike down the hillside to get into the park. There were still quite a few people in the bay, swimming and snorkelling, so we decided to have a look around. We walked part way down the roadway, then took a steep path that cut through the grass and brush down the side of the mountain.

When we reached the bottom of the hill, Tina hurried over to the washroom. I was waiting outside when I heard Tina scream, and I rushed into the bathroom, fearing she was being attacked. As I entered, I saw her exiting a stall with her shorts still halfway down her legs.

"What's wrong?" I demanded. "What is it, honey?"

She pointed towards the stall and told me to look in it. I cautiously approached the door, trying not to show any fear in front of Tina. I peered into the dimly lit stall, but I couldn't see anything.

"Honey," I said. "There isn't anything in here."

Tina had composed herself by this time and walked slowly towards me, her eyes searching the floor and ceiling as she got closer. Finally, she peered into the stall and pointed.

"Look! Right there! There it is!" she screamed.

I looked at where she was pointing. It was a gecko, a small little lizard about six inches long. I turned to her and told her that it was a lizard and that the poor little thing was probably more afraid of her than she was of it. She then proceeded to tell me what had happened. When she reached back to flush the toilet, the gecko was sitting on the handle, and she touched it. I roared with laughter as we left the bathroom.

Tina slapped me on the shoulder and said it wasn't funny. "What if it had happened to you?" she asked.

I replied, "If it had happened to me, I wouldn't have said a word. I would have just died on the spot."

We strolled down to the beach and looked around. It was probably one of the nicest bays we had seen yet, and Tina was adamant that we had to come back and go snorkelling. I promised her we would, and we hiked back up the hill to catch the next bus.

By the time we got back to the hotel, we were both feeling tired from the day's journey, so we decided to go for dinner across the street at the Hilton Hawaiian Village. We chose to dine in the patio restaurant that overlooked the private beach. Tina heard drums beating and shouts coming from the beach. She asked our waiter what was going on, and he told her that it was a luau for the hotel guests. Tina wanted to know if our hotel had a similar event. I told her that I would check it out when we returned. We ordered dinner and drinks and began to make plans for the next day. I suggested that a relaxing beach day was long overdue and Tina agreed. She suggested that we return to Hannumah Bay and spend the day snorkelling and swimming.

Back at the hotel, I stopped at the tour desk and inquired about luau's for the public. The tour agent told me there was one the next day at five o'clock. She stated that the bus would pick us up at the front entrance of the hotel, and it was about a forty-minute ride to the beach where the luau was held. The cost was $38 per person. I purchased the tickets, and we headed up to our room. Tina wanted to go for a swim but I didn't feel like it. I was ready for bed. Tina pleaded with me to go down with her so that she could have a swim, so I gave in and grabbed a towel and pulled on my swimming shorts, just in case. I went to the lounge and ordered us each a mai tai for a nightcap, and I decided to join Tina in the pool after all, placing our drinks within reach at the pools edge. We played around in the water and sipped away at our drinks, but I was done in, the sea air and sun had totally drained me. Tina asked me to wait for her as she wanted to swim a few laps. *Where did she get the energy?* I wondered.

I had arranged for a 7:00 a.m. wake-up call so that we could get an early start. However, when we awoke, it was raining, and it didn't look like it was going to clear up anytime soon. We were both disappointed, but we set our sites on touring the museum at Fort Needham instead and then drifted back to sleep as there was no hurry. We woke up again at around nine, got dressed, and went down for breakfast. It was raining very hard now, but it was a warm rain, so it wasn't so bad. By the time we reached the entrance to the museum, we were drenched. We spent a couple of hours touring the museum and then walked down to the Waikiki Mall to do some shopping. The rain was starting to let up, so we headed down to the pool for a swim. The rain had caused the snails to come out of the flowerbeds around the pool. They were everywhere! Tina, never missing an opportunity, reminded me of the story I had told her about the girl I met in college who got me turned on to eating escargot. I had used that story to convince Tina to try them back home on one occasion when we were out to dinner.

"Well, David," she teased. "How do your escargots look to you now without all the garlic butter and cheese covering them?"

"Yuk," I replied. "They look so gross, I will never eat escargot again."

We had our swim and kept hoping the rain would let up in time for the luau that evening. We spent the afternoon playing backgammon and sipping local cocktails. It cleared off quite a little bit, so we dressed for the luau and waited at the entrance for the bus.

The bus crossed through a pineapple field to a beach that was different from any we'd seen so far. The sand was black. The pig had roasted all day, shielded from the rain by large tarps. The pits were dug into the ground and filled with hot coals used to bake the pigs, which were wrapped in banana leaves and covered in earth to keep the heat in. The smell was definitely more appetizing than the look of the poor pig, but everything else looked great. We dined and participated in the limbo contest. Then we watched the fire-eaters perform. We danced and drank and had a great time.

The sky was clear when we arrived back at the hotel just before midnight. Tina flung her arms around me and thanked me for such a wonderful evening. She had been right. What had started out as a rainy disappointment had turned out to be a fantastic day.

"Shall we plan on going to Hannumah Bay tomorrow?"

"Sure," Tina replied. "Whatever you want."

We headed back to the room where I suggested that we shower together. That shower led to one of the wildest nights of passion I ever had. We both collapsed in a lifeless clump, every last ounce of our energy now spent and quickly drifted off to sleep.

We awoke to a beautiful, sunny morning, got up, and readied ourselves for a day at the beach. With our beach bag packed, we went down to the lobby to rent a car for the day. When we reached the car rental office, next door to the hotel, Tina noticed that they also had mopeds for rent and suggested that we rent a couple of those instead. She said that she had never driven one before, so the attendant gave her a quick instruction and told her to take a test drive to see if she could drive it. She returned all excited, telling me how much fun it was to drive. With our beach bag fastened on the back of my moped and a small map in hand, we set out for Hannumah Bay. It was only 19 miles away, the attendant told us. I lead the way, with Tina close behind. We turned off the highway and went through a very posh neighbourhood, then returned to the highway. As I crossed through a set of lights and started up a hill, I casually looked back. Tina wasn't behind me anymore! I pulled over to the side of the road to wait for her. *She must have missed the green light and had to stop, I told myself.* But, after about five minutes, she still hadn't caught up, and I thought that something might be wrong with her bike. I turned around and went back to look for her. I turned the corner and saw her bike lying at the side of the road. I looked around for her. She was over by the beach. *Now Tina, you can't just drop your bike at the side of the road and go sight seeing on a whim,* I thought to myself. I put both mopeds on their stands and walked over to where Tina was sitting. As I approached her, I could see that she was trembling and crying. I called out to her. When she turned around, I was shocked to see that she was covered in blood.

"Oh my God!" I exclaimed. Tina, are you ok? What happened?"

"I don't know," she responded, sobbing. "I think I'm ok. I don't know how it happened. I was just enjoying the bike ride, taking in the sights, and bam! I wiped out. Oh, I'm such a klutz. I've spoiled your day. I'm so sorry."

"Oh, honey, don't worry about that," I told her as I took her into my arms. "You didn't spoil the day. I'm just glad that you weren't hurt any worse."

"Just let me clean myself off in the water," she said. "Then, we can carry on."

As soon as she entered the water, she screamed in agony. When the blood was washed away, I took a closer look at her wounds. We weren't going anywhere but to the hospital. I could see that her plastic sandals had been torn off her feet, both knees and both arms had considerable road rash and several deep cuts on them. I wasn't sure what to do about getting help, but I had to do something. I looked around and saw a pickup truck parked by the beach, but nobody was in it. Then I spotted a guy sitting on a large fallen tree, on the beach, eating his lunch. I told Tina to stay put while I went for help. I ran over to the guy on the beach and asked him for a ride to the hospital. He hopped up and looked over to where Tina was standing. He said there was an emergency clinic not far away, and he would take us there. On the way, he cursed about how they shouldn't be allowed to rent out mopeds. He helped me get Tina inside the clinic and they took her into an examination room immediately. I offered the man some money for his trouble but he would not accept it. Instead, he told me to go and look after Tina.

I thanked him and went back to the admitting nurse to inquire into Tina's condition. She told me that the doctor was still patching her up but that she would be fine. I filled out some forms and then realized that I should be worrying about how I was going to pay for this. We didn't have any travel insurance, I explained to the nurse. She told me not to worry as we probably had medical coverage through the moped rental company. I called the rental office, and the agent that I spoke with assured me that they would pick up the bikes and take care of the medical bill. A nurse came out and said that Tina was asking for me, so I went in to see her. She said that she wasn't in a lot of pain, but she seemed almost drunk. The nurse informed me that they had given her some pain medication. Before long, we were laughing about what happened. Once she was stitched and bandaged, I went to the pharmacy to fill a prescription for pain medication while Tina rested. The doctor told me that Tina would have to stay out of the sun for a few days.

We attracted a lot of attention as Tina limped into the hotel lobby. The bellman emerged from behind the desk with a wheelchair for her. The front desk clerk called me over and told me I had a message from the rental company. They wanted me to go over to see them whenever I could. After Tina was settled in the room, I gave her a kiss and told her that I wanted to go see what the rental agent wanted but that I would be back shortly.

The rental agent was extremely concerned about how Tina was doing. I reassured him that she was going to be okay and that it was nothing serious, just a few cuts and scrapes. He indicated that he needed me to fill out an accident report and then he passed me my beach bag. After completing the form, I went across the street to pick up some supper for Tina and me. When I returned to the room, Tina was fast asleep, but she awoke when the door closed behind me. We ate and then I helped Tina change out of her bathing suit. I made her as comfortable as I could in one bed and then I stretched out on the second bed. We watched a movie on the television and both eventually drifted off to sleep.

She was still pretty sore in the morning, but she wanted to get outside and try to enjoy the day. I helped her put on a pair of shorts and a t-shirt, and we slowly made our way down to the café in the lobby for breakfast. After breakfast, Tina tried to convince me that I should go off and have a good time and leave her to sit in the shade reading. It was our last day of vacation, she said, and she felt guilty about ruining it for me. I told her that I was happy right where I was and that I wasn't going anywhere. We spent most of the day playing games and reading. The pain medication was making Tina sleepy, so we went back to the room in the afternoon so she could rest. With Tina resting comfortably, I packed our things and then went out to pick up a few souvenirs that she wanted. I stopped off at the hotel lounge, on my way back, for a few drinks. Back at the room, we ordered room service for dinner. The trip home was going to be a long one as we wouldn't land in Calgary until around 9:00 p.m., so we needed to get a good night's sleep. Around eleven o'clock, Tina was feeling a little more mobile and decided that she wanted to go to the beach one last time. I didn't think it was a good idea, but when I saw the disappointment on her face, I got an idea. I made up an excuse to leave our room, and I went down to the lobby and inquired about borrowing their wheelchair again. I returned to our room, wheeled the chair in, and told Tina to hop on. I took her downstairs and wheeled her out the lobby, down the sidewalk and across the street to The Hawaiian Village. I knew that I wouldn't be able to take her on the beach in the wheelchair, but I did manage to wheel her around the swimming lagoon and through the gardens of the hotel. The fragrance from the tropical flowers filled the night air as we held hands and stared up into the clear night sky and at the stars. This was what I wanted Tina's last memories to be of our trip to Hawaii.

Our last morning was beautiful; there wasn't a cloud in the sky. Tina asked me to come closer and as I leaned into her, she put her arms around me and kissed me. She told me how much she loved me and how thoughtful I had been the night before. A tear welled up in my eye as I told her how much she meant to me and how lucky I felt to have her in my life. We went down to the poolside café for breakfast and to wait for the bus to take us to the airport.

They treated us like royalty at the airline counter. They put Tina in a wheelchair and escorted us through customs. They boarded us first, taking us to the back of the plane. Tina was given the whole centre row of seats, five in all. The flight attendant brought pillows and blankets to ensure her comfort. I found the seven-hour flight long and boring, but Tina slept most of the time. We arrived in Calgary a few minutes before nine and were the last to disembark. By the time we made it to the baggage claim, it was 9:30. Both my parents were at the airport to pick us up, and when they saw Tina being wheeled through the doors, they were upset. We retold the accident story on the ride home. My mother showed genuine concern for Tina's well-being and felt sorry for our misfortune.

Back to Work

After a good night's rest in our own bed, we both felt ready to tackle the day ahead. Tina had a pretty good sleep and wasn't bothered as much by her injuries. They were quickly starting to heal, and she was much more mobile than the day before. After a light breakfast, we went into the office to see what work Julie had and what she had been up to while we were away. She had very little work left for Tina to do that morning but had been quite busy while we were away. She had made photocopies of what she had done so I had a reference for billing. With the billing complete and a couple of jobs sitting there for delivery, I told Tina I would drop off the customers bills and the jobs that had been typeset and needed delivering, and pick us up some lunch while I was out. She said she would call Julie to see how everything went and tell her to take the day off since there was little work to be done.

"Sounds good," I said as I left our apartment to do the deliveries.

After dropping off the jobs and bills, I swung by B&D Printing to see what was happening there. My brother was surprised to see me. Our mother had told him about Tina's accident and that I probably wouldn't be in today. He asked about Tina and then asked me to go into the office with him because he had something he wished to discuss with me.

"Sure," I said. "No problem."

We sat there and made a bit of small talk. Finally, I spoke up and said, "Okay, what's on your mind?"

"Well," he said. "I was thinking while you were away that things haven't been going all that great lately with us working together, and you seem to be more interested in working with Tina than putting in an effort here, so I want to buy you out."

"What do you mean you want to buy me out?"

"Well," he said as he passed me an envelope, "there is a check in there for $8,000."

I stared at him as he uttered those words and then told him he was crazy if he thought I was going to walk away from the business for a lousy $8,000.

"No, no, no," he said. "Hear me out."

"Well, go ahead," I replied.

"Eight thousand is all I can afford to give you at the moment. In addition, I'll give you another $1,500 a month for six months making your buyout $17,000 in total."

I looked at him in disbelief. I didn't know what to think. I hadn't expected this to happen, but I really wasn't happy being there any more, and his offer was reasonable. I told him I would think about it over the weekend and left.

When I got back to our apartment with lunch, Tina was finishing up a small job in the office.

I said to her, "Come and eat and finish that later. I have something to talk to you about."

As we sat down at the table she asked me, "Okay, what do you want to talk about?"

I turned to her said, "After I made all the deliveries, I swung by the shop and had a chat with my brother."

"What did you chat about?"she asked.

"Well, he doesn't think he and I can continue to work together anymore, so he offered to buy me out."

"What do you think about that?" Tina asked.

"Well, I really don't know what to think of it. His offer is fair, and I haven't been happy there."

"So, take his offer," she said. "You know with Julie leaving soon to have her baby, I could use your help here full time. You have been doing a lot of the work around here anyway."

"So you think I should take his offer?" I asked her.

"I think you should do whatever will make you happy," she said.

With that said, we ate our lunch and discussed how her morning had gone. Meanwhile, I kept pondering his offer in the back of my mind. With lunch over, Tina finished up a couple of small jobs, and I did up some book work. It was still early Friday afternoon, so I took the last of the jobs and left to deliver them, leaving Tina to rest and take it easy. After making my last stop, I had reached a decision. I would stop by the print shop and see my brother.

I knew what I was going to do now. When I walked through the front door my brother was standing behind the counter.

"Well," I said. "Where is it?"

"Where's what?" he asked.

"The check," I said. "I've decided to accept the offer and put everything behind us."

"Just a minute," he said as he walked back to the office. When he returned, I passed him my keys to the office, and he handed me the check.

"Put down the agreement on paper," I said, "and I'll sign it." Then, I turned and left.

When I got home, Tina was smiling from ear to ear. "What are you so happy about?" I asked her.

"I had a special delivery this afternoon" she said.

"From who?" I asked.

"From my lawyer," she replied.

"Oh, what did she send you," I said sarcastically. "A bill?"

"No much better than a bill," she replied.

"Well, what then?" I asked, somewhat impatiently.

"It's my decree nici."

"What's a decree nici?" I asked.

"It's my final divorce from Frank."

I looked at her somewhat puzzled, and she explained it to me. Under her previous separation from Frank, she had filed for divorce, then reconciled with him. Her lawyer had placed advertisements in Ontario notifying him of the filing of divorce, but he failed to respond, so her lawyer managed to get her final divorce processed on her previous filing. I asked her when she had done all this, and she replied she had been working with her lawyer on it for quite some time and was hoping to surprise me with it before Christmas. However, she felt she couldn't wait since it arrived today, and with everything else that had happened she thought it would cheer me up. I gave her a great big hug and kiss and told her that it was fantastic then told her I had some news for her as well.

"What's that?" she asked.

"I stopped at the shop and saw my brother and took his offer."

"Are you sure that's what you want?" she asked.

"Yes," I replied.

"Well, in that case, we have some celebrating to do tonight, don't we?" she stated.

"Yes, we do, honey," I said.

With work finished for the day, we decided to have dinner downstairs in the steakhouse to celebrate her freedom and mine. At dinner, I felt like splurging a bit and ordered a bottle of Mumms Cordon Rouge Champagne, and we both ordered filet mignon steaks with stuffed potatoes and mushroom caps for an appetizer, followed by New York cheesecake for dessert. After a nice, leisurely dinner, we walked back outside and along the walkway back to our apartment lobby. I promised Tina a nice massage when we got back upstairs. She said the massage would be great but asked for a rain check as her injuries still concerned her a bit, and she wanted to let them heal over a bit more before we got too frisky. I didn't mind not having to give the massage, but I was suffering from our lack of physical contact the last couple of days and didn't know what I would do if it lasted much longer.

Tina looked at me as we made our way back upstairs and said, "If you want, we can give it a try and see how we make out."

As much as I wanted it, I was more concerned about her health and healing and told her I could handle a couple more days until she was feeling more up to it. I couldn't believe how dependant and obsessed I had become with having sex with her over the last year.

As we cuddled on the couch watching a movie, the phone rang. It was my mom, inviting us over for breakfast the next morning. She and my dad wanted to hear how our trip was.

"Just a minute," I said and turned and asked Tina if she would like to go to my parents for breakfast in the morning.

"Sure," she said.

I asked my mom what time, and she told me about 10:00 a.m.

"Okay," I said. "We'll see you then." I hung up the phone.

After our movie was over we decided to go to bed as we both still had a bit of jet lag. As we lay side by side, I turned to Tina and told her what a surprise it was that she was divorced. "I can't believe you kept it secret from me."

"Well, I really didn't know how things were going to work out so, I thought I wouldn't say anything till it was done," she said.

"Well, honey, I can't tell you how happy I am that you aren't married to that asshole anymore, and now, with me free from the print shop, we can maybe have a fresh start together."

Tina turned to me and said, "You know I love you so much, but don't forget I still miss and want to get my kids back somehow, someday."

"I know, honey, I know," I said, but in the back of my mind I was relieved to not have the responsibility of three kids to look after, but I did feel sad for Tina because I could see how much it hurt her not to have them in her life at this time.

It was a beautiful sunny Saturday morning; the sun glistening off the snow and an immense amount of light was shining through our bedroom window. I couldn't help but wake up happy. I got up first and went to shower. Meanwhile, Tina lay in bed and rested a little longer. She did enjoy laying in on the weekends. When I walked back into the bedroom, she was all snuggled beneath the sheets, looking so young and beautiful to me. At that moment, I wanted to slip beneath the covers and snuggle with her and hold her in my arms forever, but I knew we had made prior commitments for the morning. I got dressed and then leaned down and gently kissed Tina on the forehead.

"I'm going down stairs to get a newspaper. You'd better get up and get ready, honey."

"I will," she replied. "Just five more minutes, okay?"

"Okay, honey, I'll see you shortly." I turned and went down to get a paper at the coffee shop in the lobby. I bought the paper and a coffee and sat there for a while, drinking my coffee and reading the paper, figuring that by the time I got back upstairs Tina would be ready to go.

When I got back upstairs to the apartment, Tina was dressed and ready to go. She was talking on the phone and from the bits of conversation I knew it was her mother. When she got off the phone, she told me she had wanted to phone her mom and tell her about our trip to Hawaii.

"How did that go?" I asked.

"Oh you know, the usual…'it must be nice to travel all around the world and not care where or what is happening to your kids.'"

I could feel a rage building up inside me. I had never met Tina's mom, but I couldn't understand how she could be so hard and hurtful to her daughter. Her mom had no idea how much it hurt her not to be with the kids.

When we returned later that afternoon from having breakfast and playing cards with my parents, Tina noticed our answering machine light was blinking. There was a message from her mom to call her. *Now what?* I thought to myself. As I went into the dining room to finish the paper while Tina went into the bedroom and called her mom back. To my surprise, Tina came out of the bedroom all smiles.

"What made you so happy?" I asked.

"You won't believe it," she said.

"What?" I asked.

"Frank is taking the kids to my mothers for Christmas."

"What do you mean?"

"Well, he called my mom and asked if he could bring the kids down tomorrow and leave them with her for their Christmas break while they are out of school."

"What, he just called her out of the blue and decides to take the kids down there," I stated.

"No, she confessed that she has talked to him on a couple of occasions in the past."

"What? She knows how worried you have been about them and only now decides to tell you that she has had contact with him and the kids?"

"Listen, it doesn't matter why or how, the important thing is I'll get a chance to talk with the kids over Christmas."

She paused for a moment, then said, "I only wish I could be there and see their smiling faces on Christmas morning. Anyway, I want to go out and buy them some presents and ship them by courier on Monday so they will get them in time for Christmas."

Having spent the rest of the day traipsing through the malls in search of the perfect gifts for the kids, I was exhausted, but I knew how important it was to Tina to get this done. We returned home with our trunk full of gifts and wrapping paper. The pure look of excitement on Tina's face made it all worthwhile. While Tina started the wrapping process, an idea occurred to me. I made an excuse and took the portable phone into the washroom and began my search. I called a couple airlines and made inquiries on flights to Rochester or Toronto. Flights were very expensive on such short notice, and even though I had received my payout from my brother, it just wasn't practical to spend close to $4,000 on plane tickets.

Time for plan B. We could possibly leave late Tuesday afternoon and drive to Rochester. With a pen and paper, I did the math and it was about 40 hours of driving straight through, but with us both driving and good weather, it could be done. I went out to the dining room where Tina was busy wrapping the gifts.

"Honey," I said to her.

"Yes?" she said.

"I have an idea."

"What?" she asked.

"Well, instead of sending these presents through the post, wouldn't it be better to deliver them in person?"

The look of delight and the thought of getting to see her kids for Christmas overwhelmed her. "Oh, honey," she said, "can we go, really?"

"Well," I told her, "I checked into flying, and it would be too expensive, but I think we could drive if we leave after work on Tuesday. We would get there in time for Christmas eve."

"What about the business?" she asked.

"Well, we aren't going to get much work to do a day or two before Christmas, and Julie could always handle any emergency work, but we would only be able to stay for a couple of days and then have to drive back as quick as we can. We will probably leave Rochester Sunday morning at the latest but I think, depending on how the drive down goes, it would be wiser to leave late Saturday evening."

After discussing it a bit further, we decided to make preliminary arrangements to leave Tuesday afternoon by about four o'clock, but first, we would wait to see what happened on Sunday with Frank. I was very skeptical about him actually following through with his intentions to take them to her mom's and thought it might just be his way of trying to lure us down there. Tina said she doubted it because when she talked to her mom, she was telling her that Frank wanted her personal guarantee that Tina wouldn't know they were going to be there, and there was to be no contact. That was why her mom was apprehensive about telling her they were coming in the first place.

"Well, in that case, how is your mom going to feel about us being there?"

"I don't know," she said. "I don't really care…I just want to see the kids."

"Well, it's getting late. Let's finish up with the wrapping and go to bed. You can call your mom tomorrow evening and see if the kids are there."

Tina nuzzled up to me in the bed; her hot breath steamed around my neck as she playfully bit my earlobes. She teased my hot shaft to life with a few rubs from her warm hand. I told her she had better stop what she was up to. "You're playing with fire, honey," I said, "and if you're not careful, you're going to get burned."

"Are you saying you don't want me?

"Oh, yeah, I want you, but what about your injuries? I don't want to hurt you."

"Baby, the way I feel right now, nothing is going to hurt me," she replied.

Those were the magic words I had been waiting to hear for days now. I carefully slid her nightshirt up around her neck and eased it over her head, and then with my right hand I gently eased her panties past her hips and carefully over her fragile knees, down to her ankles. With a well-placed flick of her ankles, the panties slid off and down to the floor. While she continued to nibble on my ear lobes and rub her warm body against mine, I caressed her warm full mounds with my hands and then began caressing her hardened nipples ever so gently. With one hand caressing her nipples, I reached down between her thighs and teased her with my fingers. She continued to wildly tease me with her hot tongue, working from one ear to the next, all the while still stroking ever inch of my hardness. I could no longer take the teasing and gently positioned her on the pillows and entered into all her warmth with my anxious member. Still wary of her wounds, I inserted myself in and out of her ever so tenderly till we were both worked up into an uncontrollable fit of passion. Tina, now unaware of her injuries, wrapped her legs tightly around my back drawing me deeper within her. Oh how I had missed the warm feel of her body and the intense lust we had for each other. The thought of hurting her still in the back of my mind helped to prolong our enjoyment of one another. Tina released her warmth all over me first, then within minutes, I returned my warmth deep inside of her. We continued to kiss passionately, still intertwined, and I could feel myself beginning to grow and swell within her again. Once again, we devoured one another till our bodies were nothing but hot sweaty mounds of steamy flesh. Tina cried out. I thought I'd hurt her and looked to her and asked if she was okay.

"Oh god, yes," she screamed.

I resumed unabated by her wild cries of ecstasy. I devoured her body with my tongue and continued driving myself deep within her warmth till I released a second time and then collapsed in pure exhaustion. We both lay still, side by side, unable or unwilling to move.

When I awoke the next morning, our bodies looked like we hadn't moved all night. I looked at Tina and smiled. Her luscious eyes were just beginning to open, and she smiled back at me, then she went to move, and she cried out in pain.

"What's wrong?" I asked.

"Oh," she said. "I can feel every bone and muscle in my body aching this morning."

"Well, honey, just lay here and rest. I'm going to have a fast shower, then I'll draw you a nice hot bath, and you can have a good long soak."

After my shower, I filled the tub with piping hot water and added some Epsom salts and bath oil. I went into the bedroom, and Tina had drifted back to sleep. I tapped her lightly and told Tina her bath was ready, but she didn't have to hurry because the water was probably a little too hot. She eased herself out of the bed and into the bathroom. I heard the water running again and figured she was probably adding some cold water to cool it down a bit. After I got dressed, I knocked at the door and entered. She was submerged in the tub, enjoying the heat around her aching body.

"Can I get you anything?" I asked.

"A glass of juice and a crossword book would be nice," she said.

I left and quickly returned with her juice and book, then asked her what she would like for breakfast.

She said, "Some bagels and cream cheese would be nice."

"Well, in that case, I have to run to the store and get some. I'll be back soon. You just relax and enjoy your bath.

I bent down and gave her a quick kiss and left. When I entered the mall to go to the grocery store, I passed a jeweller and something made me stop and look at rings. Before I knew what I was doing, I had picked out a beautiful engagement ring and put a deposit down on it, and they placed it on lay-away. Then, I looked around for a Christmas gift for Tina. We had said that the trip to Hawaii was our Christmas gifts to each other, but I couldn't help myself. Then I spotted the perfect gift, a diamond tennis bracelet. I told the clerk I would take it, and while she wrapped it up, I went to the bank machine to withdraw the money to pay for it. I knew the gift was a bit extravagant, but I was feeling a little flush with cash having just received the buyout from my brother. With the bracelet safely tucked inside my coat pocket, I entered the grocery store and picked up a few items that we needed in addition to the bagels and cream cheese. When I opened the trunk to put the groceries in, I decided to stash the bracelet under the spare tire so Tina wouldn't find it and thought it would be safe there.

When I entered the apartment, Tina was lounging on the couch with her crossword book.

"How are you feeling now?" I asked.

"Oh, much better," she responded.

I fixed the bagels and cream cheese for us both, and we sat at the table and ate them and played a few games of backgammon. Tina was anxious to call her mother and see if Frank had brought the kids down.

"Well, I think it is to soon, even with the two hour time difference. It's only one o'clock there, so why don't we go for a walk and then you can call when we get back."

"Okay," Tina said and she went and got dressed to go out.

I really enjoyed going for walks with Tina. Aside from the exercise, we could talk and talk for hours. It still amazed me how two people from such different backgrounds could have so much in common and the same dreams about life. We must have walked for a good two hours, and Tina was feeling much better now; all that walking helped her healing process. I think all we talked about was her going to see the kids, and she told me more about Rochester and her family and what to expect when we got there. I hadn't really thought much about meeting her family and the repercussions from that when I suggested we drive down. All I had thought about was how happy Tina would be to see the kids. When we got home, Tina phoned her mother right away. Her mom was very short with her on the phone and told her she would call her back later because she had company.

"Are the kids there?" Tina asked.

"Yes," her mother replied.

"And Frank?"

"Yes," was the reply again, then her mother hung up.

Tina was so excited when she got off the phone and could hardly contain herself.

"Have you called Julie and talked to her about us going away again?" I asked.

"No," she said.

"Well, why don't you call her and let her know?"

"Okay," Tina said and she went into the office to call her.

"How did it go?" I asked when she came out.

"Well," she said. "She was hoping to take some time off, and her husband didn't want her to have to work anymore until the baby was born, especially just before Christmas."

"Well, I can understand that," I said. "I think the business will be fine; we're only going to be closed for a couple of days anyway."

I was feeling a bit chilled from the walk and decided to go downstairs to the pool and have a swim and then a sauna. Tina said it sounded like a good idea and wanted to know if I wanted company.

"Sure," I said.

After a nice relaxing swim and sauna we went back upstairs. Tina was anxious to phone her mom again and check on the kids. Her mom answered and told her she would call her back in about fifteen minutes she had someone at the door. Tina figured Frank was probably just leaving her mother's house now and heading back to Toronto. It seemed like the clock stopped as we waited patiently for her mom to call her back. Finally, the phone rang, and it was Tina's mom. Tina hit her with a flurry of questions. How are the kids? Have they grown? Did they ask about me? On and on she went, but I couldn't blame her: she was really excited. Then, she told her mom that she was planning on coming down to see the kids. I don't know what was said at the other end of the phone, but Tina's mood changed from happy and excited to a bit more sombre.

When she got off the phone, she filled me in a bit. Her mom was already complaining that he dropped the kids off and didn't bring any Christmas gifts or any money for her to get them gifts with. Everything with Tina's mother always seemed to be about money. I know that her folks were retired, and her mother had disabilities, and her stepdad had Parkinson's, but I just couldn't understand their way of thinking.

"Did you talk to the kids?" I asked.

"No," she said.

Her mom thought it would be best if she waited to talk to them when we got there. A lot had happened in the last six months to the kids, and her mom thought they needed some time to adjust to things before Tina talked to them. All this confused me, but it really didn't matter as we would be there in about four days anyway, and all the mysteries would be cleared up then. We went into the office, and I put a message on our answering machine advising our customers of the hours we would be open for Christmas and New Year's, and Tina did up some work that had come in over the weekend by fax machine so we would keep on top of the work and be able to get away as early as possible on Tuesday afternoon. Later Sunday evening, I heard Tina talking to her mom and sister on the phone again. She must have asked them a million questions. and I took it they had a few questions of there own what with them going to be meeting me for the first time.

After a restless night sleep, we both got up fairly early and got a start on the days work. The customers I encountered during the day were informed about our closing for Christmas and some didn't seem too bothered, while others were quite nasty about the whole thing, and if they had their way, we would stay open on weekends, too. In my travels, I picked up a road atlas, and later that day, I planned our route to Rochester. We would leave Calgary and go east on the Trans Canada highway as far as Winnipeg, Manitoba, then turn south and enter the United States into North Dakota and take highway 29 south to the 94 east which eventually would put us on the I-90 and that would take us all the way to Rochester. It was the fastest simplest route and very little chance of getting lost. The Trans Canada was a pretty good highway as far as Winnipeg, but I didn't wish to take it into Northern Ontario, as there was too much fog and poor visibility. Tina finished working on the few jobs that had come in that day, and I started to pack our stuff. We weren't taking much for clothes since we would basically be driving all day and night to get there in time and then spend a couple days there and have to drive like crazy to get back.

After another restless night, Tuesday had finally arrived. I was both nervous and anxious to get our trip underway. I checked the fax machine in the morning to see if we had much work come in overnight. I figured with everybody knowing we were going to be closed after today, there would be a lot of last minute orders come in, and I was right. The fax machine had seven rush orders waiting to be done. Tina didn't even bother to get dressed. She wanted to start and get the work done as quickly as possible. I finished up our packing and loaded the Christmas presents and our suitcase into the car. Tina had gotten the work for up north done first so I could deliver it first, then by the time I got back, she hoped to have the stuff for our customers in the south end of the city, where we lived, ready to go. When I got back, she had received an order for downtown that was a rush as well. *Great…the last place I wanted to have to go.* We decided I would deliver the orders in the south end first, and Tina was going to do the order for downtown and then get showered and dressed, and we would drop it off on our way out of town. Although we had planned to leave by about four o'clock, it had started to snow and a small storm was moving in from the west, so I figured we had better get away a little earlier than planned.

I had quickly made the last of the deliveries, and it was almost two in the afternoon, so I went back to the apartment to pick up Tina, and we would be off after a quick stop downtown. Tina was ready to go. She had proofread the copy for the last delivery and away we went. The city streets were already getting a bit slippery from the freshly fallen snow, and Tina was starting to worry about the roads. I told her not to worry: we only had one quick stop, and we would get ahead of the storm in no time. Tina took the order in to the customer downtown while I circled the block. As Kim quickly looked over the work, she noticed one small typo that Tina had missed, even though she had proof read it a couple of times. The last thing she wanted was to have to go back to our place and fix it, but being a resourceful girl, she took it over to their light table and managed to fix it with a quick cut and paste job. They were happy and so was Tina. We were on our way, finally, just before three o'clock.

By the time we reached Chestemere Lake on the eastern outskirts of the city, there was only a light dusting of snow, and we had managed to get ahead of the snowstorm. It was just a bit past 6:30 when we reached Medicine Hat. We were both feeling hungry, so we pulled into a Kentucky Fried Chicken restaurant and had a bite to eat, and then gassed the car up at the service station across the street. Tina offered to drive from there, so I climbed into the passenger seat and decided to try to get a bit of sleep so I could take over from her in a couple of hours. I guess I must have been really tired because Tina had driven for about three hours when I woke up.

"Where are we?" I asked.

"Just outside of Moose Jaw," she replied.

"Are you okay or do you want me to take over for you now?"

"I'm fine," she said. "You can take over just before we get into Moose Jaw, it's about a half hour away."

It was a perfect night for driving. The sky was clear; the moon was out illuminating the darkened countryside; there was not much around but a long flat stretch of highway. Tina pulled into a gas station on the outskirts of Moose Jaw, and we used the facilities and gassed up and bought a couple of snacks to munch on. I was back behind the wheel, and with little traffic around, I set the cruise control at 70 miles per hour, and we zoomed along in the still of the night. I encouraged Tina to take a nap so she could take over from me in a while, but she was hesitant to sleep because she said she wanted to keep me company. I had only been driving a little over an hour when we could see the night sky lit up from all the lights of the city of Regina. It was about the same time that Tina noticed the police car lights flashing behind us. *Where did he come from?* I wondered. I couldn't believe he was out there in the middle of the night and was pulling me over for going a lousy ten miles over the speed limit. As I slowed down and pulled to the side of the road, the cop car zoomed past us and continued down the road. *Whew!* I thought, *That was lucky*, and pulled back onto the highway. A few miles down the road, the police car was on the opposite side of the road with an ambulance pulled in behind him. A big rig was lying on its side in the ditch, but no other cars were involved from what we could tell as we passed. It was 1:30 in the morning when we passed through Regina.

"Next stop, Winnipeg," I told Tina.

It was a good five hours plus away, but I thought if we were going to have to stop and sleep anywhere, I wanted to at least make it as far as Winnipeg. We only made it as far as Brandon, Manitoba, and I couldn't drive any longer. Tina had drifted off and slept a little but not enough to want to drive, so we pulled off into a rest stop called Orbit and reclined our seats and cuddled together under the sleeping bags we had brought with us.

I had slept for maybe two hours and was cramped and had to pee. I got out of the car as quietly as I could and used the outhouse at the rest stop we had stopped in and stretched my legs. Back in the car, I looked at the map, and as near as I could tell, we were about two hours from Winnipeg. Tina had stirred, and I told her to go back to sleep, and she could start driving in a couple of hours once we passed through Winnipeg. As I entered the city of Winnipeg, I took the off ramp to highway 75 south which would take us to the U.S. border where it turned into the 29 south. I stopped at a truck stop for fuel and to get something to eat. Tina was awake now and took her toothbrush into the restaurant with her as did I. We both couldn't wait to brush our teeth and clean up a bit. Refreshed, we sat down at a booth and ordered a big breakfast: eggs, bacon, sausage, and ham with home fries, toast, and coffee. There was nothing like a good truck stop breakfast to get you going.

Once we'd eaten, we were back on the highway again, and Tina was driving, giving me a chance to rest for a bit. We were about seventy miles from the U.S. border. I dozed in and out until Tina stopped just short of the border and had me take the wheel again. When we pulled up to the border crossing, the American customs officer turned out to be a real redneck. I don't think he ever saw a racially mixed couple before in his life, the way he gave us the third degree and kept asking the purpose of our trip. Then he asked us to step out of the vehicle, and he proceeded to search our car. He wasted a good 20 minutes or more questioning us and searching the car before he allowed us to proceed.

As we drove off, we still couldn't figure out what his problem was and why he detained us so long, but it didn't matter. We were zipping along the number 29 highway on our way to Grand Forks, North Dakota and then to Fargo where we would turn east on highway 94. I continued driving until we reached Grand Forks then Tina took over again.

We were both really feeling tired and decided when we got to Fargo to stop and get a room and have a shower and change our clothes and try to sleep for about four hours. Tina pulled into a small motel just off the highway in Fargo, and we rented a room and both crashed for a few hours. I had slept just over three and a half hours and was feeling rested, so I left Tina sleeping and had a shower and changed my clothes. Tina woke up while I was dressing and got up to shower. I told her I would be in the lounge/casino while she was getting herself ready.

The lounge had three blackjack tables and a wheel of chance in it, so I decided to play a little blackjack while I waited. I heard it was a "Big limits at the table. Bet between a dollar and five dollars." It was nice to have a diversion from all the driving. Tina entered and was quite amused by the little backwater casino. She wanted to try her luck, and so while she did, I went up to our room and put our bag back into the car and checked us out of the hotel. Judging by the look on the desk clerks face and the briefness of our stay, he probably thought we only rented the room to have a quickie. I wish we had.

When I collected Tina from the blackjack table, she had won a whole $36 and was having a blast, but we were on a pretty tight schedule and had about a thousand miles more to go. At least we were headed east once again on Interstate highway number 94, and it was a nice divided highway that we would be able to make pretty good time on. We had just passed through Minneapolis and St. Paul, Minnesota, and pulled into a service area for gas and something to eat. We had made pretty good time on this leg of the trip. There was hardly any traffic, and we cruised along at about seventy miles per hour. Back on the road again, Tina was feeling well rested and drove all the way to the outskirts of Chicago, then pulled into a rest stop. After a quick bathroom break, I got behind the wheel again. I drove straight through with a quick stop in Cleveland and then continued on to Buffalo, New York. Tina was very excited now that we were only about two hours away from her mom's house, and she took over the driving again. She took the exit off the interstate into Rochester and pulled over after the tollbooth and had me drive the rest of the way. She was too excited and nervous to drive anymore. Her mind was racing with questions, and she was worried how the kids would react when they saw her after such a long break. I followed her directions, and it was just a little before 11:00 p.m. Christmas eve when we pulled up in front of her mom's house. Tina started to cry and held me tightly.

"I'm scared," she said.

"Don't worry, honey," I told her. "Everything will be fine."

We got out of the car and went up to the door. Her sister answered and gave her a big hug, then Tina introduced her to me, and we went into the kitchen where her mom and step dad were playing cards. They hugged and cried and then introduced me to everyone.

"Where are the kids?" she asked.

"They are in bed," her sister said.

Tina went to the door and looked in on them. Odelia was still awake and shrieked when she saw her mother. Odelia's shriek of excitement woke up her brothers, and they couldn't believe their eyes. Bedlam ensued as they cried and hugged and kissed each other. Tina's daughter and oldest son seemed indifferent to my presence, but Kofi, her youngest son, came over and gave me a big hug and kiss. I left them to visit and went out and brought our things in from the car. Her sister took me upstairs to the room we were to stay in and then helped me bring in the kids Christmas gifts and put them under the tree. Tina emerged from the kid's room to check on me and could see I was exhausted.

"Honey," she said. "Why don't you go to bed? I'm going to stay up and visit for a while."

I said goodnight to everybody and went up to bed and gave Tina a chance to visit with her family. It was around 3:00 a.m. when I felt Tina slide into bed beside me. I gave her a reassuring squeeze and drifted back to sleep.

When I awoke, I got dressed quietly and went downstairs and put on my coat and shoes and went outside for a walk and some time alone to think. I felt like an outsider at Tina's mother's house. I was happy to see the joy on her face that being reunited with her kids and family brought her but was worried where I would fit into the whole scheme of things now. When we arrived, her family was polite and welcoming to me, aside from Odelia and Ekow, who had demonstrated to me that they weren't really happy about my being there. As I walked, I thought maybe I should go book myself into a hotel and leave Tina to visit with her family and see how things went. I was getting cold and walked back to her mom's house. When I entered, the house was bustling with noise and excitement. Everyone was awake, and the kids had begun to open their presents. Tina came over to me when I came in and asked me if everything was okay.

"Oh, yes," I replied. "I just needed to go out and stretch my legs after that long drive."

I didn't want to give Tina anything more to worry about. Her mom was really friendly this morning towards me. Whatever they talked about last night, I felt more comfortable and accepted by her mom and stepdad and sister now. Even Ekow had softened towards me a bit, but Odelia still looked at me with hatred in her eyes. After the kids and everyone had opened their gifts, Tina and I offered to go and get McDonald's breakfast for everyone.

That was what the kids wanted, so that's what they were getting; besides, the kitchen was in such turmoil. They had already begun preparing Christmas dinner the night before, and I don't think I have ever seen such a huge Christmas dinner being prepared before. There was ham and ribs and capon chicken, sweet potatoes, collared greens, baked beans, rice, peas, and mashed potatoes, carrots, and turnip. On the drive to McDonald's, Tina filled me in a bit on what they had talked about the night before. Frank had told the kids that she was dead.

"He told them what?' I said.

"Yes, he told them I was dead and that's why they moved to Toronto. I couldn't believe even he could be so cruel and thoughtless," she said.

When her mother found out about it when the kids came down, she was only then realizing how hard it had been for Tina to stay with him as long as she did, and she was beginning to understand why she had done what she did. Hearing all this was unbelievable. I felt like we were living a bad dream in a terrible soap opera. I was feeling so stressed out at hearing all this and really didn't know how to handle things or what to do next. When we got back into the car, Tina looked at me and could see I was troubled.

"What's wrong, baby?" she asked.

"I don't know," I replied. "Just everything is so overwhelming, it's like I just got a big shot of reality."

Tina looked at me with worry on her face. "You probably wish you never met me now don't you?"

"No, baby, never" I replied.

Then she said, "You realize I don't know what I would have done without you, David. You've been my rock through all this."

We embraced one another. I looked at Tina and told her I just wish things didn't have to be so complicated. As I started to pull away to drive back to her mother's house, I stopped the car and got out and went to the trunk. With all that had been going on, I had forgotten all about the package I had put in the trunk for Tina. I got back into the car and passed Tina the lavishly wrapped box. "I'm sorry," I said. "I forgot to give this to you earlier…it slipped my mind."

Tina unwrapped the box, stunned by the beautiful diamond tennis bracelet it contained. "I thought we said no gifts this year," she said.

"I know," I replied. "I just couldn't help myself."

Tina had me put it on her wrist and told me it was beautiful and that she really loved it and couldn't wait to show it off.

When we got back to the house with breakfast, the kids devoured their food and went back to playing with their gifts. Tina showed her mom and sister what I had given her for Christmas, and they commented that is was very nice and that I must love her a lot. Just then, Odelia walked into the room, having been eavesdropping on the conversation, and wanted to see her moms bracelet. She was not happy and demanded to know why she didn't get one. While her mom tried to explain things to her, she became very emotional and threw a huge temper tantrum. She accused her mother of not loving her and that she was more interested in travelling around the world with her new man than she was in being a mother to her kids. As I heard the words uttered from her mouth, I knew this wasn't a typical comment from a ten-year-old girl and figured she was just repeating conversations that she had heard in the house earlier in the week. I had just started to feel more at ease but with this latest wrangle, I felt really uncomfortable and excused myself and went out for another walk to give Tina more time to be alone with her family. As I strolled down the block, I felt bad for thinking it, but I wished I hadn't brought Tina here. I was worried that before we returned to Calgary, our relationship would suffer irreversible damage, and all my dreams would come to a crashing halt.

When I returned to the house, some family friends had stopped over, and Tina's mother asked me to sit with them and play cards while Tina and her sister continued cooking and preparing dinner. Her mom asked me if I would like a drink, and when I answered yes, she had Tina make it for me as well as one for herself. I hadn't bonded much with Tina's stepdad. He seemed like a nice man but was very quiet and basically sat and watched television or tried to follow the conversation and spent a lot of time just drifting off to sleep. I guess it was one of the side effects of his medication for Parkinson's or the disease itself. We played cards for a while, and after a few more drinks, I was relaxing more and began enjoying myself. As more family and friends arrived, I was introduced, then Tina's mother would get impatient and say that we should get on with things…she did love her card games. It must have been about three in the afternoon, and the cards were put away. It was time to eat. I thought we had big Christmas dinners in my family, but it was nothing like the feast we had in Rochester. By now, there must have been close to twenty people in the small house, the noise was overwhelming, everyone scattered about eating buffet style, and as some people ate and left, more kept arriving.

With dinner finished and most of the guests gone, Tina, her mother, the three kids, and I sat down and played a game of monopoly together. Her stepdad sat in the living room in his lazy boy chair, watching television, and her sister went upstairs to her room with one of her best friends who had come from out of town and visited with her. It was really nice sitting there with the kids and her mother spending some quality time together and watching her mom and Odelia squabble over the game of monopoly like two little kids. When the game was over, I helped Tina finish cleaning up the dishes from dinner, and the kids and her mom played cards together. I fixed myself another drink and went into the living room with her stepdad while Tina helped Kofi play cards with the rest of them.

Tina's stepdad had few words to say, but he looked at me and smiled and said, "They sure can make a hell of a racket, can't they?"

I nodded in agreement and sipped on my drink and watched the show that was on, keeping an ear on the noise in the kitchen. It wasn't very long, and I don't know if it was the long trip or the drink, but I was feeling really tired and went into the kitchen and said goodnight to everybody and made my way upstairs to go to sleep. I wasn't in bed very long when Tina came up and checked on me. She asked if I was all right.

"Yes, I'm fine, honey, don't worry about me. Just enjoy your time with your family."

Before she left, she looked at me and asked if there was anything she could do for me. I looked at her with a sheepish grin on my face, and before I said a word, Tina said to me, "Not in my mother's house." We both had a chuckle as she left to go back downstairs.

The next morning, I was the first up and got showered and dressed. As I was about to leave our room, Tina awoke and said she would like to take the kids shopping today if I didn't mind.

"Why would I mind?" I replied "Take them…it will be good for you to have some one-on-one time with them."

"Aren't you going to come with us?" she asked.

"Well, I will if you want me to, I just thought you'd like to spend some time with them alone."

"I do, but I think it would be nice for all of us to go."

"Okay," I said. "Why don't we take them for breakfast when they get up and then some shopping."

"Sounds good," Tina said, and I left to go downstairs.

Kofi was up watching television when I went downstairs he looked up and saw me and asked me to watch cartoons with him. I sat down on the couch next to him, and he snuggled up beside me. He was such a precious little boy; it was hard to believe he was only five years old.

When a commercial came, on he looked at me and said, "I remember you know."

"You remember what?" I asked.

"I remember you teaching me to swim and taking me to the park to fly a kite and eating pizza with you and mommy in the middle of the night and playing with the soccer ball in the basement."

I gave him a hug and kissed him on the forehead. He looked back up at me and told me he didn't care what Odelia told him, he still liked me. I asked him what Odelia had told him. He replied that it was because of me that his mommy wasn't with them and his daddy, then he said he missed his mommy, but he was glad his daddy couldn't hit her anymore 'cause it made him cry. I struggled to hold back the tears that were welling up in my eyes. No kid, let alone a little five-year-old boy, should have had to go through what he went through, and all I could think about was that we should pack those kids up and take them back to Calgary with us, even Odelia and her *miss thing* attitude. I told Kofi his mommy and me were going to take him and his brother and sister for breakfast and then shopping, so he should go wake up his sister and get himself dressed.

"Okay, David," he said as he crawled off the couch and went running out of the room to wake up his siblings.

Tina was dressed and came down the stairs and sat beside me. I told her about the conversation I had with Kofi and that we should just pack the kids up and take them with us back to Calgary. A look of horror swept over her face.

"My god," she said to me. "Do you know what he would do to my mother and sister and stepfather? We would have to go somewhere else besides Calgary."

"But you have custody. Don't forget that. The law is on your side."

"Don't you remember what a great help the law was before?" she said. "Besides, he wouldn't care what would happen to him. He would just make sure he hurt my family and me first before the police ever caught up with him."

I said, "You can't let him control you with fear and threats."

"Look, David, you don't have any idea what he is capable of and what he would do. You think I want to go and leave the kids here with him? I don't, but at least this way they're safe, and nobody will end up being hurt or killed. Honey, he is crazy, and his threats aren't just empty threats. I know he would carry through on them, so get any idea out of your head about taking the kids with us when we leave," she said.

We took the kids to breakfast at McDonald's again and spent the rest of the day going through the mall buying them clothes and toys. Odelia was great at laying on a guilt trip and getting what she wanted from her mother. The tension between Odelia and I kept building all day long. I knew she was only ten, but she was crafty and smart. I sensed her trying to drive a wedge between her mom and me and hated myself for feeling that way but couldn't help it. I was worried now more than ever that I was going to lose Tina long before we ever got back to Calgary. I suffered through a couple more days at Tina's moms house, and when Tina and I went to bed together for the first time in days, I talked with her and told her that we would have to leave early in the morning if we were going to get home in time to open the business up before New Year's, in case some of our clients needed some last-minute work done before the end of the year.

The truth of the matter was that we probably really didn't have to be home until New Year's day, but I was really starting to panic that Tina wouldn't want to come back with me. When Sunday morning came, Tina and I awoke about the same time. We discussed what we talked about the night before, and Tina agreed with me that we would have to get back on the road that day, but she begged me to wait until after supper to leave.

"Fine," I said, "but no later than six o'clock."

After we got up and were showered and dressed, Tina and her sister cooked breakfast. While they were doing that, I started to pick up our clothes and pack up our luggage. Tina called me to come down to breakfast, and I could feel the tension in the air. I quickly ate and announced that I was going out for a stroll. When I got back, things were worse. Tina and Odelia had a huge argument and yelling match, and Tina was trying to get Odelia to come up from the basement where she had gone and locked the door. I decided to go upstairs and get our bags and put them in the car. I knew it wasn't going to be easy for us to leave, no matter what day we decided to leave, and had dreaded this moment. When I went back inside, the fireworks were still going off, the kids were crying, and Tina's mom was yelling. I quickly told Tina I was going to drive to the coffee shop and read the paper and that when I got back, we should leave then rather than waiting until after supper.

"So take care of business and be ready to leave when I get back. Good luck," I told her as I slid out the door happy to escape the fracas that was going on inside.

I was a bundle of nerves at the coffee shop. I was really worried whether Tina would actually leave with me, and if she did, what about the kids? Would they hate her for going or me for taking their mom away from them? I was overwhelmed now and just wanted to get as far away from Rochester that night as possible. After many cups of coffee and a leisurely read of the paper, I knew it was time to go back and face the music. If Tina decided to stay there and be with the kids, I couldn't fault her for that. It would have been so simple to just take the kids with us, but even that didn't seem like an option anymore. When I arrived back at the house, there was still a lot of crying and arguing going on. I went in and said my goodbyes to everyone and thanked them for the hospitality. Kofi was the only one of Tina's kids to give me a hug and say goodbye, tears streaming down his cheek. I thought I was going to have a heart attack or stress attack or something. I just felt sick to my stomach and was having pains in my chest. I sat in the car for about twenty minutes and could hear the racket coming from the house, and Odelia begging her mother to leave me and stay with her. I couldn't take it anymore and went inside and talked with Tina upstairs. I asked her what she wanted to do and told her I would understand if she wanted me to leave without her.

"What are you saying?" she said to me. "You know how much I love you? Don't you want me anymore?"

"Of course I do. You know I love you more than anything else in the world, but I just can't go through this any longer." I looked at my watch and it was quarter to five, then I turned to Tina and told her I would make this easy on her.

"What do you mean?" she asked.

"Look, it's quarter to five. I'm going out to the car, and if you're sitting beside me by five o'clock, I'll know you want to come with me. If you're not in the car, no hard feelings. I still love you, but it just means it wasn't meant to be." I gave her a huge hug and kiss and told her I would always love her no matter what her decision, then turned and went down stairs and out to the car. I watched the digital clock in the car slowly count down closer and closer to five o'clock. With only two minutes to go, I started the car, and as I looked up towards the doorway, I saw Tina coming through the door with Odelia holding onto her arm begging her to stay. As Tina stepped outside, Odelia let go of her mother's arm.

Tina got into the car and looked at me and said, "Drive away, drive away now."

I put the car into drive and pulled away. Ekow and Kofi were looking out the living room window, and Odelia was standing at the door, still crying. Tina was now sobbing uncontrollably beside me. I felt like a piece of shit and didn't know what to do next. I drove several blocks away then pulled over and tried to console Tina.

"Just keep driving," she said to me. "Some day they will understand what I did. I only hope they don't hate me for it because I do love them so much."

With that, I put the car back in gear and headed for the connecting highway to the interstate.

Home Again

As we crested the hill, we could see the lights of Calgary in the distance. We were entering from the south end of the city. The drive had been a long, quiet trip with Tina and me barely speaking to each other. We had driven the whole way home through the northern U.S. states and had stopped for little besides gas and the odd bit to eat. For all I knew, Tina had only come back with me to get her things and leave to go back to Rochester. If this is what she wanted, I had decided I wouldn't try to step in her way. I had no kids of my own, so there wasn't any way I knew what she was feeling at this very moment. I figured it was God and fate that had brought us together, so it was up to God and fate to decide our destiny, and I would have to accept whatever it brought. We entered the parkade to our apartment, and I pulled into our parking spot and turned off the car and got out and took our luggage out of the trunk. Tina was still sitting quietly in the car. I gently rapped on her window, and she looked up at me and got out still not uttering a word. We got into the elevator and went up to our apartment. I placed our bags in our bedroom, and Tina went into the bathroom. I was in the living room when I saw her emerge out of the corner of my eye in her nightgown, and she went into the bedroom, a few minutes later I saw her night stand light go out. I went into the bathroom and freshened up a bit then went back into the living room and got undressed and covered up with a blanket that was on the couch and stared at the ceiling, wondering what was going to happen next.

I awoke to Tina tapping me on the shoulder. As I awoke and looked up at her, she asked me to come to bed.

"Are you sure you want me to?" I asked like a spoiled child who had been scolded.

"Of course, I do," she said.

With that, I got up and went into the bedroom with her. I kept my distance and lay on my side of the bed; Tina was over as far as possible on hers. Before too long I felt her snuggle in next to me and put her arm around me, and we drifted off to slip without uttering another word.

I slept quite late the next day, and when I got out of bed, Tina was already in the office getting some jobs finished up.

When I entered the office, she said, "Oh, good, you're up. These jobs need to be delivered right away. They are both rushes."

"Do I at least have time to shower and get dressed?" I asked, being somewhat sarcastic.

"Of course," Tina replied.

I hastily got shaved, showered, and dressed, then went into the office to see if Tina had the jobs ready for me to deliver. She had them bagged and ready to go. I picked them up and started for the door to the elevator when Tina called me back.

"What?" I asked as I poked my head back inside the office door.

"Where's my kiss?" she demanded.

I had almost always given her a kiss before I left in the mornings but hadn't thought it appropriate today. "Are you sure you want it?" I asked.

"Of course," she replied.

As I leaned in to give her a small kiss on the cheek, Tina grabbed me and pulled me into her lap and gave me a huge hot lingering wet kiss.

"What was that?" I asked. "A goodbye kiss?"

"What are you talking about?" Tina asked.

"I mean, I'm not stupid. Will you be here when I get back from these deliveries?"

Tina looked at me puzzled like she didn't have a clue what I was talking about. "We need to have a long talk when you get back," she said. "Now get those deliveries made and hurry back."

When I returned from dropping off the deliveries, Tina had a light lunch set on the table and asked me to join her so we could chat and clear the air. As I joined her at the table, she started by telling me that she didn't know what was going through my head but that she loved me more than ever. She said she had only been quiet on the trip home because she was trying to figure out what to do next about Frank and the situation with the kids and that it was hard for her to leave them at her mothers and return to Calgary without them.

I spoke up and said, "Didn't I tell you to bring them back with us?"

She looked at me and said, "You know that wouldn't have worked, and you know that wasn't what you really wanted to happen."

"Look, I know Odelia, and I don't get along, but we would work it out somehow."

"You're forgetting one other major problem."

"What's that?" I asked.

"Frank," she replied. "Can we really take a chance on what he may or may not do? What do you think he would have done to my mom and sister and stepdad if he showed up and the kids weren't there?"

"So, is that how you're going to live for the rest of your life? In fear of what he might do, so you do nothing."

"No," Tina replied. "But for now, no action is better until I figure out a way to get the kids away from him without involving my mom and sister and have somewhere safe to go where he can't find us."

"You sure are making me feel good. I see you have a lot of confidence in my ability to protect you and your family."

"Oh, baby," she said as she stroked her hand through my hair. "I know you have good intentions, but you really have no idea how crazy he is and what you would be up against. Just leave it for now. God will show me the right path to take when it is time."

We then embraced one another and held each other for what seemed like an eternity, softly whispering to each other how much we meant to each other and how nothing would ever separate us from being together forever.

Our tender moment was shattered by the sound of the fax machine spitting out reams of paper in the office. We let go of each other and went into the office to check the fax machine.

I looked at Tina and told her, "I guess our customers heard were home."

There were plenty of small jobs waiting to be done for most of our customers, last minute jobs for New Year's Eve. I hadn't given a second thought about what we were going to do for New Year's Eve, and it was the next night. While Tina was setting the jobs, I took a quick scan through the paper to see what was happening around town New Year's Eve. After the long trip and ensuing chaos, I was happy to just go for a nice dinner and maybe stay in a fancy hotel room with a Jacuzzi and then order breakfast in bed on New Year's Day. I called a couple of ads out of the paper and got lucky on my second call. The Bonaventure still had tickets for dinner and dancing, so I booked it, then called the front desk of the Hospitality Inn where the Bonaventure Restaurant was located and tried to arrange for a two-story

Jacuzzi honeymoon suite that my brother and his wife had booked on their wedding evening. No luck. It was booked solid. However, they had a jetted tub in a regular room available for one night only.

"That's fine," I said. "I only wanted it for one night anyway. How much is it?"

"Two hundred and twenty five dollars."

"That's fine," I said and gave him my credit card number to confirm the reservation. With the confirmation number tucked away in my wallet, I went into the typesetting room where Tina had some work for me to proof read. When I finished proofreading, I asked Tina what she wanted to do for New Years Eve.

"Oh," she replied. "I don't really care. After all that driving, I'd be content to stay home and have a pizza and watch a movie."

"Oh," I replied. "I made dinner reservations at the Bonaventure Room for tomorrow at eight followed by a little dancing, and I rented a room so we don't have to worry about driving home."

"That actually sounds nice, honey," she said as she leaned over and gave me a kiss on the forehead.

There was a couple of rush jobs that had to be delivered right away, so I took them and left, hoping to get back soon. I didn't want to get caught in the holiday traffic. The deliveries took longer than I had planned; everyone was offering a belated Christmas drink and an early New Year's Eve drink, so I was hospitable and drank them. I finally got back, and Tina asked what took so long.

I replied, "Oh traffic and stuff you know."

"Yeah, I know," she said with a grin on her face.

I guess she could smell the rum. I finished proofing the last of the jobs she had typeset, and while she made corrections, I got caught up on my year-end billing. We were finally finished for the night. As we looked outside, a light snow was starting to fall.

"Are you hungry?" Tina asked.

"A little" I replied.

"Well, if you're not that hungry, why don't we go down to the pool for a quick swim and then have a nice hot sauna?"

"Hey, that sounds good," I replied.

We both put on our bathing suits and robes and went down to the third floor to gain access to the pool. There was nobody else in the pool area, so we turned the sauna on before we went into the pool so it would be nice and warm when we finished our swim. As we swam and canoodled, Tina told me she had called her mom to say that we had arrived home safe and sound.

"How did that go?" I asked.

"Fine" she replied. "She couldn't talk too long. She said Frank had come down and was with the kids. He had planned to stay for New Year's Eve and then take the kids back to Toronto on New Year's day."

I didn't ask Tina if he knew we had been there, and I really didn't want to know too much. I had enough stress to last a lifetime. We swam for a while and did a few laps then showered off in the change room and entered the sauna, where the hot dry heat felt nice and relaxing. After about ten minutes in the sauna, we both had enough and went upstairs and ordered a pizza from downstairs for supper. We hadn't gone for any groceries since we came home so the cupboards were pretty bare. I told Tina I would pick up a few groceries in the morning. After the pizza arrived, and we had finished eating, we decided to go to bed. It was early, only seven o'clock, but we were both pretty exhausted. It didn't take long, and we were both in a deep slumber.

We finished another day of work and both got dressed for dinner: Tina in a very stylish khaki matching skirt and jacket and a cream-coloured silk blouse, and me in a blue suit with a navy blue shirt and tie. Then we packed an overnight bag and went downstairs to the car in the parkade. We checked in at the front desk and got our room key and went up to the second floor to our room. I couldn't help but notice how sexy Tina's legs were as she climbed the stairs ahead of me. It had been about a week since we had made love and with everything that had happened, I had lost my desire to even try. But watching her every move in that outfit and seeing her beautiful legs gracefully ascend the staircase stirred all the feelings back inside me. We entered our room, and all I could think about now was how bad I wanted to be inside of Tina. Tina looked around the room and was quite happy with it. Then she disappeared into the bathroom and called me in a couple minutes later. To my surprise, the bathroom was the nicest thing about the room. It had a large, double vanity and a separate shower, and in one corner a very large, square jetted tub. My mind wandered for a minute, and I envisioned Tina lying in a huge wall of bubbles with a glass of champagne in her hand and candles gently illuminating her curled locks of hair that she was wearing up that evening, and one of her legs drawn to her chest and folded to the surface through the glistening bubbles covering her sexy…

"Are you ready to go to dinner?" she said, bringing me out of my fantasy moment.

"Oh, ah, yeah, sure. Let's go," I replied still feeling aroused from my momentary mind wander.

We left our suite and went down the staircase that overlooked the Bonaventure Room and could see through the glass wall that they had it decorated with black and white balloons and streamers and party favours on each table. The maitre d' seated us at our table and within minutes our waiter brought us each a glass of champagne that was part of the set menu for the evening.

Tina was sitting next to me and gave my leg a squeeze then she said, "Thanks, honey. I think we really needed this to get back on track."

I leaned in and gently kissed her neck and cheek, and then her lips. Her hand was still under the table, and she worked her way up my leg and was now teasing my erect member that was straining to be released from the confines of my blue dress pants; the poor guy was feeling the strain of being closed up in such tight quarters. I wanted Tina so bad at that moment, I thought I was going to explode into my trousers. I continued working my tongue and lips around her neck and gently kissed her lips then gave a light bite on her lower lip. I felt her tremble and let out a quiet moan. *My god, there was no way we were going to make it through dinner.*

I whispered into her ear, "Do you want to go back to the room and eat later?"

"O god, yes," she uttered. With that, we stood up, Tina in front of me to help conceal the excitement I was showing. I threw a twenty dollar bill on the table to cover the champagne that had arrived, and we exited the restaurant telling the maitre d' that we had forgot something and would be back later, then raced like school kids up the staircase to our room.

As we burst into our room, Tina wildly kicked her high heeled shoes off, and I quickly undid my shoes and tossed my suit jacket onto a chair. I grabbed Tina back into my grasp and passionately kissed her while I unbuttoned her skirt and slid the zipper down, allowing her skirt to fall freely to the floor. Tina reached down and released my belt buckle, then unbuttoned my trousers and eased them down my legs. I quickly removed her khaki jacket as I slowly steered her towards our king-size bed. Her knees buckled when she bumped the edge of the mattress, and she fell back on to the down-filled comforter. I struggled to remove her pantyhose while she undid the buttons to her blouse, then I collapsed onto her, fitting snugly between her thighs, our hot tongues darted wildly into each other's waiting mouths. Tina flipped me over onto my back and straddled me, grinding her warmness on top of me while she proceeded to unbutton my shirt. I reached up and slid her blouse off her shoulders, then proceeded to unhook her bra and release her warm, plump bosom's from their constraints. I flipped her over onto her back and was back on top, slipping my shirt off my back with her help, and then nestled back between her thighs, grinding my hard rod against her moistened white cotton panties, feverishly ravishing her neck with my hot, steamy tongue. She reached my waistband and roughly pulled my shorts down, releasing my member that was already glistening with a light coating of love fluids. I dropped down on her and quickly moved my tongue from her neck, to her warm bosom, then her navel, and finally, teased her with my mouth as my teeth pulled at her sweet-smelling cotton panties. I could wait no longer and reached up and removed them with a quick wild pull of my hand, my hand briefly touching her warm, quivering lips. Before I could stop, I thrust myself deep inside her, and we pounded into each other with uncontrollable desire. Tina's moans of ecstasy were driving me into her more wildly and at a fevered pace. I felt myself release inside of her.

"Don't stop," she begged as I continued thrusting my softening member into her.

Seconds passed, and Tina screamed out in total satisfaction as her body writhed and trembled in one massive explosion. I collapsed on top of her, and she dug her fingernails into my back and held me tight inside of her as I continued to grind my now-lifeless organ against her. Finally, she released her death grip, and I rolled over onto my side, my arms firmly wrapped around Tina, and we gazed into each other's eyes with a total look of awe and satisfaction.

Tina was the first to break the silence when she mumbled, "Honey, I'm confused."

"What are you confused about?" I asked.

"Well," she said. "I don't know whether I want to eat first or have a nice long soak in the jetted tub."

"Tell you what," I said, "room service is probably really busy, so why don't you go and draw yourself a bath, and while your doing that, I'll order us up something to eat."

Tina grabbed her make up bag and disappeared into the bathroom. I grabbed the room service menu and perused it for a few minutes, then decided to order us a mixture of items: a fruit and cheese platter, some wings, a plate of veggies and dip, and a bottle of champagne. When I called it into room service, he advised me that they also had chocolate dipped strawberries for dessert.

"That's fine," I said. "I'll take six of those as well. Ah, how long will that be?" I asked, anticipating it to be about an hour, but I was wrong.

"About twenty minutes," he said.

"That's great," I responded and said thank you and hung up the phone.

I went to the bathroom and knocked. Tina told me to come in. The tub was almost full, and she had placed lit candles around it and on the bathroom vanity, and I could smell the scent of lilacs in the room. She had used lilac bubble bath. "Are you going to join me?" she inquired.

"Well, that sounds great," I replied, "but I called room service, and they said it would only be twenty minutes."

"Well, in that case, why don't we have a quick shower and use the tub after we eat?"

"Sounds good." I put my hand into the tub to feel the water. It was quite warm, but I drained out some of the water and refilled it with scalding hot water, so it would probably be just right by the time we ate. We slipped into the shower and washed each other playfully, then got out and towelled off and slipped on the thick white terrycloth robes hanging on the bathroom door. Tina was still primping a bit when I heard a knock at the door and went to let in the room service waiter. The presentation looked incredible, and everything was presented on crystal and silver serving dishes, and the champagne sitting in a silver-serving bucket with a white linen napkin wrapped around the neck of the bottle.

"Would you like me to open the champagne for you, sir?"

"No, that's fine," I replied and signed the bill and slipped him a ten dollar bill for a tip.

"Goodnight, sir," he said.

"Goodnight," I replied, and he turned and left.

I took the "do not disturb" sign off the doorknob and placed it on the outside of the door then chained and locked the door. I knew we were in for the night. When I turned around, Tina was standing there in her warm robe with her wet hair hanging over the collar and just enough of her leg was revealed between the slit in the robe to get my heart pumping wildly again. Tina slinked onto the bed, and I popped the champagne and passed her a chilled glassful.

"A toast," I said, "to continued happiness and a stress-free, turmoil-free New Year and to the greatest woman and friend and lover a man could ever have the joy to know."

"I'll agree with that," Tina said as we clinked our glasses and drank to what we both hoped would be a happier year to come.

We sat at the table and devoured our dinner with the exception of the strawberries, which Tina thought we should save for later. After both feeling satisfied from our feast, we decided to go have a nice romantic sit in the tub and let the jets work their wonders.

"Oh my god!" Tina exclaimed as she opened the bathroom door.

"What?" I said as I peered past her and saw what had caused the excitement in her voice.

There were bubbles from the floor to the ceiling with a tunnel leading to the tub and a dim light at the end. Tina had turned on the jets to the tub when she left the bathroom so we would have lots of bubbles and lots of bubbles are what we had. We made our way through the tunnel of bubbles to the tub and entered into the cavern of bubbles that was created over the tub. The candles had created tunnels and caverns in the bubbles, and it was the neatest and most romantic setting we could have ever hoped for. It was going to be a huge mess when the bubbles collapsed, but for now, we sat in the tub, resting our heads on the sponge pillows at each end of the tub and gently massaging each other's feet and calves. As we sat there relaxing and peering through the maze of bubbles, we could hear the candles sizzle each time some of the bubbles got close to the flames. The heat of the tub water quickly drained every last ounce of energy from our bodies and turned us into mounds of jellied mush. I heard the timer ding as it automatically shut off the tub and reached down and popped the tub stopper to allow the tub water to drain out. We forced ourselves to get out of the tub and grabbed the bubble-laden towels off the rack and towelled off out in our room.

"What do we do about the bathroom?" Tina asked.

"For now, nothing," I replied. "By morning, it shouldn't be too hard to clean up."

We made our way to the bed, both exhausted, and slipped beneath the cool cotton sheets. It was pure heaven as we cuddled up to each other and drifted off into the most peaceful slumber. When morning came, I was the first to enter the bathroom, needing desperately to pee. I had forgotten about the bubbles and slipped across the floor and banged my knee into the tub.

"Aw, fuck, that hurt!" I said out loud as I made my way over to the toilet and wiped it off with a hand towel so I could sit on it and do my business.

As I sat there, I surveyed the room and luckily it had a large floor drain in the centre of the room so when I completed my task at hand, I took the empty waste paper basket and began filling it with water and sloshing it around cleaning the soapy mixture off the ceramic floor and sopping up the water with the towels. The tub was totally disgusting; the candles had created a black, sooty mixture with bubbles, and I decided the maid could handle that mess. With the wet towels spread across the floor to keep me from slipping all over the place I made my way back to the bed. Tina looked at me sheepishly.

"What's the grin for?" I asked.

"Well," she said, "I have been holding a pee in for a good thirty minutes, hoping you'd go first and clean it up a bit in there. I peeked in earlier and came back to bed hoping you'd wake up soon. That's why I kept bumping against you."

"You're evil," I said to her as she hopped out of bed and ran to the bathroom, no longer able to hold it in.

When she returned, we lay there momentarily then both erupted in uncontrollable laughter.

I looked over on the night stand and poured the last of the flat champagne into our champagne flutes and got up and took a can of orange juice out of the mini-bar and poured that into the flutes as well and then grabbed the chocolate dipped strawberries and climbed back into bed. Tina grabbed a berry first and proceeded to feed it to me. Oh my god, it was good. Then I returned the favour, made a toast to the New Year, and proceeded to eat another berry. My mouth turned and puckered.

"What's wrong?" Tina asked.

I managed to mutter out that chocolate and orange juice does not go; she laughed at me. Before long, we were canoodling together, and I found myself once again deep inside her, feeling all her warmth and splendour and then we drifted back into a light sleep, both drained of the small amount of energy we had managed to reacquire since the night before. Awakened by the noise and movement in the hallway, I looked at the clock radio beside the bed and realized we had less than an hour before check out. We sprang out of bed and hurriedly rinsed off in the shower and got dressed. We quickly packed our belongings, and remembering the mess in the bathroom, I left the maid a twenty-dollar tip as we headed down to the front desk to checkout.

When we got home the answering machine was blinking, and I played the messages from a couple of friends, all drunken up, wishing us a happy new year and a call from my parents inviting us to dinner.

"Want to go?" I asked Tina.

"Sure," she replied.

I called my parents and accepted the invitation. "What time?" I asked.

"Well, we are going to eat at five, but you guys can come over anytime, and we can play cards."

"Fine," I said. "We'll be over in about an hour to an hour and a half. Bye."

We arrived home around eleven o'clock, having had a pleasant afternoon at my parents', playing cards and eating a delicious ham dinner. I was quite relieved to find out when we got there that my brother Brad and his wife, Jane, weren't coming, as they had accepted an invitation at Jane's parents' house. Brad and I still had a little tension over our business dealings. Tina and I went to bed and watched television until we fell asleep.

We spent the rest of the weekend visiting friends and family and were both looking forward to getting back to normal on Monday morning. Tina had noticed in the paper that they were looking for a temporary typesetter to help with their overload created by the Winter Olympic games being held in Calgary and thought she might apply. The pay was good and the hours would allow her to keep up with our own company demands, but as she pointed out, things were a bit slow right now anyway.

"Hey, whatever you think. I'll support you 100 percent," I said.

I got up as usual on Monday and went about my normal routine. When I got back at around noon, Tina was excited. She had called about the job at the paper, and they wanted her to come in that afternoon for an interview and demo.

"Hey, way to go babe."

"You haven't heard the best part yet."

"What's that?"

"Well, they are paying $28 per hour, and the hours are from noon to 8:00 p.m., with the chance for overtime at double time."

"Well, I can see why you're excited. Good luck. I know you will knock them dead."

Tina took the afternoon deliveries and went to her interview while I stayed at home and did some work in the office. I couldn't help thinking how great it would be if she got the job. Between Hawaii and the trip to Rochester, we had spent a lot of cash and had little coming in when we were away. I was doing the math in my head. Twenty-eight dollars an hour times at least forty hours per week by ten weeks...that was over $11,000, not to mention any overtime she might get on top of what we could make with our business.

Tina called me, all excited. "Hey guess what?"

"What?" I asked.

"I got the job, but they want me to start now. They are so far behind that they're desperate."

"Well, go ahead. Not much going on here, so good luck and make the big bucks, babe."

I decided to try to be a little more helpful and set some of the simple stuff I had waiting for her to do when she got home. Tina had been trying to get me more involved, but I wasn't having much luck before, but now, I was determined. As it got later and later, I wondered how Tina was making out and when she would be home. Eight thirty came and still no sign of her. By ten, I was really starting to get concerned. The phone rang and it was Tina.

"Hi," she said. "Sorry I didn't get a chance to call you before this, but they left me with a pile of work and said I shouldn't leave until it was all finished. It's going a little slower than I thought, and there is nobody here who can answer my questions, so I have to teach myself as I go."

"Well, just do your best, honey; I'll see you when you get home."

It was just after midnight when I went to bed and still no Tina. I watched television, trying to stay awake till she got home. It was quarter to one when I heard her keys in the door. I got out of bed and met her when she came in. She was so excited.

"Oh, honey, you don't know how nice it is to work on such modern equipment and the things you can do." She went on to tell me a lot of technical crap, and I tried to feign interest, but I was tired and finally told her I was going to bed. She said she would be in, in a couple of minutes. When she came in she smiled and kissed me. "Thank you, honey," she said.

"For what?" I asked.

"For trying to typeset those jobs in the office. It means so much to me that you tried."

I felt like such a heel. I wish I could have been more excited about all the technical jargon she was spewing earlier, but I really didn't know a lot about it. She slipped into bed, and we both fell asleep quite quickly.

The next ten weeks were very hectic. I had to admire Tina's stamina. She kept on top of our work, plus put in close to fifty-two hours per week at the paper, including Saturdays and sometimes Sundays. I was both happy and sad to see it come to an end. Our time together and sex life suffered for that ten weeks, but Tina really amazed me at what a hard worker she was and how, when she set her mind to something, nothing could stop her, plus she really helped our financial situation. We were sitting pretty well now. I had picked up all the household chores: cooking, cleaning, shopping, and laundry, and kept the business going while Tina worked her fingers to the bone.

I figured she really deserved something special, so I booked us a night in the Crossroads Hotel Polynesian Suite. We had a night of total pampering room service; a nice, round, deep bamboo hot tub; and one of the wildest nights of lovemaking we ever had. I even arranged for a dual massage Sunday morning in our room followed by a champagne brunch.

Inspired by Tina's ambition, I started looking for an evening job so I could finish paying for the ring that I had put on lay-away months earlier. As luck would have it, I was picking up a pizza across the street and noticed they were looking for delivery drivers. I had done it before when I was in high school and made pretty good money doing it, so I figured, why not? It wouldn't interfere with my day job. We had goals to build the business even bigger and that wasn't going to happen working with the antiquated equipment we had and working from home, so Tina was agreeable to me doing it a few nights a week. Within six weeks, I had made enough to pay off the ring and bank a tidy sum away as well, without Tina even noticing the amount I had held back to pay the ring off.

It was Saturday morning, April 23, and Tina was sleeping like an angel. We had a nice, quiet Friday evening at home and enjoyed a movie and a couple of bottles of wine. Tina was getting some well-deserved extra rest, and the moment just seemed right. I got dressed and slipped out quietly and picked up the engagement ring that the jeweller was still holding for me. When I got home, Tina was still sleeping, so I placed the gold-wrapped ring box on her pillow beside her then opened the blinds to our bedroom flooding the room with sunlight. Tina opened her eyes and immediately noticed the ring box glistening in the sunlight.

"What's this?" she asked.

"Oh just a little something for someone who means the world to me and who I can't live without."

As Tina began to unwrap the box, I knelt at the side of the bed. When she opened it, I popped the question. Without a seconds hesitation, her answer was a profound YES, then she had me slip the ring onto her finger. She surprised me when she jumped up onto the bed and did a creative little dance and shouted out, "I'm getting married," as tears welled up in her eyes. After several minutes, she lay back down, and I lay beside her. She kept reaching over and hugging me and then would outstretch her hand allowing the sunlight to catch the stone and project a rainbow of light around the room. I think part of the attraction to Tina was that life was never dull. We had really exciting and happy highs, and when things were bad, they were real bad, but we always managed to stick it out together and work through whatever problems and obstacles arose. We were both dreamers, but that was what kept the fire and spark in our relationship.

Tina hopped out of bed and returned within minutes with a calendar in tow. She looked over at me and said, "Have you thought about a date?"

"No," I replied, "I haven't."

We looked through the calendar and ruled out up to September. We talked a bit about where to have the wedding, Calgary or Rochester, then considered Las Vegas. We talked about a large wedding or small wedding. Tina said she had already had the big, formal wedding, so it didn't matter to her if we had a small, intimate ceremony but there was one thing she really wanted.

"What's that?" I asked.

"I would like my Aunt Eula to be there. She wasn't at my first wedding, and I really felt bad about that," she said.

"I have no problem with that." I liked her Aunt Eula, and she liked me, and she made me laugh with her wit and sense of humour.

Then we started thinking about how our parents would react to the news and the kids and things suddenly started to feel a little more complicated.

"Well, honey, you know we just got engaged. We don't have to set a date this minute. We can take our time and figure out the best time and where later. For now, let's just enjoy the moment, and I'm sure the right date and place will come to us."

"You're right," she said as she hugged me again and again.

Tina was too excited to hold off any longer and wanted to phone her mom and tell her the good news. When she came back into the room, I could tell by the look on her face that she probably didn't get an overwhelming warm response from her mom.

"Well?" I said wanting her to tell me how it went.

Tina said her mom said it was her life, and she hoped she knew what she is doing this time, and that they already paid for one wedding.

"Aw, honey, don't worry...they will warm up to the idea in time. Well, I guess it's my turn to call my folks."

"Oh, that reminds me," Tina said.

"What?" I asked.

"Your mom called while I was on the phone, and she asked if we wanted to go to their place for lunch and play some cards. I told your mom I was on the phone long distance and would have you call her when I was finished."

"Well, do you want to go?"

"Sure," Tina replied. "Go call your mom, and I'll get in the shower and get dressed."

Tina came out into the living room where I was reading the paper. "Did you call your mom?"

"Yes, I did, and they said come over anytime."

"What about our news?" she asked. "What did they say?"

"Oh, I didn't tell them. I thought we would just see if they noticed your ring when we are over there."

"Coward," Tina remarked.

I was shocked to pull up in front of my parents house and see a for sale sign on the front lawn. *What's that all about?* I wondered. I knew they had talked about wanting to buy a bigger place, but I didn't think they ever would. I knew my mom wanted to move, but my dad hadn't seemed too keen. When we went in, I asked about the sign.

"Oh," my mom said with a grin on her face. "We bought a new house."

"Yeah, right," I said.

"No, really, we did," she said.

I looked at my dad in disbelief, and my mom pulled out the plans for a nice executive-style home in Riverbend, then she said, "That's why we called you to come over. We thought we'd have lunch then take you over to see the show home."

Tina and I told them congratulations and asked when they were moving.

"First week in August," mom replied.

After lunch, we drove to Riverbend with them, and they took us to the show home. It was really a nice place; they told us their house was pretty much the same, only with a reverse layout, from the show home they took us to their new lot. To my surprise, they were building only a couple of blocks down the street and around the bend from where my brother and his wife lived.

"Hey, you will be real handy to baby sit when Brad and Jane have the baby."

My mom replied, "We don't baby sit."

"Yeah, right," I said. "We'll see."

We drove back to my mom and dad's house and played cards for a while when my mom finally spoke up and said, "It looks like you two have some news as well."

"What do you mean?" I asked.

"Well, that's quite the rock on your finger, Tina," mom said.

Tina smiled, and we told them our news. My mom and dad congratulated us and asked when the big day was.

"We haven't set a date yet," I replied.

On the drive home, I asked Tina what she was talking to my mom about in the kitchen.

"I just asked her how she felt about us getting married."

"What did she say?"

Tina told me my mom said she had apprehensions when we first started seeing each other, but over time, she could see how happy we were together, and so it really didn't matter how they felt as long as I was happy with what I was doing. They would welcome my choice for a wife into the family with open arms.

The next two weeks went by rather quickly, business was picking up, and I was out really pushing to build up our clientele. Things were going pretty good. My mom called me on the May 5 to tell me my brother and his wife had their baby the day before.

"What did they have?" I asked.

"A little girl, so that makes you Uncle David now," she said.

"Well, tell them congratulations from me."

"Why don't you call them and tell them yourself?" Mom suggested, knowing full well that my brother and I hadn't spoken in a while after the break up of the business.

Time was going quickly, and my mom was hoping we would set a date soon. She said we could have the wedding at their new house if we wanted and started giving us lots of suggestions of what and how we could do things. We could have it at Carburn Park in Riverbend, and they would host a small reception at the house. I know she was being nice and trying to be helpful, but it just made me remember how things went at my brother's wedding. My mom's feelings got hurt when she felt they were making all their wedding plans and included Jane's parents, and she felt left out of the process. Then, we started to experience grief from Tina's mom that we would have to have the wedding in Rochester because they, her parents, were both in poor health and couldn't travel to Calgary. We finally decided on a month. December was a good time from a business point of view because things were slower, so we decided on December, and from there, we agreed on December 10 to coincide with our trip to Hawaii a year earlier. We had a date, and all we had to decide was where. We had begun looking at travel brochures now for a warm spot to honeymoon, and I remembered how excited Tina had been in Hawaii and how things reminded her of Jamaica, plus the fact she had never been back since she was 17. Why hadn't we thought of it before? It was the perfect choice: Jamaica. Tina was so excited at the prospect of going home to get married and the fact that her older sister Claudette in Kingston and her Aunt Eula in Jericho would be able to attend. They had both missed her first wedding. Now that we had a date and destination, we looked through the travel magazines all weekend and finally decided on Sandals in Montego Bay. We would fly in a week before the tenth and stay at Sandals Negril, which was close to Aunt Eula's home, and then spend the second week in Montego Bay at Sandals Royal. They had a wedding package, which would simplify the whole process.

Things were going great. The wedding plans were proceeding, and now with a date and venue decided, my parents wanted to throw us a small engagement party—nothing fancy—just a few friends and relatives. It was Labour Day weekend, and my parents were now settled nicely into the new house and had about twenty people over to celebrate our engagement. My brother and his wife showed up with their baby girl, my niece, Susan, who I hadn't laid eyes on yet. It was almost nine months since my brother and I had seen each other, and it took the better part of the day, but we were soon conversing and had buried the hatchet, thanks to little Susan. By the time we left, my brother had offered to print us our wedding invitations and napkins and matches as their wedding gift to us, and we resumed doing his typesetting.

We sent out the invitations as soon as we got them. With the wedding being so far away, we didn't really expect many, if anybody to come, but we wanted to send the invitations as a way to announce our upcoming marriage. To our surprise, my parents and my dad's sister, Shirley, and her husband, Ivan, from New Brunswick were coming, as well as my mom's brother, Reg, and his wife, Alma, from British Columbia with my cousin Wade, their son. Of course, Tina's sister from Kingston, Claudette, and Aunt Eula who was overjoyed. Tina's family from New York was unable to make it for a variety of different reasons, which we both understood, so we arranged to spend five days there on the way home. We had to fly from Calgary to Toronto to catch the charter from Toronto to Montego Bay, so it was easy to arrange the side trip on the way back, and everyone was happy this way.

We worked hard the next two months, saving every penny we could, cutting back on eating out and ordering in, and by the end of November, we were ready to go. Tina had arranged for Julie to look after things while we were gone, and she was happy to earn the extra money just before Christmas but would only work for us up to a week before Christmas, which is why we could only stay at Tina's parents until the 18th on the way back. We were busting with excitement when the November 30 finally arrived. Our white limousine arrived early that morning to pick us up and whisked us to the airport. We had both been having a hard time sleeping the week before. I don't know if it was the excitement of the wedding or the fact that Tina had cut me off and said not until our wedding night would we resume intimate relations. We arrived mid-morning in Toronto and were booked into the Sheraton Airport Hotel overnight in order to catch our early morning flight to Jamaica on the first of December. Tina had also hoped to go to the kid's school and see them. The kids were shocked when Tina showed up and had them pulled from class. They were so excited to see her, and they already knew about the wedding from their grandma when they went there for Thanksgiving.

We had a great afternoon and took them to the mall and played pool and pinball with them and then took them out to an all-you-can-eat Chinese restaurant. Tina was a bit concerned about Frank finding out, but Ekow and Kofi had after school activities, so they weren't expected home until after five anyway, and Odelia and her father were constantly fighting, so she just did as she pleased anyway. It was sad when the time came to drop the kids off around the corner from their home, but they all seemed to be handling it fine. Tina and I had sat there in the car for a few minutes when she said drive by the house. I want to get another look at the kids and make sure they are okay.

As we neared the house, Kofi came running out and said, "Stop! Dad isn't home. He left a message that he would be late."

I parked a couple of houses ahead of Frank's and Tina went inside with the kids to see their rooms, and they had lots of things they wanted to show her. It had been about thirty or forty minutes, and I was getting nervous about Frank showing up, but Tina appeared, and after another tearful farewell, we pulled away. Tina had me circle the block again. She was so excited.

"They still love me," she cried.

We pulled in behind a van that blocked our rental car and yet still enabled Tina to watch the house and the back driveway. Maybe twenty minutes passed, and Frank pulled into the back driveway in an old dark brown van. I sensed fear in Tina just at the sight of him. She had me sit there a little while longer, and we shivered because Tina insisted on keeping the car window down hoping to be able to hear if there was any trouble in the household. Before long we saw, Frank and Kofi get in the van and pull away. We pulled out and drove to the front of the house, and Odelia came out and said everything was fine and that her dad had taken Kofi to the corner store to get some scotch tape for his school project. Tina gave Odelia another quick hug, and we left to go back to the hotel.

Neither of us could sleep that night. We just laid beside each other and talked and talked. Tina was so happy to have seen the kids and felt that things were all going to work out in time. I was nervous about the wedding but still very excited and also anxious to escape the cold and spend a couple weeks in paradise. We both looked over to the clock—3:00 a.m.

"Well, I should cancel our 5:00 a.m. wake up call," I joked.

We had a 7:00 a.m. flight and were supposed to be at the terminal an hour an a half ahead of our flight. We resumed talking, and Tina was telling me more about where she grew up and the things she wanted to show me. There were people she couldn't wait to see when we got to Jamaica. It gave me so much pleasure to see the excitement and joy this trip was bringing her, and we hadn't even left Canada yet. The phone rang and startled us both. I guess we had finally drifted asleep but probably for less than an hour. We sprang out of bed after hearing the wake up call, and both had a quick shower and got dressed in our Caribbean-wear shorts and light shirts.

We didn't have to go outside to get to the airport, as the hotel had a covered walkway connecting to terminal three at Pearson International so off we went. After checking our bags and clearing through security, we looked for somewhere to get a bite to eat, and Tina wanted to phone her mom before we left. Her mom had asked her to, and she promised she would. When she got off the phone, she was still smiling, her mom had just told her to make her proud and say hi to the family. She wished her all the best and told her they were looking forward to seeing her and her new husband on the way back. Then she leaned in and kissed me on the cheek and told me that was from her mom.

Jamaica

We landed in Montego Bay just before noon. Tina had taken the window seat, anxious to see her home country and was a bit disappointed at what she saw. Hurricane Gilbert had hit the island back in September and had been quite devastating, but the hotel assured us they were repaired and ready for guests. We exited the aircraft and walked down the stairway to the runway and walked across the tarmac to the airport terminal. The humidity and heat felt great, and I was just enjoying the warmth. Tina was pointing and explaining what this tree was and that plant. The terminal was hot and sticky and not air conditioned, and I couldn't wait to clear customs and get back outside where the cool, Caribbean breeze made the humidity and heat so much more enjoyable. Tina was wildly chatting away with the customs officer, telling him how she had left over sixteen years ago and this was her first trip back. She discovered through their conversation that he had grown up in a small town called Lucea not far from where Aunt Eula lived, and he told her how the high school had been damaged by the hurricane, and so on and on they went. I had my first lesson in Jamaica time right there and then, when "every-ting was no problem, man." Nothing is ever done in a rush, people just took their time.

We found our tour operator and loaded into the bus. We had, what I thought, would be a half hour ride to our hotel in Negril, but boy, was I wrong. The narrow road winded and twisted as it followed the coastline, and the road was crowded with people, people walking everywhere. The whole bus would ooh and aah together as we passed people, and we were sure the bus must have hit this one or that one, as it seemed like only inches separated the people that were walking along the side of the road from the bus. The bus ride got better and better. Tina had wanted to sit up front so we could look out the front window and she could talk to the driver and ask him things along the way.

I mentioned to Tina I was thirsty, and our driver, Jackson, told me to open the lid on the cooler that was at the front of the bus and told me to, "Have a Red Stripe, mon." He asked me if I would pass them back to the other tourists.

"No problem, mon," I replied.

I kept passing the beer back to everybody on the bus, and it wasn't too long before the whole bus had picked up their Jamaican accent and the local mantra, "no problem, mon." Tina excitedly continued to play tour guide to me along the way and pointed out the different posh and famous resorts, and what I thought were oil refinery holding tanks turned out to be molasses tanks for loading onto cargo ships. It was great having my own personal interpreter and tour guide. The bus slowed to make a hairpin turn and cross a tiny little bridge.

Jackson said to Tina, "You must know where you are now, mon."

Tina hesitated.

"Right back at that big mango tree is where you turn to go up to Jericho where you said you grew up" he said.

She looked back and said, "It all looks so different. That means were coming into Lucea." She was right. Tina pointed to a large building that sat on a cliff overlooking the sea. "That's my old high school," she said with delight.

I could see workmen on the roof replacing it with corrugated tin and some debris still scattered about.

Jackson commented, "Gilbert done did all that, mon."

The combination of the beer, the lack of sleep, and the twisting road was starting to make me feel nauseated. The bus slowed down and stopped at a general store in a place called Green Island. Jackson needed a bathroom break; he had been drinking the Red Stripe like they were water. "Ten minute break, mon," he announced to everyone, and most everyone got off the bus to stretch and use the facilities.

Back on the bus, Tina asked Jackson how much longer before we reached Negril. When she had left Jamaica, Negril was a tiny little hippie town carved out of swampland where artsy-type people and hippies went to hang out with the Rasta's and smoke the gangi (marijuana).

"About twenty minutes," Jackson replied. Jackson told Tina that Negril was a really nice place now, probably one of the nicest places on the island, famous for its seven miles of uninterrupted white sandy beach and the town fathers had kept a law in place that didn't allow any hotels or structures to be higher than the tallest palm trees, so it wasn't spoiled by skyscraper hotels.

Finally, we arrived at Sandals Negril. We passed through the guard gate and pulled up under a huge, white stucco dome that led into the impressive open-air reception lounge and front desk area. A hostess who offered us complimentary rum punch greeted us. We sipped several while we waited for our names to be called, then went and registered at the front desk and received our room keys. We were told our bags would be placed in our rooms within the hour. We weren't too far away from the main hotel area, and our room was on the ground floor and the patio opened up right onto the beach. It was paradise! Our back door faced the ocean and the best beach I had ever seen, and the front door opened into a garden like setting with bamboo and a trickling brook filled with exotic fish.

We decided to go look around the property while we waited for our bags to be delivered to our room. We strolled along the stone walkway back to the main complex and saw the main pool with swim up bar, then proceeded through the property, noticing that all the pools were connected by a canal with little bridges that allowed us to cross over as we walked. As we reached the end of the property, we saw a smaller restaurant and bar with a huge hot tub just to the side of it. There were a couple of couples in the tub, and we started a conversation with them and before I knew it, we were both quite tipsy from the endless supply of all-inclusive alcohol. I had been taking advantage of the Grand Marnier and Tina the banana daquiris. We sat there chatting and listening to the steel drum band that was playing in the restaurant. Before long, we felt like Brad and Margaret and Tim and Shelly were old, long-lost friends we had known forever. They were from New York City and were sad to be leaving in two days but proceeded to tell about the resort and things worth seeing and things that weren't. They thought it was neat that we had come to Jamaica to get married and every time a couple passed, they had to stop and have a toast to our upcoming nuptials.

Darkness had befallen us now and we could hear the crickets chirping in the background and the crash of the surf against the shore. We were in full party mode, and the fact we hadn't slept in well over twenty-four hours didn't faze us a bit. It was about four in the morning, and our bartender asked if it was alright for him to go home if he set us up with a half dozen drinks each. The hotel rules were that they never close a bar until the last guest has left the area. We told him, "no problem, mon."

Brad gave Tina and I a hard time about not getting into the hot tub, they had been in and out all night, so Tina and I jumped in clothes and all. Slowly, our small party group had started to disappear with the exception of Brad and Margaret and Tim and Shelly and another couple who weren't married and seemed to be having a tough time getting along. The sun had started to come up, and Tina thought we should go back to our room and get some sleep.

"Hey that's a great idea," I replied and invited everyone left back to our room to continue the party. We walked along the beach and passed the BBQ hut as it was just starting to open up. The attendant asked me the time, and no matter how hard I tried to read my watch, I couldn't, so I took off my watch and gave it to him. By the time we reached our room, only Tina and I and Michelle, the girl who was having a hard time with her boyfriend, were left. Everyone else had the good sense to go to their rooms as they past them. Tina wasn't all that happy that we had a straggler with us and didn't know what was going to happen next. Once in the room, Tina had to use the washroom and I laid down on the bed and started to chat with Michelle.

It was two o'clock in the afternoon when we woke up. I was still dazed and confused and was now paying for my excessive consumption the night before. Tina was feeling pretty good other than still being tired and a little miffed at me.

"What's wrong?" I asked.

"You mean aside from the fact that when I came out of the washroom, you were passed out and I had to find a way to get rid of Michelle."

"Who's Michelle?" I asked inquisitively. Tina proceeded to recount the events of the night before and filled in as many of the blanks in my memory as possible.

"Oh, honey, I'm so sorry," I said and begged her forgiveness.

It wasn't the romantic start to our time in paradise I had wanted and certainly wasn't how I had hoped we would spend the week before our wedding. Tina put it down to a lack of sleep and nerves and above all over consumption of all the evil temptations our island paradise had to offer. I opened the curtains on our patio doors, and the sun filled our room with its magical, healing rays. The wooden slats of our louvered patio windows opened easily allowing the fresh ocean breeze to fill the room. Tina and I lay side by side on our stomachs looking out at the inviting Caribbean Sea and the white powdered beach just begging us to come play on it.

Tina turned to me and said, "You know, a dip in the sea will probably be the best cure for both of us."

Tina tipped her hand that she wasn't feeling as spry as she had let on. She had been drinking more heavily as well, and I realized that because she would have been in the water by now if not.

"Shall we go for a swim?" I asked.

Tina looked at me and replied that she was starving and needed something to eat first. In my worst Jamaican accent, I said, "No problem, mon. Me 'ungry, too, mon. I'll call room service and get us something to eat."

I searched around the room for a room service menu and couldn't find one, so I picked up the phone and it automatically rang the front desk.

"Room service, please," I said when the voice on the other end announced the front desk.

"Sorry, Mr. Beals, we don't have room service available."

My heart sank at the news. "How come?" I asked.

"Our rooms are spread out across the property and are too far from the restaurants to offer room service." Then she informed me that it was permissible to go to the main pool buffet and take a plate of food back to our room.

"Thank you," I said and hung up.

I filled Tina in on the conversation I had and offered to go and get us something to eat. "No, that's okay," she replied. "Let's just put on our bathing suits and go have something to eat and then have a swim."

"Okay," I replied.

We quickly got ready to go and made our way to the main pool buffet. Tina was excited again at the sight of some of her childhood favourite Jamaican foods: curried goat and rice and peas, ackee, and salt fish. I wasn't feeling as adventurous and stuck to the North American fare and endless glasses of ice tea. As we sat and ate and chatted, people passed by and said good afternoon and made small talk with us. I asked Tina where she knew all these people from. She laughed at me.

"What?" I asked.

"You talked and partied with all these people last night."

At that moment, I swore I would never drink so much again in my life. I didn't like having no recollection of the previous evening.

Eating had made me feel a little better, and we went back to our room briefly to grab our beach towels and entered the beach from our room through the patio doors. The sand was so hot and yet soothing on the bottom of our feet. We placed our towels into a hammock strung between two coconut trees on the beach and entered the water. It usually takes me some time to get in past my bellybutton, but this was the warmest water I had ever swam in my life. It made Hawaii now seem like a distant, poor man's land. The Pacific Ocean and Waikiki beach had nothing on the Caribbean sea and Negril's powdery white beach sand. The salt content in the water was so high you could lay on your back and float as though you were on a raft. This was truly paradise.

Tina swam up to me and gave me a very deep and passionate kiss; my hand caressed the curve of her tight buttocks below the water line as I drew her body tightly into mine and pressed myself against her. No words needed to be spoken. I knew what she was feeling, and I was glad to have been able to bring her such happiness bringing her home to Jamaica. Our intimate moment ended quickly with two snorkels breaking the surface of the water beside us and startling Tina and me. We swam for a little while longer, then made our way to shore and lay in the double hammock, enjoying the sounds of the ocean and the rustling breeze through the palms and leaves of the trees and plants and the strolling quartet band that went up and down the beach of our resort.

As we lay in our hammock gently swaying back and forth in the building breeze, we made plans of what we needed to do in the next couple of days. Tina wanted to go see her Aunt Eula the next day. She told me Saturday would be a good day to go to the country, as almost everyone who she wanted to see would be home on the weekend. It was a tradition to visit family on the weekend. If a person worked and lived in the city he would spend the weekends in the country with family.

"Hey, that's fine with me," I told her. "Whatever you want to do."

She started to prepare me for Aunt Eula's place, telling me things were different than in Canada.

"Don't worry," I reassured her. "I've been camping and to cottages. How rough can it be?"

Tina was concerned because, unless things had changed, the washroom was outside, as well as the shower and the kitchen or cookhouse, as she called it.

With our plans made for the next day, we went into our room and showered and got dressed for dinner. We chose the Italian restaurant as our themed dining for that night and had an intimate table on the railing on the second floor overlooking the beach and sea. The service and food was incredible. Both feeling a little over filled, we thought a walk into town might be nice and made our way to the front gatehouse. We stopped to ask the guard how far it was to town, and he told us it was quite a far walk, maybe three or four miles, but he could get us a taxi. We declined his offer and told him we wanted to walk a bit. As we strolled along the edge of our property towards town, a couple of kids in a beat up old car stopped and offered us a ride. We politely declined and continued walking. We came across a second guardhouse at the other end of the property; it was the staff and delivery entrance. The guard stepped out and asked us what the kids in the car had asked us. I told him they offered us a ride to town, and he advised us not to accept rides from anyone but the taxi's with the hotel plates on their cars but then went on to say he knew the kids and that they were just going up and down the road waiting for their mom to get off work to give her a ride home. She worked in the office of the hotels he informed us. We thanked him for the tips we said and continued on our way. The same kids passed us a couple more times and when they offered us a ride again, we decided to accept. We chatted on the way into town, and they told us about where to go and what to see and said we should make sure we see the sunset at Rick's Café before we went back home to Canada. They dropped us off at a bar in town, and I offered them a couple bucks for gas, but they declined it and said they would be happy to give us a ride back if we knew when we wanted to return. Again we thanked them but said we didn't know how long we would be and parted company with them.

We entered the bar and knew instantly it wasn't the bar we were looking for. It was a local's bar, and the characters in the place looked rough and mean, not to mention the fact that there were two girls up on stage stripping. We quickly turned around and left. The road we were on led up to Rick's Café that we had heard so much about, so we continued on, and although we missed the sunset, we thought we would check it out anyway. As we strolled along we passed several different restaurants and many small hotels and guesthouses. This section of Negril was nothing like the beachfront luxury hotel section we were staying in. This section was looking like a pretty hard-core section, with street hustlers and prostitutes and drug dealers and hard-core party people. It definitely wasn't our scene, and yet, we were stuck in the middle. It was just as far to go back to the centre of town now as it was to continue on to Rick's. Our pace quickened now. I was trying to put on a brave front for Tina but was scared as hell, and she just wanted us to get the hell out of there.

Two Rasta's pulled up on dirt bikes and asked us if we wanted to go party. We said no.

"Well, den wer do ye want to go? Mi tink we shood give ye a lift."

"No, that's okay," we said again then started to walk trying to avoid them. I was muttering under my breath, "Never again, never again."

The Rasta's were revving their dirt bikes and racing past us then turning around and coming back towards us over and over. We finally reached Rick's and raced inside the place, it was empty with the exception of a couple of staff that were cleaning up.

"We're closed" they informed us.

"Closed!" I repeated. "It's only ten o'clock."

"Yeah, mon, people come for the cliff diving during the day and sunset dinner at night, then they all go into town to party, so we close at ten."

"Do you mind if we look around a bit?" I asked.

"No problem mon, da cliffs is over dat way," he said and pointed me off towards them.

We sat and regained our composure and then started laughing at what had happened and how, if we were home, we wouldn't set off walking through the worst neighbourhood in Calgary late at night. What made us lose our common sense here? We wondered how do we get back to the hotel. We had not seen any taxis up this way.

"Ask the bartender," Tina said, so I went and asked him about a taxi.

"Where you staying?" he asked.

I told him Sandals.

"Oh," he said. "I'm going that way, but me car is already full, or I would give you a lift but if you call the hotel they will send somebody."

He pulled a phone out of a locked drawer and called for us, then told me the guard at the gate said he would send a taxi for us, and it wouldn't be long. He said they were leaving, so we would have to wait out in the parking lot. With the staff loaded into the car and gone, we impatiently waited for our taxi.

"I hope he hurries," Tina said, as we could still hear the dirt bikes racing up and down the road. It was probably 20 minutes before we saw a set of headlights turn down the driveway into Rick's. A white mini-bus pulled up to us, and the driver asked if we were staying at Sandals.

"Yes," we both quickly replied and hopped in.

"My name is Vincent," he said, and he passed us his business card, then he asked what we were doing way out in the middle of nowhere this time of night and told us it wasn't really safe to be down in this area this time of day. Feeling safe, now we chatted with Vincent and told him of our ordeal. He just laughed and looked at Tina and said, "You should know better."

She told him it was over seventeen years ago since she had been back, and he told her things have changed, and people generally won't bother the tourists, but this end of Negril was very different at night than during the day. On the drive back, he told us if we wanted to go sight-seeing to tell the guard at the gate, and he would call him. We proceeded to tell him that we wanted to go to Jericho in the morning.

"What time?" he asked. We told him about ten o'clock, so he said, "I will be here at ten o'clock to pick you up."

"How much?" I asked him.

"Don't worry," he said. "I know you will treat me fair."

I didn't like not having a set price, but Tina liked him, and he seemed very trustworthy. As we exited the mini-bus, I asked him how much for the ride back.

He looked at me and said, "Whatever you think is fair."

I passed him $20 Canadian, and he seemed more than happy with that, and then offered to change any money that I needed to change for Jamaican with him rather than the hotel or banks. He said he travels to Canada once a year and it is hard to get Canadian money to take due to the government's restrictions on the movement of currency in and out of the country for residents.

Tina lay beside me, buzzing with excitement. She couldn't wait to show me where she grew up, and she talked to me excitedly in anticipation of the next day and who and what we would see. Seeing the excitement on Tina's face made me realize we had made the right decision to get married in Jamaica. I was feeling so happy inside just watching and seeing the joy this trip had given her. My angel had been through so much in the past, I couldn't begin to express how good it made me feel knowing what this trip and our wedding meant to her. I lay in the bed, listening to the sounds drifting into the room, from the distant thump of the waves lashing against the beach to the sound of the palm and coconut tree leaves rustling in the gentle evening Caribbean breeze and the chirping of the crickets from the bamboo gardens just outside our door. Tina had drifted off to sleep, anxious to be well rested for tomorrow and not wanting to sleep too late, fearful we would miss our ride. I, on the other hand, was in paradise. I had missed the opportunity when we first arrived to enjoy the simple sounds of the sea and the wind moving through the tropical vegetation. I stared into the veins of the swirling ceiling fan dreaming about the next day and the exciting days ahead.

I awoke well rested and could hear Tina in the shower. I slipped on my bathing suit and exited through our patio doors and went for a quick dip in the warm Caribbean Sea, and then I stopped at one of the fresh-water showers located along the edge of the beach and rinsed off the salt water from my swim, then made my way back to our room. When I entered ,Tina said she wondered where I had gotten to, and I told her I had gone for a quick swim.

"Well, you better get ready,"she said. "I want to get to Aunt Eula's as soon as possible."

I looked at the clock radio and it was just 8:30. "Did you forget Vincent isn't going to pick us up until ten?" I reminded her.

"I know," she said. "But by the time we have breakfast and stop at the gift store for a couple of things, it will be time to go."

"No problem," I said and went into the bathroom to shave and brush my teeth. Tina knocked on the door and told me she was going to the gift store to pick up a couple things and would meet me for breakfast in the restaurant in 15 minutes.

"Okay," I mumbled with my mouth still full of toothpaste.

I searched around the breakfast buffet restaurant for Tina and didn't see her anywhere. Still shopping, I thought to myself and sat down and ordered a Blue Mountain Coffee and a freshly squeezed glass of tangerine juice. Tina walked in the same time as my coffee and juice arrived.

"Where's mine?" she asked, so I passed her my glass of juice and ordered a second coffee and juice.

"Sorry, honey, I didn't know how long you would be." Tina sat down and placed two full shopping bags down by her feet.

"What did you buy?" I asked.

"Just a few knickknacks," she said. "A couple of bottles of rum for my uncles, and some perfume for my aunts, and candy and other treats for Myrna and her kids and the Perkins's and on and on…"

"Oh, so something for everyone in town."

Tina laughed and said, "No, it's just when you come from away, people expect some kind of gift."

"No problem," I said. "But I thought that's what the extra suitcase of stuff we brought was for."

"Well, yeah, but that's things for Aunt Eula, then last night I got to thinking about my other uncles and aunts and cousins…"

"Hey, it's okay. Don't be so defensive," I said.

With a couple of coffees and juices into me and some scrambled eggs and bacon and toast, I was stuffed, and we were out of time. We hastily went back to the room to pack Tina's shopping in with the other things she had brought from home, and we both quickly freshened up again. With the heat and humidity, it didn't take long to feel all sweaty and grungy.

When we made our way out front, Vincent was standing outside his mini-bus all smiles and took our bags and placed them into the bus.

"Good morning, good morning," he boomed. "Are we all set to see God's country today?

"Yeah, mon," I replied, and he opened the door, and Tina and I sat on the front seat beside Vincent.

As we made our way towards Jericho, Vincent and Tina reminisced about how things were when Jamaica was still under British rule and how much better they both thought things were then. In between their political discussions, they pointed out different things of interest to me. When we entered the town of Lucea, Tina had Vincent drive down by her old high school Rusea High, and we got out and looked around. I was fascinated how the schools were so open and different from Canadian schools. The building that we had seen coming down that was damaged was the old boarding school quarters, but Vincent told us nobody boarded their kids at the school anymore. That was a thing of the past. From school, we made our way through town and then crossed the bridge and turned right by the big banyan tree.

"Seven miles" Tina said.

"What do you mean?" I asked.

"It's seven miles from here to Aunt Eula's house."

With that, we began the slow winding trail up the rough mountain road, Tina pointing and reminiscing as we passed this house and that, her excitement was bubbling again. As we passed the post office at Jericho, Tina yelled out to a girl she recognized and the girl yelled back and asked her something I didn't understand.

Tina yelled back, "It's me, Prim, Primrose."

The girl came running alongside us, and Vincent stopped so Tina could get out. There was a bunch of hugging and kissing, then Tina introduced me to her cousin Pinney. They talked for a couple minutes, and Pinney ran off to tell her uncle and her brothers and sisters that Primrose was home. Back into the bus, we crept along the road. Tina was sitting beside the window, shaking hands and chatting with people as we drove the last half-mile to her aunt's driveway. There were people popping out from everywhere welcoming Prim, as they called Tina. We had to walk into Aunt Eula's house, as it was back from the road, and the heavy rains from Hurricane Gilbert had put huge ruts in the long grass driveway, and Vincent was afraid of getting stuck. He pulled off to the side and sat there while we walked the 500 feet into Aunt Eula's place.

As we walked along the path into Aunt Eula's, two little boys came running down the hillside and asked who we were.

"Who are you?" Tina asked.

The boys replied, "I'm Chris," and, "I'm Devlin."

Tina asked them something in Patois and they answered her with the name Myrna.

"Oh," she said, "you're John and Mary's little brothers."

As we crested the top of the path, there was a hard-looking woman standing by an outside fire pit next to a smaller house, I assumed that must be Myrna. She was a lady Tina's aunt had taken in many years back who was one of Tina's great-uncle's illegitimate daughters, and she now helped Aunt Eula out and in exchange Aunt Eula let her rent one of her houses for very low rent. Aunt Eula stepped out onto her porch, all smiles, when she saw us coming up the pathway to her house. It had been a fairly cool walk coming up the trail, but the dry heat was stifling as we crossed out into the open to go up onto the porch. Aunt Eula and Tina hugged and hugged, and then Aunt Eula gave me the warmest smile and wrapped her loving arms around me and squeezed me tight into her ample bosom. I could tell Aunt Eula was a real beauty queen back in her day. She motioned for us to come inside, but I was very comfortable on the porch. It faced the ocean, and there was a nice breeze that came out of the trees and onto the porch, so I sat there and cooled off while Tina went inside with her Aunt. A couple minutes passed and Aunt Eula appeared with an ice-cold Red Stripe beer for me.

"I been saving these for you, young man," she said. She always called me young man.

I graciously accepted her beer and sat in the big comfy deck chair on the porch and quenched my thirst. I couldn't get over how the heat affected me and drained my energy. As I sat there drinking my beer, the two young boys were firing questions at me left and right. Their mom, Myrna, came over and introduced herself to me and shooed the boys away, then another girl about twenty, Mary, appeared with a baby from inside the house. This was Myrna's daughter, and she and her baby Shanique lived with Aunt Eula, and in the other house, Myrna lived with her two young sons and her oldest boy, John, who was about twenty-two. She said John would be by soon. He had gone to help someone in the field for the morning. Mary seemed to know all about Tina and me and that we were there to get married.

She explained that she worked at the post office in Lucea and helped Aunt Eula write her letters since her eyes weren't so good anymore. When Aunt Eula was in Calgary, Tina had taken her to have her eyes looked after and had kept sending her a special eyewash, but Mary said she had spilled the last bottle and that's why her eyes had deteriorated so badly. We brought four big bottles with us, and Aunt Eula was grateful to have a new supply. Mary said she wanted Aunt Eula to go to town and see the doctor at the clinic, but it was really hard for her to go into town anymore. Tina came out and asked Mary about Aunt Eula's eyes ,and I quickly explained what had happened and why she hadn't been into the doctor. Mary quickly mentioned that the clinic in Lucea was open until 3:30, and if we could take her into town, it would be great. Tina went inside and told Aunt Eula that we were going to take her into town to see the doctor.

As Tina emerged back outside, her Aunt got dressed into her Sunday clothes, and a frail-looking old man made his way up the hill.

The old gent called out to Tina, "Prim, is that you?"

She went off the porch and greeted the old fellow. It was her Great Uncle Lester, Aunt Eula's brother. Tina brought him up onto the porch and introduced me. We shook hands, and I offered him a cold beer.

"Oh, no thanks," he said.

Tina disappeared and returned with a bottle of Appleton Estate Rum and passed it to her uncle.

"Oh, Prim," he said. "You didn't forget." They both had a laugh. He cracked the bottle open and took a swig, then wiped the rim and passed it to me. I took a small pull and passed it to Tina, who feigned a drink from it, wiped the rim, and gave it back to her uncle.

Aunt Eula, all gussied up, came out onto the porch and was surprised to see Lester there. We all sat and visited for a bit, and then checking the time we thought it would be a good idea to get Aunt Eula into town to see the doctor. Lester took one arm and I took the other, and we helped Aunt Eula down the pathway to the road. She was introduced to Vincent, and he treated her with great respect immediately. It was quite nice to see how people treated the elderly in Jamaica. We gave Uncle Lester a ride down the road to his house, and he invited us in, but we declined and told him another time we wanted to get Aunt Eula to the doctor.

Vincent found the clinic in town with no problem, and we walked Aunt Eula upstairs into the waiting room. I could feel all eyes in the room on me, people wondering who was this white man with these three Jamaicans. We only had to wait about five minutes, and they took Aunt Eula in. Tina went in with her, and I told her I was going to look around the hardware store across the street. Vincent came with me. I chatted with Vincent, and he asked if I minded if he looked for a wax collar for his toilet while we were in there.

"No problem mon," I said.

He commended me for taking care of Aunt Eula, and I put that down to Tina, and he replied that it was nice to see how we cared for her. With Vincent's purchase made, we spotted Tina and Aunt Eula coming down the stairs from the doctor's office and made our way across the street to them. Aunt Eula's eyes looked so much better, and Tina said as long as she used the drops we brought her everyday, she shouldn't have much trouble. Vincent helped Aunt Eula back into the mini-bus, and I was curious how much the doctor cost. Tina told me $80 Jamaican, which was about $16 Canadian. I couldn't believe how cheap it was.

Aunt Eula asked if we could go down the street to the bakery where she wanted to get some hard dough bread. Vincent pulled the mini-bus up nice and close, and Aunt Eula haggled with the baker and got three $5 loaves plus some Christmas buns for $15.

From the bakery, we went to the grocery store and took Aunt Eula in to buy some supplies. We stocked her up on canned and other dry goods. She was quite happy to get to shop in town instead of the local grocer in Jericho who charged twice as much and had little selection. From the grocery, we took Aunt Eula out for an early supper at a Chinese restaurant. It was only around four o'clock, but the sun was already setting, so we finished our meal and made our way back down to the mini-bus to head back to Jericho.

On the drive back to Aunt Eula's, we continued the discussion from the restaurant we had with Aunt Eula about our upcoming wedding next Saturday in Montego Bay and how would she get there. We hadn't given it much thought back in Canada. We just assumed someone in the area would drive her. Vincent interrupted and said he would consider it a great honour if we would allow him to pick up and escort Aunt Eula to our wedding. Tina and I thought what a generous and kind offer. Vincent spoke to Miss Eula as he had always addressed her and asked her for the pleasure of escorting her to our wedding next Saturday. He told her he would pick her up early in the morning so she could spend the day helping Tina prepare for the big day and would see her home safely that evening. She was all smiles and accepted his offer.

As we pulled back up to Aunt Eula's driveway, she invited Vincent up to the house, but he declined graciously saying that it would be dark soon, and he wished to stay with his vehicle to keep it safe. We retrieved the shopping from the van. Myrna's two young sons were standing beside us by the time we had everything unloaded. Aunt Eula said something in Patois that I couldn't make out, and the next thing I knew, they had the grocery bags in hand and were running back up the hill. John arrived a couple minutes later and helped me get Aunt Eula back up to her house. The trip to town had taken a lot out of her, and she sat on the porch and had a cool drink of water from the jug in the fridge. She called Prim over to her, and they talked quietly for a couple of minutes. Tina came over to me and told me that Aunt Eula had asked us to stay the night. She said that while we were gone, she had asked Mary to make up the guest bed with a pair of brand new sheets never used before and that she would be truly honoured if we would stay. I asked Tina to walk with me back to the road, and we would discuss it more privately. We left the porch and made our way down the path. Myrna's boys were following us closely, and Tina sent them back up to the house. We discussed the idea of spending the night, and I said as long as we could arrange a ride for tomorrow and she was sure we would be safe, then I was game. We spoke to Vincent, and he said he would come back for us tomorrow, but it would have to be later in the day as he had commitments in the morning, taking his family to church. We agreed on 1:00 p.m. and then I went to pay him, and he refused saying we could settle things tomorrow, that way we would know we could trust him to come back for us. I shook his hand, and he left.

With Vincent gone, we made our way to the front gate of the house located beside Aunt Eula's driveway. A little dog was in the yard and was barking at us none stop. An older gentleman came out of the house and shooed the dog into the back yard and put him inside a pen, then returned and asked us our business.

"Uncle Ted, it's me, Prim," Tina said.

He scratched his head and thought for a minute or two. Meanwhile, a well-dressed lady appeared out of the house and made her way up to the gate.

"Prim girl, is that you?" she said.

"Yes, Aunt May." Her aunt spoke to the older gentleman, and he now seemed to remember who Tina was.

Tina introduced me, and we chatted for a few minutes over the gate, and when her Aunt May invited us in, we politely declined and said we had to get back up to Aunt Eula's before it got too dark. Her Aunt May seemed surprised we were staying over night at her sister's house. On the way back up the hill, Tina filled me in. May was Aunt Eula's sister, but they never got along too well. She said May always thought she was so much better than Eula and Lester, but Tina said the real reason was probably because Myrna was Ted's illegitimate child, and May didn't like the fact that when she turned up with no place to go a lot of years back, Aunt Eula took her in and took care of her.

Back up the hill, Aunt Eula was delighted that we were staying overnight, and she gave us a quick tour around the property. First was the outhouse, which surprised me. It was the cleanest odour-free one I had ever been in. Then, Aunt Eula showed us the bathing area. They had an outside sink and outside shower area, which was quite neat. Around back was the outside cooking kitchen. We went back into the house from the backyard and entered a pantry area that led to the inside kitchen and off that was Aunt Eula's bedroom, then through the living room, we went into another bedroom that was ours for the night, and off of this bedroom was another one that had its own outside entrance. That was where Mary and her daughter stayed. It was really interesting to see such a different way of living, everything really focussed more on living outside and only sleeping inside, along with a small amount of cooking in the kitchen when it rained, plus doing dishes in the kitchen. Other than that, they pretty much lived outside or on the porch.

Aunt Eula, Tina, and I sat on the porch and talked about her trip to Calgary and how the visit went when she left Calgary and went to Rochester to see her sister and the rest of the family. She was so thankful to Tina for making the trip happen for her. We sat on the porch, enjoying the cool evening breeze and drank the nice, cold Red Stripe beer while Eula and Tina talked and talked about people in the area and who was still around and who married who and moved where and generally gossiped and laughed to no end. Myrna's young boys interrupted us and asked Miss Eula if it was okay to watch her television. She told them to go on in, but keep the sound low so she could hear herself think. It wasn't long after that when Myrna and Mary and John joined us up on the porch and enjoyed hearing about Canada and the places we had travelled. Our little group kept on growing, word had spread that Prim was at her Aunt Eula's, and Tina's cousins and family slowly made their way up the hill to see her. John was the first to mention to me that the beer was almost gone and the canteen closed at ten, so I asked him if he would go with me to get some more beer. He told me to stay put because the pathway was dark and people would be stopping by to see Tina and me. He said he would take his brothers Chris and Devlin with him and get the beer. I asked him how much a case of beer was, and he told me $60, then I discretely slipped him $60 for the beer. I calculated that to be about $10 Canadian, which didn't seem too bad, but when John arrived back, I found out what he meant by a case was 24 stubby-nosed bottles. My good deal just got better.

As the night wore on, people slowly dissipated back to their homes and finally Aunt Eula excused herself and went off to bed leaving just me and Tina and John and his sister, Mary, chatting. Myrna rounded up the boys from Miss Eula's parlour and took them home to bed. All those beers had caught up to me, and I made my way to the outhouse and took care of business. I still couldn't get over how an outhouse could be as nice as a bathroom. When I got back to the porch, Mary and John had left, so Tina and I stood there, looking out into the darkness and shadows lightly illuminated by the moon in the sky. We kissed and hugged each other and without another word being spoken, I knew exactly how Tina felt at this moment.

What the hell! The most god-awful, annoying, blood-curdling noise awakened me. Tina opened her eyes and looked up at me and laughed.

"What's so funny?" I asked.

"You should see the look on your face," she said.

"Well didn't you hear that?" Before I could finish my sentence, the noise repeated itself.

Tina looked up at me again and said, "You crazy fool, haven't you ever heard a rooster before?"

"No," I replied. "I guess not. I thought they only crowed at the crack of dawn, and it's still the middle of the night."

In reality it was about quarter to five. I covered my head with the pillow and went back to sleep. After a couple more hours of sleep, I got up and went out to the outhouse and then washed up and went around to the kitchen. Tina, Mary, and Aunt Eula were cooking breakfast and having a nice little chit chat. They stopped when I walked up, and Mary let out a laugh. I figured they were having a laugh at my expense about the rooster, but Mary looked at me and with a wide-eyed smile said she heard me last night. I didn't have a clue what the heck she was talking about. Tina and I didn't make love last night, so what was it that she heard or was talking about. I was still confused as Tina showed me some of the herbs and fruits that were growing around Aunt Eula's house.

When we were out of earshot of Mary and Miss Eula, I asked her what Mary was talking about.

"Oh, that," she said with a laugh. "Don't worry about it."

"About what?" I asked again.

Then Tina told me that I had snored rather loudly and that's what Mary and Aunt Eula had gotten such a chuckle out of. I didn't know whether to be relieved or embarrassed. When we got back to the kitchen, Aunt Eula had a fresh bath towel waiting for me and told me I had time to go shower before breakfast.

"Oh, yes," Tina piped up. "I had one earlier, and you've just got to try the shower."

Tina and Aunt Eula were right—the outdoor shower was fantastic. There was something magical about standing naked under a mango tree, listening to the birds chirp and feeling the warmth of the sun on your body as I cleansed myself with the homemade soap and then rinsed off under the air warmed shower water. It was truly invigorating and peaceful.

Breakfast was ready, and Tina, Mary, Aunt Eula, and I sat down and had a feed of sausage and something like pancakes and a variety of fresh fruits. Oranges and grapefruits, I recognized, the rest of the fruits were a mystery to me, but I tried them all. Aunt Eula asked Tina and me if we would accompany her to church later on, but Tina and I declined, telling Aunt Eula that we didn't bring proper attire to attend church with her but that we would be sure to bring suitable clothing to attend next time. Tina and I started to wash up the breakfast dishes while Aunt Eula went to get ready for church, and Mary went to get her daughter up to feed and dress her and get her ready for church as well.

We walked Aunt Eula out to the roadside where she was picked up by Mr. Purkiss, who was a nephew or related to Aunt Eula somehow, but I wasn't sure how. He looked to be only ten or fifteen years younger than Aunt Eula himself. He was happy to see Tina, and they chatted briefly. He told us to stop up and see them and that Mrs. Purkiss would be sad if we didn't. He said she was sick this morning, or she would have been with him. Tina told him we would try to come by but that it may be difficult to do this trip. Tina and I were sitting on the porch, enjoying the breeze and view when we saw Chris and Devlin helping Aunt Eula back up the hill to her home.

"It's too bad about the rut and washed out roadway," I told Tina. "It must make it hard for Aunt Eula to have to walk in from the road."

Just then, John rounded the corner and must have overheard our conversation because he told us he had fixed the roadway several times and what it really needed was a load of rock brought in and a new culvert pipe to fix it properly. Our conversation ended there with Aunt Eula now sitting on the porch resting and telling Tina about the people she knew from church asking about her. I didn't realize the celebrity status Tina had obtained by just coming back for a visit, but I guess everybody figured that when people go abroad, they became rich, and the fact that she was with a white man just added to this myth.

We visited with Aunt Eula for a short while then heard the toot from Vincent's mini-bus. While Tina said goodbye to her aunt, I grabbed our things from the bedroom. I remembered Tina had brought her aunt a dress to wear to the wedding and had forgotten to give it to her, so I passed it to her, and she quickly showed her aunt before we left. Vincent was smiling when we met him at the roadside, then he asked if we still wanted him to escort Aunt Eula to our wedding next Saturday, and we told him yes. He put us in the mini-bus and started it so the air-conditioning was running and told us he would be back in a minute. He just wanted to go talk to Aunt Eula and finalize her pickup for next Saturday, if that was okay, and away he went. While we sat there, enjoying the cool air conditioning, Pinney, Brownie, and Paupau, three of Uncle Lester's children, came over and chatted with us asking about Tina's mom and sisters and mainly wanting to know about Momma, Tina's grandmother, who was in a nursing home in Rochester. She was Aunt Eula and Uncle Lester's and Aunt May's sister and the matriarch of the family. She had always been the most successful and wealthiest of the family and had always helped provide for her siblings and their families.

Vincent arrived back at the mini-bus, eager to get us back to the hotel. He told us he usually doesn't work on Sundays and told his family he would only be about two hours. He said he could tell we were special people, and he liked the fact that Tina kept looking out for her aunt all the way from Canada and that showed great respect and earned great respect from him. When we got back at Sandals, I settled up with Vincent and was shocked that he only wanted a hundred Canadian dollars for taking us to Jericho and to town the previous day and then picking us up and returning us to our hotel. We again confirmed that he was picking up Aunt Eula next Saturday and bringing her to Montego Bay early that morning. He had been good to his word so far, but I didn't want anything to go wrong on our wedding day. He understood this and told me not to worry.

Tina stopped by the front desk and inquired about sending a telegram to Kingston. She had not heard from her sister Claudette since we arrived and had tried to contact her at work but she never seemed to be available or in when she called. To be on the safe side, she thought she should send a telegram to her sister's house to make sure she knew what was happening.

With that all taken care of, we dropped our stuff in our room and put on our swimwear and spent the rest of the afternoon relaxing on the beach and sipping banana daiquiris. Tired from the afternoon in the sun, we showered off on the beach, hoping to get a burst of energy but all it did was get me excited for Tina watching the water droplets cover her hot tanned body. She was tanning a lot quicker than me, and it only added to her sex appeal. Back in our room, I approached her like a rabid dog licking her and kissing every inch of her body. Although we showered, I could still taste the salt from the ocean on her body and that only drove me into a more frazzled state of desire and passion.

Tina had planned abstinence or as little contact as possible before the wedding, but she was as desirous of me now as I was of her, and I pushed her onto the bed and roughly removed her bathing suit to expose the lighter colours of flesh that had yet to be tinged by the warm Jamaican sun. I feverishly worked my tongue over her warm, salty heaving breasts, licking and biting her nipples. She reached down and slid her hand beneath my swim trunks and playfully teased the head of my straining penis. It was only a few minutes, and I felt my whole body quiver as I shot my juice onto my belly.

Tina pulled away and with a wicked look said, "That's all your going to get to our wedding day." Then, she got up and went into the washroom while I drifted off to sleep.

When I awoke about 90 minutes later, Tina was laying beside me reading a magazine. I looked up at her and couldn't help but ask, "How can you have such control?"

Her reply was, "What control? You have no idea what I may or may not have been doing in the bathroom while you recharged your batteries."

"Ah, another bright sunny morning," I said to Tina as we awoke well rested from the previous evening.

We had taken things easy Sunday night, went to dinner, then stayed and watched a bit of the night's entertainment and went to bed fairly early. I felt like we had been in paradise for a month, and here it was, only Monday. We had three more nights in Negril and then it was off to Montego Bay for the wedding and our final week's stay. Seeing the beauty in Negril, I now wished we had just made plans to have the wedding here and spend our second week at this property rather than transferring up to Sandals Royal Montego Bay. I mentioned this to Tina as we snuggled together for a few more minutes, but she was eager to spend time in Montego Bay and said I would like it as much as here and that their were nice beaches in Mo Bay as well. Besides, our family was staying in Mo Bay and everything has been arranged for Aunt Eula already.

"Trust me, honey, you'll love it," she said.

"Okay," I responded, and then asked if she was hungry because I was starving.

We both quickly got dressed and went to the poolside restaurant for breakfast. Over breakfast, we decided to spend the day relaxing at the resort and would get involved in some of the activities going on: pool volleyball and beach volleyball and a whole day of other beach events and activities set for the day. Sandals had a group of staff called players, and their job was to organize and get people to participate in the activities they planned, kind of like having eight to ten ambassadors at the property making sure everyone was entertained and having a good time. When people joined in an activity, they became a member of the players club and received a little pair of leather sandals to wear around their neck. With each event or activity they participated in, they received coloured beads to string on the mini-sandal necklace. At the end of the day, when they put on the evening variety show, people received various gifts and prizes, usually rum, depending on how many beads they had obtained that day. It was a really clever way to get the whole resort interacting with one another and just added to the whole Jamaican experience.

After a very active day, we went back to our room and both sacked out for about two hours before freshening up and going to dinner. As we sat eating dinner, I looked across to Tina. Her warmth and inner beauty were radiating from within her; the physical energy we consumed earlier in the day only seemed to charge her with more fire and passion. She caught me staring at her and blushed, then asked me what I was thinking.

My reply was, "I can't believe that in another five days I will be married to such a beautiful, warm, loving, caring, sexy, exciting woman."

We shared a quiet moment after that just holding hands, gazing out at the moon dancing on the darkness of the Caribbean Sea and listening to the sounds of the waves rolling up on the beach and the distant sound of the reggae beat filling the air. With dinner finished, we went strolling through the dimly lit garden pathways, the smell of hibiscus and jasmine filling the warm night air. We stopped on one of the tiny footbridges that cross the connecting pool canals and embraced one another. I wrapped my arms tightly around Tina and kissed her as she held me tight and passionately kissed me back. We stood there under the moonlight and gently swayed back and forth to the gentle rhythm of the distant beat of the music. I felt myself arousing, and Tina could feel it as well. She released her hold on me and broke free.

"No way, Jose," she said. "We worked too hard today to get our Sandals and beads. Let's go to the show and collect our prizes."

We made our way to the outdoor stage and found a bench next to the sea wall about halfway back. It was a perfect spot to sit and watch the show. The ocean breeze that was flowing over the flowering hedge and wall kept us comfortably cool and intoxicated with its exotic scents. Between Tina and I, we had been to the stage four times and collected four half-litre bottles of rum for the various activities we had won that day but held on to our beads since we found out you could add to them each day and get a bigger gift by the end of the week.

"We should have been in the players program the first night we got here" Tina said to me. She wanted enough beads to each get a pair of the full size leather Sandals, but for that, we needed another 42 beads. We had earned eight beads earlier that day, so I guess it wasn't impossible.

After an entertaining evening, we strolled back towards our room along the beach and decided to go for a late night swim to cool off before going to bed. It was easy for me take off my shirt, and I was ready to go, for Tina it required more thought. She slipped out of her clothes and put on my shirt and left her panties on. It was pretty dark, but there were too many chances of people strolling by to skinny dip, and when the clouds were blown clear of the moon, it brightened things up dramatically so we had to endure a nice cuddling swim with clothes on. It was quite enjoyable until something brushed up against Tina's leg, and we both freaked out and exited the water without a second to spare. We sat down on our patio and began laughing; the way we reacted to whatever was in the water was funny now that we were safely onshore.

We were off to bed for a good night's rest as we had decided to go rafting in the morning on the Martha Brae River. During the evening's entertainment, they informed everyone about the next day's excursions and activities, and the rafting sounded good. It was only about an hour away and, more importantly to Tina, was the fact we would be back early enough in the afternoon to compete for more beads. It was another fantastic sleep. I couldn't get over how early we seemed to go to bed, but we both were having the most restful relaxing sleeps of our lives. I think it was a combination of the full days and the fresh ocean breeze and the gentle sound of the surf lapping the shore while we cocooned ourselves together in our bed.

Surprisingly, we found out after breakfast that there was only one other couple besides us that had signed up to go rafting that morning, so the escorted trip was cancelled. We chatted with Keith and Kathy, the other couple that signed up and decided to share a cab and go anyway. When we got out front by the security hut to arrange for a cab, we ran across our old buddy Vincent, and he took good care of us all. We told him what we wanted to do, and he gave us a price per person that included rafting, and it was cheaper than the organized tour the hotel was selling. When we arrived at the starting point for the raft trip, Vincent went into the office and left us sitting comfortably in his mini-bus while he arranged our trips. He came back after a few minutes and told us we could leave our belongings in his van, and he would take care of things and wait down river for us. He said the raft trip was about an hour and a half long. Tina and I left our things with Vincent and only took our camera with us. Keith and Kathy took their day packs with them, even though we assured them that Vincent was the number one driver and could be trusted.

We met our raft pilot, Jim, who looked to be about 90 years old and had about three teeth, which added to his thick Jamaican accent. Even Tina was having a bit of trouble understanding him. Our raft was constructed out of large bamboo trees lashed side by side maybe three feet wide and probably forty feet long. About six feet from the back of the raft was a raised seat made out of bamboo as well. Jim motioned for us to sit there, and we were underway. The ride made me think of the gondolas in Venice that I had seen many times on television. We had only been underway fifteen minutes, and Tina was antsy. She was watching Jim navigate us down the river using a smaller diameter bamboo push pole about ten feet long and decided she wanted to try it. Jim accommodated us, and once he saw that Tina had the hang of things, he came and got a plastic bag out from under the seat and then sat down on the raft with his legs crossed and started to whittle away on some kind of gourd. Tina had poled us along the river for probably twenty minutes and then I took a turn and she went and sat down on the seat and started chatting away with Jim. It wasn't too long, and Jim directed me to pole over to the far side of the river where the current was slower. We emerged into a field of grass growing in the river and all we could smell was lemons. Jim pulled up some of the grass as we passed and rubbed it into his hands and passed some to Tina. She did the same, then he told her something in Patois, and they both laughed. At that point, Keith and Kathy passed by, and I heard Keith ask their raft pilot if he could do it after seeing me poling our raft I guess. Kathy seemed okay to us, but Keith was a former cop in some little town in the northern part of Florida, and he was turning out to be loud and rude and obnoxious and a know it all. Tina and I switched up, and she started poling while I sat and relaxed and asked Jim about some of the trees and things and what they were as we passed by them. He asked what day we were getting married; I figured Tina must have told him while I was poling. I told him Saturday coming.

"No, what is the date?" he asked.

"The tenth of December" I said.

"Ah," he replied and that was the extent of our conversation.

A few more minutes passed, and Jim put his carving back in the bag and placed it under the seat and walked to the front of the raft where Tina was poling. They exchanged a few words, and she came and sat down and told me he said the river was about to narrow and would become a lot faster so he thought he better take over, even though we did a good job. As we rounded the bend and picked up speed, the raft started to bob this way and that. It added a little bit of excitement to a relatively tame trip. We could hear a lot of shouting and yelling coming from around the next bend. As we came around the corner we saw Keith's and Kathy's raft on the far side facing backwards. They had spun out somehow, and Keith appeared to be reluctant to give the pole back to their guide to get them underway. Tina and I looked at each other and figured we were in for a long uncomfortable ride back to the hotel, listening to Keith's griping the whole way. I could see what appeared to be a boat dock about a half kilometre down stream, and although we had enjoyed the raft trip, I was glad it was over. It was just too hot and humid on the river, and I couldn't wait to get back to the beach and the cooler ocean air.

Vincent greeted us at the dock and told me quietly that it was customary to tip the guide.

"How much?" I asked.

"Oh that's up to you, but about twenty J would be fair."

I quickly calculated that into Canadian, and it was only about four bucks. When I turned around, Tina was showing me the gourd that Jim had been carving coming down the river. He had carved an intricate design into it with hibiscus flowers and hummingbirds and some of the other flowers we saw as we drifted down the river. He had even put our names and Jamaica W.I. on it.

"How much is it?" I asked her.

"Nothing," she replied. "It's a gift."

For a beautiful flower is what he told her. I slipped another 20 J from my pocket and went over and thanked Jim and shook hands, palming the $40 tip to him. Vincent suggested we may want to look at some of the handicrafts that were set up where we disembarked. He said the merchandise was locally made and good quality for the money. We looked around a bit, but once we made a couple of purchases, the vendors were swarming on us like bees to a hive, so we quickly made our way to the van and took full advantage of the nice cool air conditioning while waiting for Keith and Kathy, who were just pulling up to the dock.

Vincent hopped out and went over to greet them while Tina and I sat back and talked about how fun the trip was but, like me, Tina found it way too hot being away from the coast. When Vincent returned with Kathy and Keith, Kathy didn't seem all that pleased, and they bickered a bit on the way back to the hotel. As we arrived back at Sandals, they asked us if we would like to join them for a late lunch. I looked to Tina, and we made excuses that we were hot and were eager to go for a swim but thanked them anyway and said we would take a rain check. As we walked back to our room, Tina asked me what we going to do now. She was starving and so was I, but if we had gone and ate with them, we would have been stuck with them all night, and the thought of listening to them snip and bicker all night didn't appeal to either of us. Beach burger hut was our salvation, and we shouldn't run into them, so we dropped off our things and changed into our bathing suits and off we went. The selection at the beach hut wasn't like the restaurant, but they did make good french fries, and the beef patties weren't bad, either.

The sun lit up our room like a 2,000-watt light bulb. We had gone to bed, totally exhausted from the rafting and swimming and competitions we had competed in the previous day. Upon returning to our room the previous night, we left the drapes open so we could watch the moonlight twinkle and dance on the glistening Caribbean sea. Tina and I lay snuggled close together in our bed with the sheets pulled over our head to help shield our eyes from the sunlight. Tina turned to me and asked if we could just have a nice lazy day at the resort since it was our last day in Negril. The next day, we would lose a good portion of the day transferring up to Montego Bay to our new hotel and the imminent wedding day.

"Whatever you want, my little primrose," I said as I nuzzled my face between her bosom and teased her ever so gently with my tongue.

She playfully pushed me away and told me to be careful not to start something neither of us could finish. I now just wanted us to get the darn wedding over with so we could get back to being normal and resume our intimate relations. I got up and slipped on my swim shorts and opened the doors to our patio and told Tina I was going for a swim but would love some company. As I slipped out the door, I looked back and saw Tina slip into the bathroom.

I was glad in a way that we left the curtains and shutters open the previous night. I had never been out to the beach so early before, and the sand had been freshly raked and looked so manicured and pristine and perfectly untouched. As I entered the sea, I expected it to be a little cooler than I was used to, but it was actually warmer than the air temperature was yet. It felt like entering a hot bath. I swam around a bit and then flipped onto my back to relax and float for a while. I was still amazed with how easy it was to float and how I could put my hands behind my back just like I was lazing on a lounge chair. I was startled by Tina's touch as she brushed against my leg and quickly stood up. Tina was commenting how good the water felt, and we resumed floating side-by-side, holding each other's hands. It was funny, but everyday, I seemed to discover something new that we normally just take for granted and never really stop and take the time to appreciate. This truly was the greatest holiday I had ever experienced so far in my whole life. Every time I thought I had experienced a once-in-a-lifetime experience since I met Tina, I was always wrong. Just when I thought it couldn't be any nicer or better, something new would happen and stir new and deeper more intense feelings for her. How lucky I was!

We spent the day lounging and reading and taking a dip in the ocean every time the heat got to be too much to endure. As the afternoon clouds appeared, we decided to go back to our room and pack up most of our things before we went to dinner. That way, we could relax for the evening and would just have to pack a couple items in the morning before the transfer to Montego Bay.

During dinner, we noticed that most of the acquaintances we had made during the week were gone now, and there were pretty much all-new faces around the restaurant and at the floorshow later that evening. We felt like old-timers now. My sunburn had finally turned more brown than red, and Tina had darkened up and gained quite a bit of colour herself. We cleaned up that evening and earned our first pair of sandals and were working on acquiring the second pair. We had a bit of an advantage now, as most of the other hotel guests were newbies and were apprehensive at participating in a lot of the events. By the end of the night, we had both earned our sandals and several more bottles of rum and were actually excited to be heading to our new hotel in the morning and to see our family that had come for the wedding. Tina was anxious to see what they thought of her homeland. In bed, we lay awake for what seemed like an eternity as Tina regaled me with her memories of Montego Bay and things we would have to do and see once we got there.

We both awoke early, and I got up first and showered then packed up the last of our belongings in the suitcases other than what we would take in our carry-on bags.

I called the bell desk to have our bags picked up. Tina was in the bathroom when the bellman arrived at the door. He had a message with him from Corinne, who was the special events coordinator. After the bellman left with our bags, I opened the letter from Corinne. She wanted to see us before we left for Montego Bay, and the second item in the letter was that our family had arrived Tuesday in Montego Bay, but they had been moved from their original hotel to Wyndam Rose Hall Golf and Country Club due to damage from the hurricane at the Holiday Inn. When Tina exited the bathroom, she asked me what I was reading. I filled her in, and she was eager to go see what Corinne wanted. I told her to relax, and we should go have breakfast first and then we could stop to see her. I've never seen Tina get ready so fast before. We picked up the last of our things and took our remaining carry-on bags with us when we left the room to go for breakfast. Tina ate quickly and asked me to hurry as well.

"What's wrong?" I asked her.

"I have a bad feeling," she said. "I just want to go see her and find out what's up."

I quickly finished, and we went to the special events office where Corinne asked us to be seated as she was dealing with another couple already. Tina was fidgety as we waited, and I couldn't get her to relax. Corinne finished up with the other couple and had us move into her office.

"Well," she said. "I have some good news and some bad news. First off, we are having some delays in finishing the repairs to the Sandals Royal Montego Bay Hotel. The hotel repairs were done, but the private island where they hold weddings in a gazebo was still missing."

"What do you mean, still missing?" I asked.

She went on to say how the hurricane had totally removed the small, man-made island that had been built at that property, and they had been pumping sand into the retaining wall to rebuild the island but it wouldn't be ready for our wedding. Tina's heart sank. It had been the private island that made us choose Sandals Royal in the first place. Corinne went on to say that things at the hotel just weren't as nice as they had hoped they would be by now, and she had two alternatives for us.

"What's that?" we asked.

"Well, the first option is you could stay here for your second week and have the wedding here, or we can have you still go to Mo Bay, and you can stay at the Sandals Montego Bay, or if you really have your heart set on the Royal you could do that and move the wedding to the hotel but I really can't guarantee the condition of the hotel yet."

I was in favour of staying right where we were and having our wedding here. Tina had a good point, though. She hadn't reached her sister, so she would show up in Montego Bay, plus we would have to contact our family and have them travel down to Negril for the day. Corinne showed us some pictures of the Sandals Montego Bay, and it was nowhere near as nice looking as the Royal had looked in the brochure, nor was it as nice as Negril, but it had suffered very little damage from the hurricane, and it was located quite close to the Golf and Country Club our family had been moved to. Corinne assured us that she would make all the necessary changes for us and notify the minister and photographer and videographer of the change in venues. We weren't happy about having to make changes at such a last minute but decided it would be for the best; at least, we would still be in Montego Bay if we had any unexpected guests show up, and it wasn't such a big deal to go from one Sandals in Mo Bay to the other. Tina was a bit upset about the changes and thought it was a bad sign of things to come. The fact that they had a hurricane back in September and now the change of venue and...I stopped her before she got more wound up and asked if she had a good time so far, and before she could answer, I asked if she had been happy to see Aunt Eula and the rest of her family and did she not want to marry me.

She looked at me and said, "You're right. It really isn't a big deal, is it?"

"No," I replied. "Now, let's go out front and wait for the bus to take us to Mo Bay. It should be here soon."

While we sat waiting, I kept an eye out for Vincent, hoping to see him to let him know about our change in locations in Montego Bay. The guard at the gate said the tour bus had passed about forty minutes ago and would be picking up guests from the other hotels closer to town, and we would be the last pickup. I turned to Tina and asked her if she wanted to avoid the long drive and take one of the small planes to Montego Bay.

"No," was her instant response.

To my delight Vincent pulled up and greeted us. "Good morning boss. Me remember ya' was goin' to Mo bay tis morning and tat I was hopin' to se ya and say by and not fur you to worry. I will be bringing Miss Eula on Saturday no problem."

"Actually, Vincent there's a small change. We will be at Sandals Montego Bay rather than Royal Sandals Montego Bay."

Vincent took a slip of paper from his visor and wrote down the name of the hotel. "No problem, boss." He kissed Tina on the cheek and shook hands with me and told us he had to go as he had a pickup down the road.

"You see, Tina," I said. "There is a good sign. Vincent stopped by and now you know Aunt Eula will be there, no problem."

As we pulled into Sandals Montego Bay, I was a bit disappointed by the look of the place. It didn't look as posh and updated as Sandals Negril, nor the pictures I had seen of Royal Sandals, but I said nothing. Tina was stressed out enough as it was. We quickly checked in and went to our room. It was actually not too bad, and we were again right on the beach. We quickly freshened up from the bus ride, which didn't seem anywhere near as long as when we arrived in Montego Bay a week ago. I guess not having been travelling for two days made quite a difference. We strolled around the property and found it to be quite a bit smaller than Negril, but it still had some nice features. It had a little piano bar and these jetties that went out into the water with hanging papasan chairs at the end covered by a gazebo and a fantastic fountain that was lit up by an array of coloured lights.

After touring the hotel, we went to check in with the events planner to make sure things had been arranged the way we had been told in Negril. We met Kimberly in the events office, and she was so sweet and helpful that she put us both at ease immediately, and we both knew we were in good hands. She finalized a few arrangements with us regarding the videographer and the photographer and also told us that due to the time we had planned our wedding, we would have to change the order of a couple things. We both hadn't thought about how early it would get dark when we had planned everything back home. It was dark here by six o'clock in the evening, and the videographer didn't have camera lights, so he basically would only be able to film the wedding ceremony and then he wanted us to do our dance and pictures before it became too dark to film it and also have the cake ceremony before dinner. In the grand scope of things, it wasn't really going to matter, and we left the details up to Kimberly as she seemed to have a good handle on things.

With the arrangements made and our guest passes in hand for the day of the wedding, we went out to the lobby, and I called over to my parent's hotel to see how they had made out and that they had all arrived safely. My mom answered the phone and said they had tried to reach us earlier. I explained about our change in hotels and then she invited us to come over and have dinner with them that evening. Their hotel was practically empty, and she said they were all receiving the royal treatment from the staff. I checked with Tina then asked my mom what time dinner was, and she said they had booked a table for everybody at six o'clock.

"We'll see you then," I replied and hung up the phone.

Tina and I spent the rest of the day hanging out at the beach, swimming and chatting with the other guests. The crowd here was older and somewhat quieter than down in Negril. A lot of fellow Canadians were staying here, and they found it exciting that we were here to get married. An older gent from Ottawa that we became friendly with serenaded us with his harmonica. They may have been an older crowd, but they were a lot of fun. Around four o'clock, Tina thought we should head back to the room and get ready to go to dinner with my parents and family. I sent her ahead and decided to go over to the hot tub for a quick, soothing soak. When I arrived back at our room, Tina was still towelling herself dry and putting lotion on her skin. I took the bottle of lotion from her and slowly began rubbing it into her back and slowly worked down her back to her buttocks.

Tina turned swiftly and scolded me. "When will you learn?" she said. "You're making this harder on both of this than it has to be." Then, she reached inside my swim trunks and dropped an ice cube she had concealed in her hand on my hard penis. "I was ready for you this time" she said as she started laughing.

I left, dejected, to have a quick shower and get dressed for dinner.

We arrived at my parent's hotel around 5:30 and took the elevator up to their floor and found their room. All we had to do was follow the noise, my mom and dad were entertaining my uncle and aunt and my cousin, Wade, having a few cocktails while they waited for my other aunt and uncle to arrive. My dad was quite red from the sun and greeted Tina with a big hug and kiss as he proudly let everyone know that his new daughter-in-law had arrived. My Uncle Reg told me how happy he was that we had invited them. It was their first trip to the Caribbean and they loved it. Uncle Ivan and Aunt Shirley arrived, so we finished our cocktails and proceeded downstairs to the restaurant. Tina's head was spinning as my family asked her 1,001 questions about Jamaica and how had the hurricane affected things, but she was thrilled to answer their questions and was so happy that they loved her little island paradise.

Our dinner took us over three hours as we talked and caught up with everybody. During the course of the evening, they had all decided to go with Tina sightseeing tomorrow and my cousin Wade and I were going to spend the day at our resort doing some water sports. They were the only problems with the resort they were staying at: it had a great golf course that hadn't reopened yet from the hurricane, and the beach area had been decimated by the hurricane and hadn't resumed any of its water activities. With dinner over, Tina and I were quite tired, but my cousin was hoping we would go into the disco with him. We three excused ourselves from the table and made our way to the disco. It was really sad, and I felt sorry for Wade. There were a couple of older couples dancing and a few of the staff, but not much else going on. He told us that the days were great, but he was starving for some nightlife and looking forward to meeting some nice young ladies. We only stayed about a half hour and decided the place was a bust. We left Wade at the elevators and made our way to the front to catch a cab back to our hotel.

On our way back, Tina was asking me where she thought she should take everybody tomorrow.

I said, "I don't know. What do they want to do and see?"

She decided she would take them back into the country areas and that on another day we would all go down to Ocho Rio's and see some of the coast.

Tina and I met my family at ten in the morning out at the front gate and said goodbye. They had hired a mini-bus for the day, and Wade hopped out, and Tina hopped in, and away they went. Wade and I went to the front desk and got him a day pass that allowed him access to the resort for the along day with unlimited food and drinks and activities for the day for just $50 U.S. dollars, which was a great deal considering how much it cost to stay at the resort for a day. The first thing Wade noticed was the abundance of hot, bikini-clad women around the pool and down at the beach. We had a good day windsurfing and sea kayaking and swimming and drank our fair share of rum. Tina found us playing volleyball on the beach when she arrived back. She told Wade that the mini-bus was out front, and she was checking to see if he wanted to head back to Rose Hall with everyone else. He asked, if we didn't mind, he would like to stay at our resort longer since there was a lot more activity going on. Tina told him it wasn't a problem and that she would go tell them he would see them later.

"Thanks, honey," I said to her and gave her a quick kiss before she left.

Wade told me I was a lucky man after Tina had left. I told him I knew, and we resumed playing volleyball. We had finished our volleyball game and were laying on the lounge chairs having another rum-based drink when Tina came back with her bathing suit on. She went into the ocean to cool off, then returned to have a drink with us and told us about the day she had playing tour guide. After a couple more drinks, the three of us went into the sea for a final swim before going back to our room to change for dinner. Tina and I sat out on the terrace while Wade showered and got dressed. I gave him directions to the piano bar lounge and told him we would meet him there after we showered and got ready.

With our room to ourselves, we showered together and realized this was our last night alone as single people. Tomorrow was the big day. Tina had hoped we could have dinner alone, but she was glad to see Wade enjoying himself. He had a rather odd time up to now, being by himself and hanging out with the old folks. It wasn't bad during the day, but we knew he had hoped for more nightlife, but the hurricane had really messed things up and put an odd spin on what should have been an exciting, adventurous vacation for him.

When we found him in the lounge, he was busy chatting away with a nice-looking girl, so we sat down at the far end of the bar to give him his space.

Tina looked over and said, "Do you think Wade realizes this is a couples only hotel, and he has no chance to pick up."

We both laughed, and shortly after that, Wade came over and said, "You know, I just don't understand it. The ladies in here seem so friendly, but every time the conversation gets interesting, some guy shows up, and they leave. It's like every good looking girl in the place is taken."

Tina and I erupted in laughter.

"What?" Wade asked.

Tina explained that he was hitting on women who were already involved. Sandals was a couple's only hotel, and everyone here has a mate.

"Just my luck," Wade replied.

We had a nice dinner, and Wade decided since he was having no luck meeting anyone here and probably wouldn't, he was going to grab a cab and head back to his hotel. Tina gave him a hug and kiss and told him good luck, and we would see him the next day.

Tina and I went to watch some of the evening's entertainment and, after a short time, decided to take a stroll out onto one of the jetty's with the hanging papasan chairs. We snuggled into the chair, allowing the ocean breeze to gently swing us. We both had drifted off to sleep and were awoken by the loud laughter of a group of people on the beach not far away. Hesitantly, we made our way back to our room for a final night of sleep before the big day. I told Tina I was going to sleep in the other bed in our room and that I wouldn't see her in the morning, not until our wedding in the afternoon.

"How will you manage that?" she asked.

"Well, I will stay out of the room in the morning and will come and get dressed when you are having your hair done in the afternoon."

In the morning, I quickly grabbed a small kit bag and grabbed a few things, like my bathing suit and beach towel and slipped out while Tina was still asleep. Off for breakfast I went. Chris, my best man and a player at the resort, stopped and had breakfast with me. He asked if I was nervous or if there was anything I needed. From breakfast, I passed the main pool, and they had an announcement posted about our wedding in the afternoon and that all were invited to attend. I made my way to the far end of the resort and lounged back and forth between the pool and the hot tub. As I sat there talking with people, Joe from Ottawa, the harmonica player, offered to play for our wedding. I wasn't too sure, but he assured me it would just be in the background, so I thanked him and figured it would be a nice touch and a surprise for Tina. People were stopping and wishing me well and bringing me over drinks. The more fuss they made, the more nervous I was getting. I soon realized I had better start turning down the drinks, or I would be real messy and that was something I was determined not to let happen.

By 1:00 p.m., I went back to the room to get ready. I hung my suit on the back of the shower door and showered and shaved and primped myself. I wasn't finished when I heard Tina and her Aunt Eula and another lady enter the room. We spoke briefly through the bathroom door, and I told her she would have to go out on the patio so I could leave. The other lady was her sister who had gone to Aunt Eula's the night before and rode to Montego Bay with Aunt Eula and Vincent.

When I went back out, I saw Vincent and the rest of our guests having lunch at the buffet restaurant. I stopped to chat, and my mom asked if I was going to eat with them. I told her I couldn't and went to make sure things were ready. I found Kimberly, our coordinator, and she told me that Tina and I had to meet with the minister at three o'clock in our room to go over a few things before the ceremony. Kimberly said she would go and inform Tina of the meeting with the minister. I paced around the resort, surprised how nervous I had become and was glad that it was finally three o'clock.

I went to our room and knocked on the door. Claudette, Tina's sister, answered the door and I went in and met her and said hello to Aunt Eula. Tina had on a robe so I couldn't see the dress she was wearing. After a few minutes passed, the minister arrived. Kimberly escorted Aunt Eula and Claudette to the wedding area while Tina and I talked with the minister. We were both shocked. I thought the minister would have been Jamaican, but he was from the small town in New Brunswick where I had been born, and I knew of his brother because he ran the only photography studio in town. We started talking and filling him in about the town and what was going on in Sackville. This was surely a good omen. We had talked and reminisced for about an hour when my parents knocked on the door.

"Are you two still getting married?" they asked.

"Yes, of course," we replied.

Then they came in, and we introduced them to the minister, and they starting talking and were shocked that he was from our hometown. I left with the minister, and my mom stayed behind to help Tina. As I waited at the altar, it seemed like they were taking forever, then my mom appeared and following behind was my dad with Tina on his arm. Joe began playing "The Bridal Chorus" on his harmonica as they proceeded over the small bridge to the altar. The small crowd of hotel guests that had gathered along with family to witness the ceremony erupted in applause as Tina arrived at the altar with my dad, who was beaming like he was the proud father rather than the father-in-law to be.

Tragedy

The door bumped my chair and stirred me from my deep daydream as the nurse entered the room. She was startled to see me still sitting by Tina's bedside, holding her hand.

"Mr. Beals, you should go home. There is nothing you can do. We will keep a close eye on your wife and call you if anything changes. The doctor has told us to keep her on a rich flow of oxygen, and he will reassess her condition tomorrow."

"No," I replied. "That's okay. I am staying right here, thank you. This is our first Christmas in Halifax, and I'm not about to leave her here all alone on Christmas Eve."

The nurse turned to me and said that since it was Christmas Eve, she would relax the rules for me so I could stay all night. "Feel free to lay down in the empty bed next to your wife's," she told me as she left the room, warning me that they would be coming in and out of the room every two hours to check Tina's oxygen levels, so I wouldn't get much sleep.

"That's fine," I told her. "Thank you."

As I sat holding Tina's hand, staring at her sweet face with an oxygen mask attached while they tried desperately to increase the oxygen levels in her blood, I wish it was all a bad dream. But it wasn't. It had been just a little more than seven years ago when we had celebrated our vows in Jamaica and had our dream wedding and honeymoon, and now I was terrified. I had never been away from Tina before except when, less than three weeks after we returned from our honeymoon, Tina returned to Rochester for her grandmother's funeral. My thoughts turned to all the events of the past seven years that brought us to Halifax, the many trips and holidays we had taken the hard work of building up and expanding the typesetting business and then watching as technology made our business obsolete and sent us into a whole new career.

We came to Halifax just over seven months ago to take the positions of Table Games Floor supervisors at the new casino that had opened back in May. After selling off our typesetting business in Calgary, we both had become blackjack dealers in Calgary, which eventually led to what we thought would be a fresh start. In addition to bringing us geographically closer to Tina's family, she was hopeful that it would bring an end to the terror we had suffered from her ex-husband all these years, and once we were settled, we would have a safe haven to raise her kids. Since coming east, we had managed to visit her family three times and saw the kids two out of the three times. Previous to that we were lucky if we managed to secretly see the kids once a year. We had just visited Tina's family in November because we weren't going to be able to get any vacation time at Christmas and had planned to have a low-key holiday so we could afford to go back to Rochester in the New Year.

When we got to the hospital earlier that day, and Tina found out she was going to have to stay overnight, she sent me home to get the Christmas card she had gotten me, and I brought hers as well. She made me laugh as she apologized for ruining Christmas by getting sick.

"Hey it's not your fault," I reassured her.

We had gone to our staff Christmas party just over a week ago, and Tina had a little shortness of breath, but she figured it was just from all the dancing and the late hours we were working. When it progressively got worse over the next couple of days, she went to the doctor who gave her a prescription and told her she had pneumonia and that the pills would make her better in a couple of days. After our days off, Tina was still feeling really lousy, so she took a sick day, and I went to work. When I got home, she seemed worse again.

"The medication is doing nothing. You had better call your doctor," I said.

When I awoke later that day, having worked all night, I asked her if she had called the doctor.

"Yes," she said, "but she is off for the holidays."

"That doesn't make sense," I said to Tina. "Didn't she tell you when you saw her that if you weren't better in three days to call her?"

"Yes ," Tina replied.

I was frustrated by my first encounter with the Nova Scotia medical system— it was nothing like Alberta's.

That evening, Tina was still feeling poorly and said she was having a hard time catching her breath. "Let me stay home with you then."

"No, you go to work," she told me. "Tomorrow is Christmas Eve, and we're off for a couple of days. I just need some rest."

"Are you sure?" I asked.

"Yes," she replied. "Just go and quit bugging me."

When I returned home early Christmas Eve morning from work, Tina was sound asleep, so I quietly slipped into bed beside her and drifted off. I had only been asleep a short time when I was awakened by Tina's shivering and laboured breathing. I called the emergency medical clinic where Tina's doctor worked and left an emergency message for a doctor to get back to me. Within twenty minutes, a Dr. Maria called me and asked a few questions. I explained the situation, and she said she was covering for Dr. Lackey, and she asked me where we lived. I gave her our address, and to my surprise, she said she would stop and see her within the hour but to try and get her dressed because there was a good chance she would have to go to the hospital. I struggled to clean Tina up and got her dressed.

"I don't want to go to the hospital," she whimpered. "It's Christmas."

"You may not have to," I told her. "The doctor just said to get you ready."

The doorbell rang, and it was Dr. Maria. She went into our bedroom and asked me to step out while she examined Tina. When she called me back into the bedroom, she told me that she was on her way into the hospital and that she wanted me to take Tina to emergency. She would call ahead so they would be expecting us. A look of fear came over Tina's face, but Dr. Maria assured her it was just to get her fluid levels and things up, and since it was Christmas time, it would be better to go in sooner than later. With Dr. Maria's help, I got Tina into our van and drove her to emergency where Dr. Maria had her immediately admitted to a room. *Maybe the Nova Scotia medical system isn't so bad after all,* I thought.

Thump! The door hit my chair again as two nurses came in to draw blood from Tina so they could test the oxygen levels.

"Are you sure you wouldn't like to lie in the empty bed?" one of the nurses asked.

"No, I'll just sit here and hold her hand, thank you," I responded.

Without saying another word, the nurses wheeled the empty bed over next to Tina's. I just smiled at them as they left. The empty bed looked tempting, and I was exhausted from the previous night's work. After fighting the urge, I lay on the bed and held Tina's hand. I was embarrassed when the nurses came back in: I was sound asleep and, according to Tina, had been snoring up a storm. The nurse told us the previous sample they had taken two hours earlier showed that her oxygen levels were stabilizing and things were slowly starting to look better. With that bit of good news, I gave Tina a peck on the forehead, and we both went back to sleep.

It was Christmas morning, and I looked over at Tina. She was still sleeping. I stood up and stretched my back out. I hadn't slept all that well, but I was glad to have been able to stay the night with Tina. I walked over and looked out the window where a light skiff of snow was falling. We had both been amazed at how mild the weather was here in Halifax compared to Calgary. I sat back in the chair and watched Tina rest; I couldn't believe we were in the hospital from a case of pneumonia. I always thought it was like a bad cold, but I guess with the odd hours we worked at the casino and all the changes in our lives in the last year, Tina had just become too tired and run down to fight it off. They had kept her on oxygen all night, and the results had improved, so hopefully, she would be released today or tomorrow, and we could go to a nice restaurant and have our Christmas dinner. I was feeling a bit restless and grungy having slept in my clothes all night and was anxious for Tina to wake up so I would have someone to talk to. I waited for about a half hour and still Tina was sound asleep. I whispered in her ear that I was going to go home to shower and change. I stopped at the nursing station to tell them I was going home for a shower but would be back soon.

"Oh, that's fine. The doctor will be making rounds about eight o'clock if you want to talk to him," the nurse told me. I looked at my watch. It was only 6:30, so I had plenty of time to go home and make it back.

The streets were empty as I drove back to our condo out in Bedford. A feeling of loneliness came over me. It felt so strange to leave Tina in the hospital and come home by myself. As I turned to go up the hill to where our condo was, I noticed that the snow was falling heavier. How strange it was that by leaving the seaside and going up a couple hundred feet, the weather could change so much. By the time I had finished showering and changed and got back downstairs to the van, enough snow had accumulated that I had to sweep it off.

I had just finished when I heard someone say good morning. I turned to see Patrick, another floor supervisor from work. He and his wife and son lived in the complex ,as well as quite a few other staff from the casino, some of who we worked with in Calgary before so we had our own little community.

"What are you doing out and about so early on Christmas morning?" he asked.

I quickly filled him in on how Tina's pneumonia had gotten so bad that she and I ended up spending the night in the hospital. He extended a quick invitation for us to join them for Christmas dinner if we were home by five, and I thanked him and told him I doubted Tina would feel up to going out for dinner. A quick check of my watch and I made my apology, as it was almost twenty minutes to eight, and I had to get back in time to talk with the doctor.

When I reached the hospital, I was told I would have to wait as the doctor was just finishing up his examination of Tina and then I could go in and speak with him. I paced impatiently, anxious to see if I could take Tina home. The doctor came out and told me he still had concerns. The earlier tests had shown an improvement in her oxygen levels, but they had dropped off again. He had increased her oxygen feed up to almost 90, and he wanted to monitor her until around noon to see if that would improve things. I asked him to explain things to me again because I didn't really understand what he meant by her oxygen levels in the blood. Since she was breathing fine, what was the problem? He explained that her blood was not absorbing the oxygen due to the pneumonia in her lungs. I still wasn't sure what he was talking about but asked him what would happen if things weren't better at noon.

"Well, let's not get ahead of ourselves," the doctor said as he excused himself and went on to continue his rounds.

I went in to see Tina. She looked so tired and pale and could hardly speak. The almost pure oxygen was drying her out. She grabbed my hand as I sat on the bed next to her, and she looked worried. I brushed my hand over her forehead and told her not to worry and gently talked with her till she drifted back off to sleep. When the nurse came, she filled a reservoir attached to the oxygen mask with saline solution and explained that it would help her from becoming dehydrated, and she asked me if I had any other questions. Not wanting to wake Tina, I spoke with the nurse just outside of Tina's room and asked her what would happen next and if it was serious.

"It isn't," she replied. "But if her oxygen levels don't increase, we would have to possibly put her on a respirator."

"Why?" I asked.

"Well, it will do the breathing for her, and it forces the lungs to work and absorb the oxygen and give her a chance to rest."

I was starting to feel scared and confused but tried not to show it when I went back in the room. I sat quietly and watched Tina sleep. *Some first Christmas for us in Nova Scotia,* I thought.

At ten o'clock, the nurse came in and woke Tina so they could take more blood. I used the opportunity to go down the hall and use the bathroom and decided to call my parents to wish them a Merry Christmas and also to tell them about Tina. When I got back to the room, Tina was still awake, and I told her I called my parents, and they told me to wish her a Merry Christmas and a speedy recovery.

"That's nice, they are so sweet," she managed to say before coughing and coughing. Tina explained what the nurse said. "That's good if I cough. It will get all that phlegm out."

I asked Tina if she wanted me to call her mom and sister and let them know what was happening.

"No, let's just wait till we see what the doctor has to say. I'd rather wait and call them from home; I don't want them to worry."

"Okay," I agreed.

Tina sat up and reached over to her bed stand and opened the drawer, pulled out the unopened Christmas cards I had brought from home a day earlier, and we each opened the cards and read them to each other. I fought to keep the tears back that were welling up behind my eyes. Over the seven years that we had been married, our Christmas cards had always been a special gift to one another, each starting the search months before Christmas to find the perfect card with just the right sentiment, and we always included some type of gift: concert tickets, airline tickets, restaurant coupons, spa vouchers. It was funny this year, with the recent move and having travelled to Rochester so recently, we both took it easy, but the funny thing was we ended up each putting in a $20 celebration lottery ticket to be drawn on New Year's Day. We figured that was a good omen that we had both picked the same thing.

"Good luck," Tina said.

"You, too," I replied as I kissed her and put our cards on her bed stand.

She passed me her lotto ticket and told me to take good care of it

"I will," I promised. "I have a good feeling about it."

The nurse came in and told us she had bad news for us.

"What?" I asked.

She said, "Mrs. Beals oxygen levels aren't getting to the point where the doctor feels comfortable so he wants to move her upstairs and put her on the respirator."

"For how long?" I asked.

"I don't know," she replied. "You can talk to the doctor once we get her settled in on the seventh floor."

Tina was looking scared, and she said she wanted to call her mom. The nurse told her to wait until she got to the seventh floor as there would be a phone by her bedside, and it would be much easier to do up there. She then began explaining what was going to happen on the seventh floor. Tina would be hooked up to an IV so that they could administer fluids as well as medications without constantly sticking needles into her. They also were going to put a line into her vein for the blood draws.

"Will that hurt?" Tina asked.

"A little," the nurse said, "but then we won't have to keep sticking you to draw blood every time."

Another nurse entered pushing a wheelchair into the room with a portable oxygen tank attached to it, and the two nurses moved Tina from her bed into the chair. The nurse passed me a large plastic bag and told me I could put her clothes and coat into it, and they would seal it and store it on the seventh floor at the nursing station. I followed behind as we took the patient's elevator up to seven. I noticed the elevator listed what was on each floor, eight was surgery and critical care and seven was the Intensive Care Unit. I inquired with the nurse if Tina was going to intensive care.

"Yes," was her reply.

Tina and I looked at each other, wondering what the hell was going on. The nurse must have sensed our apprehension and quickly told us that she had to go to I.C.U. in order to go on a respirator and not to worry, and besides, on this floor, Tina get her very own nurse around the clock. I was glad for that at least. She would be closely monitored, not that I was all that worried. After all, it was just pneumonia.

Tina was put into bed number one. I quickly looked around the intensive care unit and saw and counted 12 beds. There were three rooms at the far end that were glassed in and were more private. The rest of the beds were separated by a curtain, and in the centre of the floor was a glassed-in nursing station and lots of monitoring equipment. The two nurses who brought Tina up told her to get well soon and off they went. I saw one of them stop at the nurse's station and talk with a tall brunette nurse, and she looked over and smiled. Tina noticed the phone on the table by her bed and said she wanted to call her mom now. I passed her the phone and dialled the number for her. She was acting like nothing was wrong, asking her mom if she got the presents she had sent and talked to each of the kids. When her sister got on the phone, she told her not to worry but that she was in the hospital with pneumonia but told her not to tell everyone else. She didn't want them to worry for nothing. Tina called me over and said her sister wanted to talk to me and wish me a Merry Christmas. I took the phone and kept smiling while her sister told me to phone her back as soon as I could from a pay phone so she could find out what was going on. Just then, the nurse appeared, and it gave me an excuse to hang up. Tina's family overreacted to everything.

"Hi Mr. Beals, Mrs. Beals. I'm Nurse Ward. I'll be looking after you until midnight, then we have a shift change, and the other nurse will be Nurse Blask."

She showed Tina where the call button was located and how to use it. She asked me if I would mind waiting out in the family room while she did a few tests and got Tina ready for the respiratory therapist and assured me she would come and get me as soon as I could come back in. I gave Tina a kiss and told her not to worry; everything was going to be all right. There was one other lady waiting in the family room, just sitting working on her knitting. I sat down across from her and put my head back and closed my eyes for a few minutes. I was suddenly feeling extreme fatigued; my body felt like it was made of lead. I had woken myself with my own snoring and looked around, unsure of where I was and what I was doing for a second.

The other lady was still sitting there knitting, and she spoke when she saw me awake. "Hello. Terrible way to spend Christmas, isn't it?" she said to me. "I'm Mrs. Bealson."

"Hi, I'm David Beals," I replied.

Our last names were very similar and that seemed to be all it took for us to form an immediate solidarity in the family waiting room. Her husband, Chuck, had a heart attack and had contracted pneumonia, so he was in intensive care recuperating as well. Barb, as she asked me to call her, had put me at ease about pneumonia and how common it was. I checked my watch and even with my nap, which felt like I had slept for hours, and our conversation, only 20 minutes had passed. Barb assured me that the nurses were great, and as soon as they were ready for me to go back in, they would come out to get me.

"Thanks," I replied still anxious to return to Tina's bedside.

I heard some movement coming down the hall, and as a doctor passed, Barb informed me that it was the respiratory therapist and not to worry unless they, meaning the staff, came running down the hall, it would just be a routine stop in I.C.U.. I told her that they were supposed to hook my wife up to a respirator. Another tense 20 minutes passed, and Nurse Ward came out to get me. She also told Mrs. Bealson that they were done attending to her husband, and she could go back in as well.

Tina had a mask over her face and two large tubes running from it to a large blue machine with two baffles in it that went up and down, forcing air in and out of Tina's mouth. She had a heart monitor hooked up as well as a monitor that gave constant measures of her blood oxygen levels. Nurse Ward explained what the different pieces of equipment were for and how they worked. I could see the anxiety in Tina's face increase more and more as the nurse gave me information. I sat there and held Tina's hand and gently stroked her forehead for a while then the nurse excused herself and said they had to do reports but that she would be only over at the nursing station. After she left, Tina asked me a question that sent shivers down my spine.

"Am I going to die?"

"Don't be foolish," I responded. "You have pneumonia. You'll be outta here in a couple of days."

I squeezed her hand, and she smiled at me and mouthed, "I love you," then she drifted off to sleep. I watched the oxygen monitor. Tina had been on it for a couple of hours, but I saw very little improvement in her levels. Her pneumonia must have really attacked her lungs badly to cause such a rapid decrease in their ability to function.

Nurse Ward came over and told me I would have to wait out in the family room for about forty minutes while the doctors and residents made rounds, and someone would be out to let me know when I could return. I walked by the family waiting room and went over to the payphone at the end of the hallway by the elevators to call Tina's mom and sister. They were bewildered at how she got so sick so fast and seemed suspicious of everything that I told them. I was confused by their apparent sudden mistrust of me. I struggled in all the confusion to try and relay all the information I had available, but I was really starting to feel the strain now and had become gripped with fear and worry myself. I needed somebody to be there for me, and I had no one. After I hung up the phone with Tina's family, I called my mom and dad back and updated them on the situation. My mom asked me if I wanted them to come down. In my heart, I did, but if they came, that would be like me admitting that Tina was really sick, so I told them not to come and that everything was going to be fine.

When I returned to the waiting room, Barb and her son were there, waiting to go back in. I gathered from their conversation that Chuck had a setback and wished them both well. A few minutes passed, and we were all able to go back in. Back at Tina's bedside, I noticed her vitals had not improved. The nurse informed me that the doctor wanted to do a tracheotomy in the morning if things didn't improve overnight. She went on to explain the procedure to Tina and myself.

I spent the rest of the evening sitting beside Tina, stroking her forehead and wiping her brow with a cool cloth, drifting in and out of sleep. It was just before midnight, the nurse woke and told me I had to go to the waiting room while they did rounds for the shift change and someone would come and get me when it was okay to come back in. The family room was empty, so I took the opportunity to check things out more in detail and noticed they had a small fridge and microwave in the kitchen area and washroom and some pillows and blankets in the closet. It was nicely equipped and remarkably comfortable. It was funny how the lack of sleep and the stress of the situation made my mind work; looking at the details of the room was like a mini-vacation to the mind and very restful. For a whole two minutes, I had stopped thinking about Tina and her situation. I was totally exhausted and just wanted sleep.

I grabbed a pillow out of the closet and sat in one of the reclining chairs with the pillow comfortably behind my neck. I was awoken by the noise of a gurney being rolled by and into the intensive care unit. The room was dim with only the lights from the hallway shining through the windows to illuminate it. I also now was covered by a blanket. It bothered me to think I had been in that deep a sleep and got up and went into the washroom to check my appearance. I was stopped at the I.C.U. room doors and told I would have to wait for a couple of minutes as they were just settling a new patient into her bed. I went back in and sat beside Tina and not much had changed in her vitals. The new patient had been put next to Tina's curtained off section. I was unhappy to lose the privacy I felt we had by having an empty bed between us and the other patients. I had dozed off and on through the night, not really getting any amount of sleep, but every five minutes' worth felt like an hour. I was starting to feel a bit delirious, not knowing what had been dreamed and what had actually happened. The nurse, seeing I was awake, came over and told me they would be taking Tina up to surgery in about an hour, and then she reassured me not to worry as it was a simple procedure. I went out to the waiting room and saw through the window in the door an older couple lying down on the two couches covered by blankets. I turned and went towards the elevator to go down to the cafeteria and get some breakfast and read the paper and pass some time while Tina was in surgery.

I couldn't eat much and reading the paper seemed almost impossible. I couldn't concentrate on what I was trying to read, rereading the same article over and over with no comprehension of what I had just finished reading. I went back upstairs and the waiting room was empty, so I went in and got comfortable. I barely opened my eyes at the sound of the couple across the room talking in hushed tones. It was his mother that had been brought in the middle of the night from Truro by ambulance, and from what I overheard, it sounded terminal. Feeling uncomfortable at being able to hear them discussing such private information, I shuffled my feet and straightened up and opened my eyes. The couple stopped talking. After a few awkward moments of silence, we introduced ourselves to each other, then resumed the still silence again, all just staring out the windows of the room towards the door into the I.C.U.. The doors flew open and out came a couple of nurses with a gurney. They stopped just outside the waiting room, and one of the nurses motioned for me to come out. They had Tina on the gurney on her way up to surgery. I kissed her and hugged her hand and told her not to worry and away they went. Back inside the waiting room, I began to pace around the small room, sitting down then almost immediately getting back up and pacing again.

Barb Bealson entered the room. She had gone home for the night. "How's your wife this morning?" she asked.

I explained that they had taken her up for surgery for a tracheal.

"Oh, don't worry," she said. "It's simple, and she'll be back in no time."

Still fidgeting, I announced I was going to go to Tim Horton's coffee shop in the basement and offered to get Barb, Jim, and Francis coffee. Barb accepted and the other couple, Jim and Francis, asked for tea instead. While in the coffee shop, I also purchased a box of Tim Bits, little tiny donuts. I put the coffee tray and donuts on the cupboard in the little kitchen and told everyone to help themselves to the donuts and drinks. They thanked me, and we all sat down. Barb had filled them in about her situation, and I told them about mine as well and had gotten the information on Jim's mother as well. It was strange how after less than two days in this waiting room, complete strangers suddenly become my most trusted confidants and allies.

It seemed like it had only been 20 minutes ago that they wheeled Tina into the elevator to go to surgery, and she was already back settled into her room when the nurse came to get me.

"Mr. Beals, you can come back in now, and the doctor will be around in about twenty minutes to talk to you, but he did say to tell you that it went fine."

Tina was unconscious when I approached her bedside. I immediately noticed that with the breathing tube now attached to the tracheal tube in her neck, her vitals had already begun to improve. I asked the nurse how long before she would wake up. She seemed somewhat puzzled by my question and said the doctor would be by soon, and he could explain and answer any questions I might have.

Dr. Ward came and stopped at Tina's bedside. "Mr. Beals, as I'm sure the nurse told you, your wife's surgery went fine, and it was a pretty simple procedure."

"Thank you, Doctor. Can you tell me how long before she will wake up?"

A confused look came over his face as well. "Ah, Mr. Beals, I, ah, I thought you realized that because of the amount of air pressure we have to force into your wife's airway, we have to keep her sedated in an unconscious state. Basically, she is in a medicated coma," he told me.

Stunned, I looked at him amazed. How could I not have been told that she would be in a medicated coma? "How long?" I asked again.

He replied that until her lungs were healthier and able to normally absorb oxygen that they would have to keep her chest cavity pressurized, and if she was awake, the pain from her ribs being forced to contract and expand would be excruciating.

"Oh, so as soon as her pressure is reduced, she will regain consciousness after you stop drugging her?"

"Yes, pretty much." He excused himself and went over to the nursing station.

I wanted to start yelling. I feet like things were moving so fast and out of control. How, just a few days ago, we could be having a great time at our Christmas party, and now, the love of my life suddenly is so sick that it requires a machine to make her breath, and she is in a medically induced coma.

It was time for another shift change. I was exhausted and thanked heaven the nurses didn't kick me out but allowed me to stay at Tina's bedside. I occasionally fell asleep but never let go of her hand. I wanted to be sure she knew I was there. She would be so scared if she woke up and I wasn't there. Later that afternoon, the nurse informed me that a nurse and a doctor from New York City had called earlier and wanted to obtain information on the condition of my wife. "That's her Aunt Joy. Go ahead. I give my permission for you to release any information they may want."

When I went out to use the washroom, the family room was quite crowded. It looked like Jim and Francis' family had brought them Christmas dinner. I passed Barb in the hall as I made my way to the pay phone. I called my parents house to tell them the latest, but there was no answer. I called and talked to Tina's sister Dawn and filled her in on the latest news. She informed me that Aunt Joy had tried to get some information earlier, and I told her to let her know that I had authorized the release of information to her so tell her to call back. I called work to let them know I would be off for a couple more days, and they were very accommodating and told me to take all the time I needed and if I needed anything to just give them a call. The casino felt like an extended family member; everyone we worked with was so nice and friendly. The three top managers—Mel, Ron, and Jack, from the U.S., who had come to run things—were top notch and really took care of their staff. They had already sent flowers to Tina.

With the family room still crowded, I decided to go down for a coffee. I let Jim know where I was going if the nurses came out looking for me. I felt like a mess. I didn't know whether I was coming or going. They must have told me she would be paralysed and in a coma. How could I not have heard and remembered that? I found myself shaking with chills one minute and perspiring from heat the next. I couldn't keep any food down, only coffee. I couldn't seem to get enough of that.

I exited the elevator on the seventh floor and was shocked to see my mom standing outside the family room talking to Barb, who had just finished telling her that I would probably be back soon. I put my arms around her and tears filled my eyes. When I wiped away the tears from my eyes, I saw my dad sitting in the waiting room as well.

"Thanks, Mom," I whispered into her ear. "I'm glad you came."

The waiting room emptied out, and my dad gave me a hug when I went into the room and told how sorry he was that I had to go through this and how he thought of Tina just like a daughter. He pulled away from me, and I realized his eyes had gotten teary as well and didn't want me too see it.

My mom asked if they could go in and see Tina after I had finished filling them in on her latest condition.

"I think so," I said. "Just let me check with the nurse."

"Yes," she said, "they could go in, but only one at a time."

When I informed my parents, my mom wanted to go first, but asked if I would go in with her, she was afraid of what she might see. Once at Tina's bedside, mom was fine. I explained what the different machines were and once she felt comfortable, I told her I would go wait with dad.

Sitting with my dad, I told him I was surprised to see them.

He said, "You can thank your mother. After your last phone call, she told me she was going to Halifax and wanted to know if I was coming as well. I said yes, and she booked us out on the next flight."

Mom came out, and I could tell she had been crying. I took Dad in and left him at her bedside and went back out to sit with my mom. We hugged, and she told me Tina would be all right.

"I know she will, Mom. I know she will."

It wasn't too long before my dad came out, and we took the elevator down to the lobby. My mom wanted to go outside for a smoke, and my dad had to fill the parking metre. They had rented a car at the airport. We visited for a few more minutes, and my parents asked how to get to the hotel where the casino was.

"What for?" I asked.

"Well we have booked a room there," was the reply.

"Why don't you just go out to our apartment?"

"Well, we could but we don't know our way around, and your father and I thought it would be better if we were within walking distance for now," my mother said.

With that, I gave them directions to the hotel. They left, saying they wanted to shower and such and would be back around suppertime. Back up on the seventh floor, I went into the waiting room to use the washroom to freshen up a bit and when I came out Barb was sitting on the couch.

"Your parents seem very nice," she said. "You must be relieved to have them here."

"I am," I replied. I had only known Barb a short time, and yet, she was like a life-long friend. Nurses and doctors and respiratory therapists, even the coffee shop staff: after they see a person around the clock for a couple of days, it's like they are all suddenly good friends.

I went back in to see how Tina was and hadn't been there too long when the nurse came by and asked if I wanted to help out. "Sure," I asked. "What can I do?"

"You can rub her feet and legs and help the blood circulate and avoid her getting bed sores," she replied.

I asked the nurse if they had any body lotion or cream, and she brought me several tubes. I massaged Tina's feet first with the cream as I had noticed her feet were looking a bit dry and then did her legs, arms, back and neck. It felt good to be able to do something to help her besides just sitting there holding her hand. God knows, over the years, how many times she had massaged my scalp or rubbed cream on my back or massaged my tired feet after a long day at work. Seeing Tina lie there in bed, helpless, only made me appreciate her more day by day. I felt like I had been so selfish over the years. She had always been there comforting me and taking care of my needs. Sure, I had showered her with expensive gifts and lavish trips and plenty of romantic gestures, and I did tell her happy and in love I was with her, but when was the last time that I just spontaneously gave her a massage without being asked? I felt like such a heel as I reflected over the years. It was always Tina who gave so much of herself, running her fingers through my hair till I fell asleep on hot summer nights. I just wanted her to wake up and get better so I could do more of the things for her that she had done over the years for me.

I wondered why and how could God have given her so much grief and trouble in her life when she was such a kind and caring person, but she always said her Aunt Eula told her God only gave her as much to handle as He knew she can, but I still didn't know why.

After the doctor did rounds, he told me that the pneumonia wasn't getting any better, so they were still running many more blood tests and had sent a sample to disease control. In the meantime, he wanted to try her on some aggressive drug therapy. After he explained the pros and cons, I asked if he would consult with her Aunt Joy's boss, the doctor from New York.

"Have him call me, or do you have his number?" Dr. Ward asked.

"I'll call her aunt and let you know." I went out and called Aunt Joy, who then conference called with Dr. Ward and her boss. When the doctor returned, he questioned me as to what type of doctor her aunt's boss was, and in the future, he would only deal and relay information to me, and I could pass it on to them. I called Aunt Joy, and she was quite demanding about what kind of backwoods hospital Tina was in. The high-class Park Avenue practice that she worked in had developed her into trying to carry herself in a certain manner and station, but I had never been impressed by wealth and status. Her aunt and I had butted heads a few times in the past over simple things like when I would pick up a dinner bill. She had always been accustomed in the past to her family allowing or expecting her to pay for this or pay for that. I was my own man and paid my own way.

Regardless of our difficulties, she explained in simple terms what the drug was supposed to do, and that its pros outweighed the cons, so I consented for them to start her on the drug therapy. My parents had returned from the hotel and had brought me something to eat. We sat in the waiting room, and I ate the cold chicken and had a pop to drink. My parents said the hotel had been very accommodating to them and had given them a free room and asked if we had more family coming in. The hotel would try to keep a couple rooms available, but we had to let them know soon, as it was New Year's Eve coming up.

With my parents there and my mom at Tina's bedside, I took the opportunity to go home and have a shower and change my clothes but hurried back to the hospital. I just didn't feel right leaving her there without me. Mom was tired and so was Dad, so I told them to go to their hotel and get some sleep. I would call if anything changed. We hugged, and they left, and I went back in and sat with Tina holding her hand and drifted in and out of sleep. It was about 4:30 in the morning, and my mom came in.

"What are you doing here?" I asked her.

"I couldn't sleep," she said. "I hopped in a cab and decided to come back and sit with you and Tina for a while."

"Thanks, Mom," I said.

Although we were talking in hushed tones, the nurse came over and said only one of us at a time could be at her bedside at this time of morning, so we decided to both go out to the family room so we could talk. On the way out, my mom mentioned she was craving a cigarette, so we decided to go down and get a coffee, and I went outside with her while she had her cigarette. We exchanged stories about Tina and funny things that had happened over the years.

"You know, your dad hasn't slept much since you called us the first time. He just talked about how proud he was that she asked him to walk her down the aisle in Jamaica, and I've never seen him cry so much."

We reminisced about the wedding day, and how once they crossed the bridge to the alter, Dad proudly spoke up when the minister asked, "Who gives this woman?" and remembered the tender kiss he gave her before handing her off to me. Aside from the incredible breeze, the day had been perfect. I reminded my mom how she started to laugh when she had to do her religious reading during the ceremony. She still didn't know why that happened. We signed the register and cut our wedding cake, followed by a long-standing tradition of the bride hiding a piece of the wedding cake in her mouth and the groom having to retrieve it, using only his mouth and tongue. Our Jamaican wedding had a few other subtle changes; the next process was photographs followed immediately by our dancing amongst the almond trees with the moonlight shimmering through the leaves. From there, we went to our private dinner. My mom asked if I remembered what happened during our dinner.

I said, "You mean after all the toasts were done?"

"Yes," she replied.

Our wedding guests slowly disappeared, two by two, to go watch the nearby crab races that were going on. Tina and I thought that would be the perfect opportunity to slip back to our room and change out of our wedding attire and perhaps consummate our wedding vows. Our guests foiled that plan by loudly arriving at our patio doors. We could clearly hear them listening at the door and laughing and making a big ruckus. With shorts and shirts on, Tina flipped on our lights at the same time as I drew open the drapes. They all came crashing into our room, and after a few more stories and well wishes, they left us on our own to enjoy our wedding night. The day had been absolutely perfect.

Mom butted out her cigarette and dried her eyes. Mine had tears as well remembering that day so fondly. We went back upstairs, and Mom suggested I try to get some sleep in the family room and she would sit with Tina.

"Okay," I agreed, "but promises to wake me if you are going to leave."

"I will," she said.

I had slept for almost an hour when I heard the door open. It was my dad.

"I woke up and your mother was gone, so I thought maybe something had happened," he said.

"No," I replied. "Mom just said she couldn't sleep."

Dad sat with me, and we chatted for a bit until he heard the hunger pangs emanating from my stomach and suggested we get my mom and go for a bite of breakfast.

"That sounds good, Dad," I replied and went to get Mom.

When we came out, Dad asked for us to wait for a minute. He wanted to go in and see Tina before we left. As we ate breakfast, I could tell Mom was ready for sleep.

"Listen, thanks for breakfast, Dad, but you know not much is going to happen around here until the doctor makes his rounds and the blood test results come back. That's usually around eleven, so you guys might as well go back to the hotel and get some rest."

They agreed and left, and I went back up to Tina's bedside.

I had a strange feeling suddenly come over me. I don't know what it was, but even though the doctors and everyone seemed to think things were looking bleak, I suddenly knew in my heart that Tina was going to be okay. It was more than wishful thinking. I couldn't explain what it was, but I suddenly felt a sense of relief for the first time. I was now 100 percent sure that Tina was going to recover.

The doctor, a different one than Dr. Ward, looked like a little girl barely out of med school. Dr. Nancy explained that they rotated out of intensive care every two weeks, but Dr. Ward would still monitor Tina's progress, and she assured me she was fully briefed. The nurses on duty assured me that Dr. Nancy was a good and highly qualified doctor. I wasn't so sure until, for the first time, I saw a more aggressive approach to Tina's care. She ordered an extensive number of tests to find out why she hadn't been responding to her medications. In a private consultation with me, Dr. Nancy seemed to be looking into AIDS.

"AIDS," I told her. "You are way off base and wasting time. I know that I have been faithful, and I know that she has been faithful, so there was no way for her to contact it."

"The fact remains," said Doctor Nancy, "that her strain of pneumonia, that had still not been identified, had the characteristics of AIDS." She wanted me to go to haematology to be tested as well.

Five days, and it seemed like they were still guessing what was wrong. At least the new doctor had ordered a bunch of new tests, so maybe we would finally find out what was wrong. It was just after twelve o'clock when Tina's sister Dawn and her Aunt Joy had arrived from New York. I gave Dawn a hug and told her it was nice to see her but that she didn't need to come all that way. Tina was going to be all right and would be upset that they came all that way for nothing. Aunt Joy was more to the point.

"Where is Tina? I want to see my niece and see what these quacks have been doing to her. Don't you see this place it is so old? Is this the best place for her? What kind of witchcraft doctoring do they practice up here?

I now understood more why my doctor only wanted to communicate through me. Aunt Joy meant well, and for all her hoity-toityness, she could be a little crass when it came to Canada and our "backwoods ways," in her opinion. I took Dawn in to see her sister while Aunt Joy freshened up in the family room. She didn't want the nurses and doctors to meet her in what she considered to be a dishevelled state. In all the times I met Tina's Aunt Joy, I had never, even after a long plane trip, seen her look dishevelled or have a hair out of place. The lady exuded class, and I always thought she reminded me of Patti Labelle. She was fiery, and I admired that about her. I alerted Tina's nurses to the fact that her Aunt Joy was here now; a couple of them had the pleasure of speaking to her on the phone already.

When Dawn and I went back out to the waiting room, Aunt Joy asked if I would accompany her in. She surprised me, her being a nurse, but she was nervous to see her niece hooked up to a respirator and a bunch of tubes. Aunt Joy asked me to pray with her, and she held Tina's hand and mine, and I held Tina's other hand and her aunt's while she said her piece. Then Joy asked me to leave her alone with Tina. I quickly retreated to the waiting room where Dawn immediately began questioning me. Dawn informed me that Tina's other sister was due to arrive later that afternoon, and if possible, they wanted to go to the airport to pick her up. I was a bit nervous. I hadn't met Beverly yet, and what I had heard about her wasn't all that good.

My parents arrived back and I introduced them to Tina's sister and aunt. Her aunt wanted to go to the hotel to get a room and put their luggage somewhere. My mom volunteered to take them to the hotel, and Dad stayed and kept me company. I explained about Aunt Joy's directness, and we figured with my mom's strange and sometimes unexplained violent outbreaks, fireworks were sure to follow.

Everyone arrived back at the hospital in a good mood. My mom and Tina's aunt and sister had seemed to bond. They decided to take my van to the airport to pick up Beverly, and I was happy for the solitude again. They hadn't been gone very long when a lady appeared on the floor with long braids and a definite American accent. I overheard her ask a nurse about Tina, so I spoke up to her and told her my name. It was Tina's sister Beverly. She had caught a different connection and arrived early but her luggage hadn't. The airline was going to send it to the hotel once she called to let them know where she was staying. After a few minutes of small talk, I took her in to see her sister as well. She seemed to be pleased with what they had been doing and filled me in more on what the various monitors and such were for. She also understood Tina's chart and questioned me about a notation of AIDS. I explained that she didn't have it, but she also said from all the other symptoms it appeared as though that was the probable cause.

She was also eager to go to the hotel, so I went down to the lobby with her. There were no cabs around, so I suggested we walk: it wasn't that far and not all that cold out. By the time we did walk to the hotel, Beverly was half frozen. Even though it was pretty mild, it was no Florida. I was glad we walked, though, because it gave us a chance to talk and get to know each other, and I immediately had a good feeling about her and liked her. At the front desk, they recognized me and gave Beverly a key to her sister and aunt's room. She called the airline to arrange for her things to be delivered to the hotel, and with that taken care of, I told her I had to go check in at work and then would be going back to the hospital.

"Stop by, and I'll go back with you," she replied.

"Okay," I said.

I had been running around and going in all directions that I didn't realize it was New Year's Eve, nor did I care. I walked through the casino and spoke to some of my co-workers and then went down to the table games shift office. I went into the office and Elizabeth, the day shift manager, was on duty. She took care of some business then closed the door so we could talk privately. She cleared me off the schedule and contacted human resources, who arranged for the rooms for my family to be taken care of, and she also told me how all the other departments had asked how Tina was and if there was anything they could do.

She then said, "In fact, I just got an email from food and beverage inviting you and your family to go to the pub at your convenience for dinner."

I thanked Elizabeth for her kindness and asked if she would bestow my thanks to everyone else, and she gave me a hug, and I left. When I got back to Beverly's room, I could hear laughter coming from behind the door. My mom, Dawn, and Aunt Joy were all there now, and Beverly was recanting her change in flights and lost luggage. I informed them about the offer for dinner, and we decided to do it later that evening around 5:00 or 5:30. I asked where my dad was, and my mom told me their room number, and I left and went to his room. I filled my dad in on our plans for later, and he offered to give me a drive back to the hospital.

"No, Dad, that's okay. I think I'm going to take a walk along the waterfront and clear my head. I'll see you guys in the pub later for dinner."

As I walked along the waterfront with a light snow falling, I looked for the good that had come out of this. My family had never met Tina's sisters or aunt, and they seemed to hit it off, and I got to meet Tina's sister from Florida for the first time. I'm sure Dawn and Aunt Joy and Beverly, for that matter, were curious to meet my parents after all the praises that Tina's mom and stepdad had bestowed on them after they had met them a couple times while visiting us in Calgary in the past. The hard feelings of the past, when Tina and I first met and my parents couldn't understand how they could take the side of such a violent and mean person as Tina's first husband, were now just a distant memory. They had come over time to realize just what a cruel and inhumane person he had been to her. His lies and half-truths had all been exposed, and they now supported Tina whole heartedly. I had a feeling of glee and knew when Tina woke up and learned of our families bonding because of her illness, she would get some solace out of that.

They were already seated in the pub when I arrived back from the hospital and had each already had a couple of cocktails. The mood was upbeat and jovial. They had gone into the casino and had won a couple of dollars, and they were also impressed at how friendly the staff were and how they seemed to know who they were the minute they walked through the door of the casino. My dad had met a lot of my coworkers back in September when he and my brother and my nephew had made a surprise visit for my grandparent's sixtieth wedding anniversary, and they remembered him. I had a couple of drinks and immediately felt the effects. I made my mom promise that I would be back at the hospital at least a half hour before midnight so I could celebrate with my little Pooh Bear Tina, and she promised that I would be there. Our meals came, but I couldn't eat and instead excused myself. My dad gave me his room key, and I went upstairs to lie down. I really needed the sleep. Somehow, what I thought had been the passing of one day, had turned into two days at a time, and what I thought had been a 40 minute to hour long rests had only been five to ten minutes. My mom and dad struggled to awaken me. I was out cold and down for the count. I heard my dad suggest to my mom that they just let me sleep, but she wouldn't hear of it.

"No, Robert," she said. "I promised him he would be back at the hospital for New Year and back at the hospital is where he is going to be."

I struggled to sit up but kept falling over; finally, with an ice-cold face cloth on my face, I managed to get my bearings and got up. It was 11:45 p.m. when I sat down beside Tina.

It had been three days since Tina's family left. It was nice to have the support while they were here, but it also added to the stress. Something transpired between my mom and them, and their close little bond and friendship had soured. I should have been used to that by now. Every time I let my guard down and have new trust in my mom, she comes on like she is fine, then *wham!* The big disappointment. In her defence, at this time, we weren't aware of her bipolar disease, and she wasn't receiving treatment yet.

My parents were back at the hotel with my uncle and aunt and my grandparents. They had arrived just before lunch and offered their prayers and good wishes. Tina had become very fond and close with my grandparents. She loved to go up to Sackville, and we would stay with Gram and Pa for a couple of days and play cards and visit with my other family members. There was something about that little town of Sackville that Tina really liked; I think it might have reminded her a bit of Jamaica somehow.

Tina's condition was getting no better, and they wanted to try a new drug. They thought they had finally tracked down the strain of pneumonia, but that isn't helping much. Very little was known about it as far as we knew. Tina was only the seventh person in the world to have contracted it. On the plus side, the rarity of her illness has garnered the attention of almost all of the medical staff associated with infectious diseases. My mom and dad returned to the hospital after having a nice visit with my grandparents, uncle and aunt.

"Your father and I thought we might go up to Sackville for a couple of days, if you didn't mind," my mom said.

"No, I don't mind," I replied. "There isn't much you can do around here right now. It's just a waiting game while they keep experimenting with different drugs everyday. When are you going up to Gram and Pa's?" I asked.

"In the morning, we were thinking," was the reply. "But, only for a couple days and then we'll be back for the weekend, but your father thinks if much hasn't changed, he has to fly out Sunday night to go back to work."

In the back of my mind, I was thinking if Dad went, he better take Mom with him because I can't handle trying to deal with her and everything else. I told my dad the first chance I got. We spent the rest of the day taking turns sitting with Tina and two of the three of us playing cards in the family waiting room. As my dad and I sat playing cards, he asked me if I had thought about when I should go back to work. I had been off just over two weeks but really didn't care. Tina was all I could think about.

"You know," my dad said. "It might do you some good to get back to work and take your mind off things. You have no idea how long Tina could be in this coma."

I didn't want to hear this because I knew it would only be a day or two until she turned the corner. I couldn't bear to think about this now. The three of us had dinner in the cafeteria, and Mom and Dad went back to the hotel. They told me they would stop and see me in the morning before they left.

"That's fine," I said.

I gave them my spare key to our condo out in Bedford and told them they might as well stay there when they got back. I spent the night travelling back and forth between Tina's bedside and the family room. I was very restless and craving a good night's sleep, but no matter how hard I tried, I couldn't seem to sleep more than ten minutes at a time.

I went down and had breakfast with my parents in the morning, and we had a tearful departure. They made me promise to call if things changed, and I assured them I would.

When I met with the doctor later that morning, she seemed very optimistic. She wanted to try a new drug, and then she went on to tell me it was very expensive.

"Like I care how expensive it is. We have health care and extra coverage, so just do whatever it takes." Out of curiosity, I asked the nurse how much the drug was.

"It's about $1,200 per pill."

"What did you say?" I needed her to repeat it.

"About $1,200 per pill, and she gets two a day."

Boy, no wonder our health care system is under such dire straights, I thought. *That's ridiculous for one pill.*

Two of the pit managers from work that we hung out with and had become friends with stopped by to see if there was anything I needed or if there was anything that they could do. Nina asked when I thought I might return to work. I had thought about what my dad said and was considering going back on Monday if Tina showed improvement and stabilized on the new drug, but I was dreading having to work nights. I wanted to spend them at the hospital with Tina. I told Nina this.

She said, "Let me have a word with Terry, our shift manager at work, and I'll see if he can work something out."

"Thanks," I replied. "Everyone has been so great down there."

After two more days of restless travel back and forth, we finally got a break Saturday morning. Tina's oxygen levels were climbing rapidly; the new medication appeared to be knocking the virus out of her system. I was bubbling over with excitement. I knew all along that Tina would beat this bug. My parents were do back that day, and I couldn't wait to share the good news. I went out and called Tina's mom and let her know the good news. On the way back, I ran into another pit manager, Miguel, and his girlfriend, Kim. They just wanted to come by and let me know that things had been arranged for me to return to work on day shift on a temporary basis, and I didn't need to worry if I had to leave during a shift. They would have been covered. All I had to do was give them a day's notice of when I wanted to return. I shared my good news and told them I would be there for Monday, if that was okay.

"I'll let them know," was Miguel's reply.

It wasn't much longer after they left that my parents arrived, and I shared the good news with them. They were so happy as well. We decided to go out and celebrate later that day with a nice dinner that wasn't hospital food. I felt like I had a huge anvil lifted off my chest. Later, after dinner, we stopped back at the hospital, and Tina was still improving. The numbers weren't going up as dramatically as before, but they were still going up.

"Listen," my mom said. "We are leaving tomorrow night to go home, so why don't you go back to your place with your father and get some sleep, and I'll stay here and sit with Tina so you can be rested after were gone."

"Thanks, Mom, but I can't sleep anyway."

The nurse overheard us, and Tina's doctor came by and authorized them to give me an Adavan, a sleeping tranquillizer. I took it and my dad drove me home. I was groggy and barely able to keep my eyes open by the time we reached my place. I struggled to walk up the three flights of stairs to get to our unit and immediately went into our bedroom and flaked out. It was almost 7:00 a.m. before I woke up. Wow, what a sleep! I needed more of those tiny blue pills. They worked like a miracle. I quickly showered and got dressed. It concerned me that I had been away from the hospital all that time, but I knew my mom was there and would have called if anything had happened. When I went out into the living room, my mom was sleeping on the couch. She woke up as soon as she heard me.

"Did you have a good sleep?" she asked.

"Yes, but you should have woken me if you weren't staying at the hospital, and I..."

She interrupted me and told me not to worry. Dad had come to the hospital around 3:30, and they switched, and he sent her to the apartment.

"Are you going to the hospital now?" my mom asked.

"Yes," I replied.

"Can you wait for a few minutes while I shower and get cleaned up, and I'll ride in with you and maybe the three of us can go get some breakfast if your dad feels up to it."

"Sure, but try to hurry. I'm a little anxious to get to the hospital. This is the longest I've been away since Tina was admitted."

"I'll do my best," Mom replied.

When I went in, Dad was sitting right beside Tina's bedside holding her hand. When I approached, he told me he had been monitoring her vital numbers throughout the wee hours of the morning, and they seemed to be constantly improving every hour.

He said, "I think the nurse even said they lowered the pressure on the ventilator."

I looked over the numbers on all the different machines, and they had cut back the ventilator pressure by 5 percent. A couple of weeks ago, I had no idea what all this stuff was; now, I knew how to monitor her vitals and oxygen to blood ratios. "Listen, Dad, Mom is out in the waiting room. She thought you might like to go to breakfast with us."

"I am pretty hungry," was his response, but he asked if we could go anywhere besides the hospital cafeteria. It wasn't that their food was bad, it was just after a while, it was tiring.

"Sure, wherever you guys want to go is fine."

We had an enjoyable breakfast. I was finally able to keep things down. I think it was because I was worrying a lot less now that I saw Tina improving. I always knew she would be all right, but it was nice to see the medical side backing up what my heart told me already. I was actually going to miss having my parents around: it really helped. The family members of the other patient's support helped, but it was nice not to feel so alone. My mom offered to stay, but I had to decline. Without my dad there as well, I couldn't and wouldn't have been able to deal with Mom if she had another outburst. Poor Mom. I knew she meant well. We spent most of the day together at the hospital, then they left to go back to our condo and pack their bags and stuff to get ready for their flight. I was surprised that they came back to the hospital, but Mom said Dad wanted to give me back my spare key, and They both wanted to say goodbye to Tina. We had a teary goodbye, and they were away.

I stayed at Tina's bedside throughout the night. They had reduced the pressure on the ventilator by another five percent, and each time, her vitals dipped slightly, at first, but then recovered. She was getting stronger and stronger. Around 9:30 Monday morning, I informed the nurse that I was planning to go to work for noon that day but for them not to hesitate to call me for anything. I double checked to see if they had my work phone numbers, and it was written right on Tina's chart, so there would be no mistakes. I left at ten to go home and shower and put on my suit for work but was back at the hospital by 11:15 to check on Tina again. Things were still going great, so off to work I went. It felt strange to be back at work. I felt like everyone was staring at me, and I was getting tired of the questions about Tina and how she was doing. It only made me miss and worry about her more. I couldn't wait to get on the casino floor. Hopefully, that would get my mind off things. They stuck me down in no-man's land, a quiet section of the casino, and I was glad of that. I leaned up against a post and rested one eye at a time. I felt a pen jab me in the ribs and I was startled. The supervisor from the next section had woken me up. She chuckled as she did it.

"You were snoring, you know."

I was embarrassed and quickly thanked her and apologized. I was struggling all day to stay awake and called the hospital I.C.U. nursing station on every one of my breaks. Tina was doing fine. I was relieved when the day ended.

I went straight back to the hospital. The nurse told me I looked exhausted, and I told her I was still having trouble sleeping. "Would it be possible to get some more of that sedative pill they gave me a couple of days ago?" I asked.

"No," she replied. "That was a one-off. We can't just pass out medication." Then she said to give her a few minutes, and she would check with the doctor and see what could be done.

When she came back, she told me to go down to the emergency department. There was a doctor waiting to see me, and he was aware of my situation. He could give me a prescription for the Adavan after a quick medical exam. The exam involved two questions, and he instructed me to take the Adavan when I was leaving the hospital, and by the time I reached home, I should be able to fall asleep. I looked at the prescription. It was for ten pills, which hardly seemed worth the trouble to get it filled. On the way to the pharmacy up the street, I added a zero and made it for 100 Adavan instead of ten. The pharmacist didn't bat an eye. He just filled the prescription, and I headed back to the hospital. I stayed until about two in the morning, then popped a pill and headed home so I could get a good six or seven hours sleep before I went back to the hospital and then work. With the help of my little blue pills, I was able to function on very little sleep over the next few days and managed to do it all: work, stay at the hospital, and then power sleep for only four to five hours now because I wanted to be back to the hospital in time to talk to the doctors after they did there morning rounds.

I had just come back from my break at work where I took the opportunity to get something to eat instead of calling the hospital and Kim, the pit manager, said the hospital called, and they needed me back at the hospital.

Oh, God, what happened! Why didn't I call? I rushed to the hospital and up to the seventh floor. They were working on Tina when I went in.

"It's okay," the nurse reassured me. "Just wait out in the family room, and one of the doctors will come and talk to you once they have her stabilized."

I paced back and forth in that room for what seemed like an eternity; finally the respirologist came in and told me that Tina had a pneumothorax.

"A what?" I asked. "Talk English."

He explained that her lung had collapsed but not to worry: they had put a tube in, and it reinflated. The tube entered where the hole or puncture had happened, and they used a clamp to stem the flow of oxygen through the hole. He explained that this was one of the side effects of the rich oxygen mixture and high pressure that Tina had been under; it weakened the walls of the lungs. They were going to be more aggressive reducing her reliance on the ventilator and hoped by next week they would have her off of it and on just an oxygen mask. I stayed at the hospital over the next few days and skipped going into work. Tina had three more pneumothoraxes over that time, but they soon became almost routine. Finally, after about four weeks in the I.C.U., they were ready to take her off the ventilator and allow her to breath on her own with just the help of an enriched oxygen mixture. The next step was she no longer needed the pain medication and the artificially induced coma medication was stopped; I just had to wait for Tina to naturally wake up. In anticipation of her awakening, I brought in some photos of her kids and a couple of drawings her niece had done, telling her to get better. I also brought in small boom box and played a mixed tape of some of her favourite songs. I also put a special song on it by the Proclaimers. I had heard it on the radio, and it just seemed to be a fitting song given the circumstances, the song was "500 miles," and what I liked was how it went, "when I wake up, when I wake up, I will walk 500 hundred miles, and I will." It just made me think of all the things Tina and I had yet to do.

I watched over Tina for three days, intently looking for any sign of movement. I didn't know what to expect when she came out of her coma. Maybe she would have brain damage, maybe this, maybe that—my mind just ran away with itself. Day four was the day. I think I was lightly dozing when I felt Tina squeeze my hand. I looked up, and I saw her eyes open and a small smile on her face. I watched her eyes dart around the room in confusion. I buzzed for the nurse, who came over and told me to calmly tell her where she was and what had happened; meanwhile, the nurse went to get the doctor. He came and quickly checked out Tina's responses to light and a variety of other checks and found, what he thought, were no lasting damaging effects from the medications. He explained to both me and Tina that what she would require now was a fair amount of recovery and therapy to build her muscles back up. Tina was unable to talk due to the trache in her throat that was still there to allow them to suction out her throat. She had considerable phlegm and some bleeding still in her lungs. They also were going to move Tina over to a more private room in the I.C.U. that was glassed in, instead of just a curtain, and she also had her own window where she could look directly outside. This minor change seemed to lift her spirits.

Tina and I were now able to communicate by her using a note pad and pencil. She also wanted to call her mother, and although she couldn't talk back to her, she tapped the mouthpiece of the phone with her pencil to respond. The doctor explained that it was going to take a considerable amount of time for Tina to build up her strength and energy once out of the hospital, and she might need to use a wheelchair and walker for some time. This posed an immediate problem in that our residence had three flights of stairs to walk up. Our building manager was most accommodating and was willing to let us out of our lease once I found a new place to live. I located a building that was close to work and had an elevator and pool, which I thought could help in her recovery. It was also attached by pedway to the casino so that, when Tina was finally back at work, she wouldn't need to go out in the cold to get back and forth to work.

On my way back to the hospital one morning, I was stopped by admitting.

"The hospital administrator wishes to see you, Mr. Beals."

"What for" I asked.

"I don't know," she replied, "but he is in and can see you right away."

"Fine, let him know I'm available now." I went into the administrator's office, somewhat confused. If there was extras, I was sure our work coverage would take care of things like that. He introduced himself as Mr. Burns and asked me to take a seat.

"Is there a problem?" I asked him.

"Oh, no problem," he said as he thumbed through a rather thick file that I assumed was Tina's.

"No," he said. "I just wanted to make you aware of some of the costs associated with your wife's care."

"We have sufficient health insurance, don't we?"

"Oh, yes," he replied. "But, your wife's current bill for her stay is almost at $250,000. She has received multiple doses of drugs that exceed $1,000 per dose, and a bed in I.C.U. costs just under $1,500 per day."

I stopped him there, as I really had no idea why he wanted me to know how much this and that cost, and I really didn't care. All I knew was I wanted my wife to get the best treatment possible irregardless to cost. "Excuse me, Mr. Burns, but you are keeping me from my wife's bedside at the moment, so unless you have something to ask me or need me to sign something, I would like to go now, please."

"No, no, Mr. Beals. I just wanted to make you aware of some of the costs associated with your wife's care."

"Well, thank you and good day." I left, still puzzled at what the pencil pusher had wasted my time for as I rode up the elevator to I.C.U.

I found out about a week later from two of the I.C.U. doctors what that was all about. The administration had been pushing them to move her out of I.C.U. for over two weeks to help keep costs down, and they told me they couldn't have moved her out any earlier because the infirmary didn't have a step down unit which was a level of care between I.C.U. and the general floor. It was now January 31, and Tina had been doing incredible. She still had the trache in her throat due to the constant suctioning required to remove the excess phlegm from her throat, so her only means of communication was through her note pad and pen. The doctor had informed us that as of the next day, they would be moving her down to the fifth floor and in with the general patients. Tina was both excited and a little scared at the thought of moving, but it was that one step closer to checking out of the hospital.

The next morning, the nurses put Tina in a wheelchair and told me to wait in the family room, and they would come for me once she was settled in downstairs. It wasn't long, and the nurse came and got me. When I saw Tina she did not look at all happy. They had moved her into a wardroom with eight patients, and it was busy and noisy.

"I don't like this and don't want to stay in this room," she wrote on her note pad.

"Don't worry," I told her. "I will be right back."

I went out to se the head nurse at the nursing station. I complained to the nurse about Tina's current room assignment, and she checked our paper work and said that we had coverage for a semi-private room, or, for an additional fee of $20, she could have a private room. I went back and discussed the situation with Tina. She wrote down semi-private and in bold letters wrote, "I don't want to be left in room alone." I went back to the nursing station and informed her of Tina's request for a semi-private room.

"No problem, we will have her moved shortly."

I went back to Tina's room, and she asked if I would go home and get a few of her things. She wanted her own night robe and a puzzle book that was in her night stand and a couple of other items.

"Sure," I said and kissed her on the cheek before I left.

When I got back to the hospital, she had been moved into a semi-private room, but her bed was around the corner and couldn't be seen from the hallway. The other bed looked straight out into the hallway, and I could see what was happening from it, but it was occupied from a nice elderly lady from Amherst.

Tina sent me downstairs to get her a popsicle and also asked for a thank you card so she could send it with me to work to thank everyone for all the kind things they had been doing. I was amazed when I returned. She had rung her bedside call buzzer, and I could hear the nurse asking her what she wanted.

"Excuse me, this is Mr. Beals, and I just entered the room, and my wife is calling for help and you are asking her over the intercom what she needs. Aren't you aware that she can't speak?"

Mrs. Campbell, the lady in the other bed, spoke up and said she answered for Tina. That still didn't sit well with me. They should have come in here. I told Tina I would be right back and left the room. I went to the nursing station and started to tear a strip off the nurse sitting there. Her superior came out of a nearby office and asked me to come in. She barked at me that I had better settle down, or she would have me removed and that the fifth floor wasn't like I.C.U., and they didn't have one on one nursing.

"And furthermore," she said. "We knew you were in the room, so we had no need to send a nurse, you could have answered for her."

I piped right back, not willing to take any shit off her or anyone else, that at the time of the call, I was down in the gift shop getting some items for my wife, and I had used the back stairs so they hadn't seen me leave. "And furthermore, I don't care if it is or isn't I.C.U. I expect my wife to get proper medical care."

After we both crowed at each other like two prize roosters, I left and went back to Tina's room.

Two young nurses were moving her around on the bed and attempting to change the sheets. In the process, they had pulled out her catheter and also nearly pulled out a drainage tube that was attached to her lung. Tina was not happy and was in a lot of pain.

I could hear the phlegm build-up in her trache and barked at the two inept nurses that she needed to be suctioned. Still fuming, I left to find the head nurse. This was fucking bullshit. She hadn't been there for a day, and they had no clue what they were doing. The head nurse was in a briefing, so I went back upstairs to look for Tina's doctor. It was Dr. Ward on duty again, and he listened emphatically and told me that was the problem with the old infirmary. It had no step down unit. "Why don't you let me arrange to move her by ambulance tomorrow to the V.G. They are better equipped to handle this type of thing."

"Thank you," I replied and shook his hand and went to take the stairs back to the fifth floor.

Upon re-entering Tina's room, I found the nurses cowering behind her curtain, afraid of getting any of the phlegm on themselves.

"She doesn't have aids, you know," I barked at them, seeing half the problem was the antiquated portable suction machine they were trying to use. Even I could tell it was malfunctioning. I grabbed Tina's buzzer and gave it three sharp rings.

I recognized the head nurse's voice on the other end and told her to get her ass down into that room right away. I was spitting fire and ready to tear that loudmouthed nurse a new hole. When she entered the room, she asked the nurses what was going on, then she sent them for a new suction unit, and I filled her in on everything that they had done. She was calming down and so was I, and she reassured me that she would be sure the next shift would be aware of Tina's special needs. She also thought it was unnecessary for me to go upstairs to see Dr. Ward. I guessed he must have called her.

When the nurses came back with a new suction pump, the charge nurse sent them away and took care of it herself. Once the room cleared, I spoke to Tina and told her about the doctor's plan to move her over to the V.G. tomorrow to the step down unit.

Tina scribbled a quick message. "I hope these fools don't kill me before then." She smiled when I looked at her face.

I looked at my watch. It was close to six o'clock, and I was supposed to work swing shift tonight or call in by six o'clock. I asked Tina if she wanted me to cancel work and call in.

She wrote out a quick note, "No, you go. Someone needs to bring home the bacon."

I gave her a hug and kiss and told her I would see her later. As I was leaving the room, Mrs. Campbell told me not to worry she would keep an eye on her.

"Thanks," I replied as I left.

I gave Tina's thank you card to Jennifer in the uniform room, and she posted it so everyone could see it when they signed in for their uniforms for the evening.

"I'm glad she is getting better," Jennifer remarked. "We sure miss her around here."

As I started to walk away, I turned to thank her, and she went on to tell me a little story of how she had gotten to know Tina better. One day, they were both in the locker room, and Jennifer had a rip in her nylons. She said before she could say a word, Tina opened her locker and passed her a brand new pair, and when she offered to pay her, she said Tina told her that was okay—just to do a good turn for someone else one day. That little story made me tear up. I was always finding out little things like that about her.

Work was busy that night, and it felt good to be back on my own shift with all my own friends. I would be glad to have Tina home in the next week or two so we could resume our normal life. I thought I had better call the hospital to see how things were. It was about five minutes to one. The nurse that answered informed me that Tina had been experiencing some discomfort but that she was taking her in some pain medication and sleeping pills to help and to feel free to call her back on my next break. It was around three o'clock when Paris, a co-worker, asked me if he could get a ride home with me. He and his wife lived in the same complex as me and Tina.

"Uh, I don't know," I said. "I have to call the hospital first and see how Tina is doing."

Paris came back just before four o'clock and asked again.

"I don't know. I still haven't had a chance to call the hospital yet."

He was the breaker and told me he would watch my section while I used the pit clerk phone. I quickly dialled the hospital and the nurse informed me that Tina had settled down after receiving her medication and was resting fine. She informed me, when I mentioned coming in to see her, that unlike I.C.U., which had unlimited visiting hours, floor five was more strict and liked to see the general visiting hours observed.

"Fine, if you're sure she is okay."

"She's fine," the nurse reassured me. "Go home and see her in the morning. First visiting starts at 9:30."

"Thank you," I said and hung up. I went back over to Paris and told him the ride would be no problem.

I was pretty keyed up and unable to sleep when I got home, so I thought I would call my mom. It was only a little past one in the morning in Calgary, and she was awake all hours. We talked and talked and about ten minutes to five, the operator interrupted our call.

"Hello?" I said.

It was Dave, the graveyard shift manager at the casino. "Hi," he said. "The hospital called here looking for you. They need you to come in."

I thanked Dave and called my mom back and told her I had to go to the hospital. I told her I figured Tina woke up and was pissed off I wasn't there. She asked me to call her after I got to the hospital, and I told her I would.

It had started to rain and snow, and the roads were getting pretty slick. I was taking my time and being careful when I felt a strange chill go down my back. I looked at the digital clock on my radio. It was 5:00 a.m., and I clicked the radio on. The Proclaimers were playing. I floored the van and drove to the hospital as fast as I could.

When I arrived at the door, there was a security guard waiting to escort me upstairs. We stopped at the nursing station, and a doctor I had never met stopped to talk to me. Before she got the words out, I went past her into Tina's room. Her lifeless body was laying in the bed. I grabbed hold of her and could feel the cold already enveloping her body. I screamed out and begged her to come back to me.

"Please, Pooh Bear, come back!"

The doctor and guard entered the room.

"What happened?" I cried out. "what happened?"

"I'm sorry, Mr. Beals, but the nurse came in and found her slumped over the rail. She had a massive haemorrhage in her lungs and suffocated. We tried to revive her and worked on her for quite some time, but at 5:00 a.m., we pronounced her deceased…"

"Get out," I ordered. "Get out!"

I felt sick to my stomach. I didn't know what to do next. How could Tina leave me like this? I stayed by her bedside and held her cooling, motionless body, not wanting to believe she was dead. It was a bad dream, and I need to wake up.

Nina entered the room and spoke in a soft tone to me. "David, I just wanted to let you know that me and Bob are here just down the hall, and if there is anything you need us to do, just ask."

I turned and looked at Nina, my cheeks stained from tears. "I can't believe she is gone," I told her. "I just can't believe she is gone."

"Neither can we," Nina replied. "We're so sorry, David."

I told her I would be out soon. "Just give me a few more minutes to say goodbye."

"Take as long as you like," she replied.

I'm not sure how much longer I sat there with Tina when I began to shake uncontrollably. I was suddenly so cold it was painful. I made my way out into the hallway, turning and taking one last look at Tina in her hospital bed. She did look at peace, like she was just having a nice sleep.

I saw Bob and Nina sitting in the staff lounge at the end of the hallway. Nina saw me and came over and put her arm around me and escorted me into the lounge. Her arm wrapped around me did little to stem me from shaking. Bob summoned a nurse who brought several blankets and wrapped them around me. As I sat there, trying to follow the conversation going on around me, I couldn't make out what was being said. Everything was so muffled, and it was as though they were all speaking in a foreign language. I vaguely remember being passed a cup of hot coffee and was incapable of swallowing it, and the liquid just dribbled out of my mouth and down my chin. I remember I was feeling real dizzy and asked Nina if she could call my mom, who could then call Tina's family and let them know what happened. I told her I just couldn't do it at this point

The next thing I knew, I was laying on my side, feeling so hot, so hot I could hardly breath. Bob was still sitting in the lounge.

When he saw me wake up, he asked, "Are you okay, bud?"

Still a bit dazed and confused, I told him I had this terrible dream that Tina had died.

"I'm sorry, mate," he replied in his British accent. "It was no dream."

Somehow, I guess I knew it was no dream, but I had hoped it was. I felt sick to my stomach and wanted to get out of the hospital and get some fresh air. I stood up and felt dizzy again. I slumped back onto the couch in the staff lounge, feeling like I had been drugged. Bob told me to stay put he would go and get Nina, and they would both help me get outside for some air. It wasn't long and Bob returned with Nina.

"Your mom asked me to tell you to call her as soon as you can."

I had no idea what to do now and what was I going to do with Tina gone. In all the time she had been in the hospital, I had always only made plans of how to care for her when she came home. I never imagined she would die, never. The hallways were getting busier, and the day staff had started to arrive. I just wanted to get as far away from those people as possible at this moment. I got up and steadied myself, then hastily exited the lounge. Keeping my eyes to the floor, I made my way to the back stairwell and down to the main floor and out the side door to the street. My van was still sitting parked on the street; Bob and Nina's car was parked behind it.

Nina spoke and suggested she should drive my van, and Bob would follow in his car. She asked "Where do you want to go?"

"I don't know," I told her. "I don't know."

She suggested that they take me back to their apartment, and I readily agreed. I didn't want to go to mine. I wasn't ready to deal with the phone calls that would be coming, and I just wanted to hide out.

Back at Bob and Nina's, I was going crazy just sitting there. I couldn't calm down; I couldn't relax. I fired question after question at Bob and Nina. Before they could answer one question, I was on to another topic or problem to deal with. Suddenly, my mind fixated on the funeral. I must take care of the funeral. Yes, that was it. I want to go to Sackville and make the funeral arrangements. I informed Bob and Nina of my plans, and Nina offered to go with me. Bob didn't think that either of us was fit to drive all the way to New Brunswick, and Nina thought maybe we should rest first. I needed to go then. Up I got, heading for the door. Nina quickly followed me, and with a quick thank you to Bob, we were heading to my house first, then on to Sackville.

As I arrived at our apartment an eerie feeling came over me, and I asked Nina if she would mind waiting in the van while I went upstairs.

"No, just yell if you need me," she replied.

When I got upstairs, it suddenly felt so strange to be in the apartment without Tina. I had been on my own for the past six weeks, but it was somehow totally different at that moment. I didn't like it. The place gave me an eerie feeling. I called my grandmother, and before I could say much to her, she said that my mom had called, and she told me how sorry she and Pa were about what had happened. I let Gram know I was coming up to make the funeral arrangements.

"Today?" she asked, somewhat surprised.

"Yes, I should be there in about three hours." With that, I hung up.

I called my banker just down the street and told him my news. He was aware that Tina had been in the hospital, and the bank had even sent her flowers. We had both been impressed at how well we had been treated at the bank since moving here. Back in Calgary, they just treated you like a number. With Tina in the hospital for the last six weeks and me barely working, our readily available cash was pretty much gone. Scott asked what I needed, and I told him I could use about $20,000 to cover the funeral expenses and things. He told me it would not be a problem. I asked if he needed me to stop and sign any papers.

"No, don't worry," he said. "Just go and take care of things and see me when you get back."

I couldn't believe how great he was being and thanked him for his help.

When I went back downstairs, Nina was over talking to Bobby D. Tina and I had worked with him in Calgary, and he and his wife had moved into the same complex as us as well. He came over and offered his condolences to me. It was funny. In Calgary, he was Tina's and my boss, but down here, we had all been hired at the same level as supervisors. Tina was so happy when she found out that Bobby D had been hired to go to Halifax as well. We both really had enjoyed working with him before. Nina said that Christine, Bobby D.'s wife, had offered to drive us up to Sackville, as she had a full nights sleep and was well rested. With Christine in the driver's seat and Nina in the passenger's, I took the bench seat in the back. It wasn't long, and they were busy chatting away. I stared aimlessly out the window, thinking about what had to be done. I had to take my mind off it I was feeling ill again. Christine must have seen me change colour in the rear-view mirror because she pulled over to the side of the rode, and I hopped out and emptied out what little food was in my stomach. The chills and shaking started up again, and I turned up the rear heater as high as it would go.

Christine passed Nina a pen and pad of paper that she had brought with her. "Listen, David," she said to me, "whatever you think of that needs to be done, just tell Nina, and she will write it down. We will help you deal with things."

"Don't let the situation overwhelm you. We will help you get through this. You're not alone." Christine's words had a calming effect on me, and my chills and shakes eased up.

We took the turnoff into Sackville, and I had decided to go straight to the funeral home before going to my grandparents. We had talked about it on the way up and thought, since none of us really knew what had to be done, the funeral director would be our best place to start. I had never met Will Campbell, before but my family had always spoken highly of him. He was the town mayor and also a schoolmate of my dad. He halfway seemed like he expected me when I arrived.

"You look just like your father," he remarked and then offered his condolences.

He informed me that my grandmother had called him earlier, so he was expecting me at some point in the day. He eased me into the matter at hand and discussed when I wanted the funeral to be held. I asked him what was the norm and he said three or four days after the death. He inquired if there was a lot of family coming from far away, and if that was the case, he would recommend going four days.

We looked at the calendar. It was Friday, February 2, so we counted four days, which took us to Tuesday, February 6. I couldn't think why the sixth seemed so familiar, but told him no, it couldn't be on the sixth. Our days off at work were normally Monday and Tuesday, so I really had hoped to keep it to one of those two days so our coworkers could attend. Mr. Campbell inquired as to where the body was. I hadn't even thought about just leaving her in the hospital when I left. It hadn't dawned on me. Was I supposed to take her home with me or what happens? I suddenly felt such shame for deserting her body in the hospital and all her belongings. Nina and Christine had been terrific, they had given me the space when I needed it, and they must have sensed I needed them again. They helped me finish the process of collecting the body and arranging for the death certificate with Will; then we selected to have both the service and viewing at the funeral home, and I let him know that internment would take place at the Midgic Cemetery. Will informed me that at this time of year, the bodies were generally stored until the spring thaw, at which time a small memorial would be held and internment done then. I couldn't put Tina's kids and family through that. I still didn't know if they were going to be able to attend the funeral, and if they did, I wanted to be sure that Tina was laid to rest while they were there.

"Can't the ground be thawed?" I inquired.

"Yes, it probably can," Will responded. "It will add considerably to the expense. I'm just trying to keep this as reasonable as possible for you."

"I appreciate that, but Tina was a first-class lady, and she will have a first-class funeral. I don't care what it costs."

With the last of the arrangements made and the casket and flowers selected, we left and went to my grandparent's house. It felt reassuring to be at Gram and Pa's. I felt safe as I always had when at their home. With introductions out of the way, Gram hastily put out some lunch for us, and it was the first time I was able to eat and keep it down. Gram took me into her room and passed me a small kraft envelope.

"You know Pa and I thought the world of Tina," she said.

My eyes tearing up, I told her, "I know ,and she thought the world of you guys as well."

"Anyway, after you called, Pa and I went to the bank, then up to see Mrs. Hicks, who looks after the cemetery, and we purchased a family plot for you and Tina. It is our way of helping you if you will let us."

The tears now flowed freely as I thanked and hugged Gram for her kindness. She also said that my Aunt Shirley and her daughters and Gram and Pa would like to look after the lunch for after the service. I wasn't sure what she was talking about at this point but told her that would be great and told her to thank my aunt and cousins.

Back out in the living room, I thanked Pa, and he asked if I would like him to drive me up and see where the plot was that they picked out. Nina and Christine told me to go ahead, as they were in no rush and were quite content visiting with my grandmother.

I couldn't see much as the ground was covered with snow, but it seemed fine. It was in the new section at the front. Pa informed me it was the closest he could get to where Gram and he had their plots. I told him it was fine and thanked him again for making the arrangements. The cold was now thoroughly numbing us both, and we retreated back to his car and back home.

When we entered the house, the sound of laughter could be heard from the kitchen. That disturbed and angered me. I wanted to go home. I don't know why people laughing bothered me the way it did, and I didn't care why they were laughing. I just knew I wanted to go home. Nina was starting to feel the effects of no sleep. She had worked the evening, before just like me, and she and Bob had just fallen asleep when Dave had called from work to inform them that the hospital had contacted him to contact me. I hadn't really stopped before now to think how they ended up at the hospital.

I told them both that I appreciated all the help, but I just wanted to go home and be alone for a while. They both understood. Nina hadn't decided if she would be going to work that evening or not yet, and Christine, being the sweet soul that she was, volunteered to go to the hospital and collect Tina's belongings for me.

It was around six o'clock when we got back to Bedford. Christine took me home first, then drove Nina home in her car. I felt nervous going up the stairs to our apartment. There was a large bouquet of flowers in the hallway. I was too exhausted to read the card and placed them on the kitchen table. I noticed the answering machine blinking rapidly. Lots of messages. There were several calls from Tina's mom and sister, each message got angrier and angrier, and the final message demanding to know where was I and what the hell was going on. I dreaded phoning them back. I was drained. My parents, my brother, and a few of my close co-workers had called. *Where to start?* I thought. I called my mom and told her about the funeral arrangements. She told me she had called Tina's mom and found them to be quite rude and demanding to know where I was and what the hell was going on. My parents were trying to book flights and didn't know when they would be arriving yet.

"That's fine," I said and hung up.

Then, the call I dreaded the most. I had to call Tina's mom. How do I tell her that her little girl was gone? I couldn't say much to her. She wouldn't stop crying, and it was awful. Then her sister got on the phone and started to rip me apart. *How could Dawn be so cruel at a time like this?* I thought. She started saying that I didn't have the decency to phone and tell them; they had to hear it from my mother and on and on she went.

The anger in me built to the boiling point, and I finally told her to shut up and listen. The funeral is on Monday, February 5, in Sackville. Her best bet would be to fly into Halifax and drive up from there. That opened up a new can of worms.

"What do you mean, she is being buried in Sackville? Why isn't she being buried in Rochester where her family is and..." Blah, blah, blah is what it started to sound like.

I cut her off and told her to inform the rest of the family of the time and place.

"What about the kids?" she asked. "How are they going to get there?"

I told her I had enough on my plate that the least she could do was arrange their flights and call me back with the details, and I would pay for their tickets. I was emotionally and physically drained, turned off the ringer to the phone and all the lights in the house and just sat staring out the front window at the distant lights of the city, drifting in and out of consciousness. I don't think anyone realized the effect the last six weeks had on me, let alone me. I had been running on very little sleep everyday and had hardly been eating.

The only thing that had kept me going was coffee and adrenaline. The little bit of sleep I managed to get was through the use of the Adavan pills.

I heard a very faint knocking at the front door. I went and looked out the peephole. It was Christine. I opened the door, to her surprise.

"I hope I didn't wake you," she said.

"No, I was just sitting here in the dark, thinking."

She stepped in and passed me the list of things that her and Nina had written down for me of what had to be done.

"Thank you," I told her. Then she told me she had gone to the hospital to get Tina's things, but they wouldn't release them to her because they had to be signed for by a family member.

"Oh, thanks for trying, Christine. I'll take care of it," I said.

"Is there anything I can get you or do?" she asked.

"No, I just need to be alone right now, thanks."

With that, she turned and left. I sat down with the list in my hand. There was a lot to be done before the funeral and very little time to do it. I had to select six pall bearers, pick out a dress for her to wear, select the music, pick out the hymns, select someone to give the eulogy, pick out any jewellery and special items for Tina to wear and have in the casket, bring her makeup to the funeral home and get the information to Will by Saturday evening so he could have the programmes printed for the first viewing on Sunday.

I felt bad about having argued with my sister-in-law, but I just didn't have the energy in me to figure things out. I decided to call the airlines to see what I could do to arrange the kids' flight out of Toronto first and then would call her back. With a couple of options on hold, I called Dawn back. She had spoken to Tina's ex-husband about the kids attending the funeral and, with the assistance of some other family members, had conceded to allow them to attend. I discussed the flight options with Dawn, and once we agreed, I called the airline back and booked them on a flight.

With that taken care of, I decided to go to the hospital to collect Tina's belongings. I was particularly interested in seeing the crossword puzzle book that she had been using to keep notes inside to pass to me. The streets felt deserted as I made my way to the hospital. I was trying to get in and out before midnight and the nursing shift change. I didn't want to see the staff that had been on duty when Tina had passed away. I went to the nursing station and saw the duty nurse who went to a back office and returned promptly with a sealed box and had me sign for it. Without saying much, I left. It was so eerie to be there now with Tina gone.

Back at home, I noticed the answering machine was blinking. Two messages: one from my parents saying that they would be arriving around seven in the morning, and the other was from Dawn to call her back. *Now what?* I thought.

I called her, and she said Frank didn't want Odelia to fly because she had a cold.

"Well, let's put her on a train."

Dawn didn't think she would be able to get her here in time by train.

"Couldn't the funeral date be moved to a later time?"

I replied with a terse, "No. The funeral is on Monday, and that is that. I don't give a damn who, how, or why you can't or won't come. I'm just telling you when the funeral is, and that's that." I was so full of anger over Tina's death that now I was just lashing out at whoever was at hand. Unfortunately, it had to be Dawn, and all she was trying to do was be helpful and get Tina's kids to the funeral.

I was fixated on the funeral. It was the only thing I had to do, and I put all of my thoughts and what small amount of energy I had left into making sure it happened on time on the day scheduled. I took care of a couple other items on the list and selected an outfit and jewellery for Tina, as well, and packed her makeup into a small travel bag. I could do no more today. When I stopped to think for a minute, I couldn't believe it had only been earlier in the morning that I was at the hospital finding out that Tina had passed away. *A lot had been accomplished today,* I thought as I started to drift off to sleep. The Adavan that I had taken earlier when I went to the hospital to collect Tina's things had finally kicked in.

I woke up a little before six and was very shaky. I was still having trouble grasping the idea that it was true that Tina had indeed died the day before. I was trying to remember what time my parents were arriving and then I couldn't even remember if they were flying into Halifax or Moncton, and if I was supposed to pick them up. I found my mind going a thousand miles per hour, and I couldn't slow it down long enough to focus on any one task. I didn't know what the hell to do. I saw the box with Tina's belonging's sitting on the kitchen table and thought to check her crossword book to see if there was anything written inside. As I rummaged through the box, I couldn't find it, nor could I find the cassette tape that I had made for her. I was frustrated why couldn't I find anything I was looking for, then I noticed a bag labelled nightgown. That puzzled me because it wasn't large enough to hold the blue velour robe I had taken to the hospital for Tina. I opened the sealed bag and inside it contained a pink hospital gown. *Why would they send me these?* I wondered as I went to hold it open. Rage filled inside. What the hell was wrong with these people? How…why? I was at a loss for words. I punched the wall with all my might. *I've got to get out of here,* was all I could think. I was beside myself. I wanted to burn that fucking hospital to the ground with everyone in it. These people that I had come to know and trust were now my enemies, seeing what they had done and how careless and cold they were. I felt sick to my stomach that I had left Tina in their care for one more day.

I grabbed my coat and car keys and headed downstairs to my van. As I bolted out the downstairs door, I ran into Christine. She had just returned from McDonald's with her daughter, and she could tell I was hopping mad. She passed the bags of food to her daughter and told her to take them inside.

"What's wrong David?" she asked.

I was biting my lip and trying to regain enough calm to speak to her. "Those sick fucking bastards. I hate them." A sudden feeling of shame came over me. I couldn't help but think how mad Tina would be if she heard me cursing and swearing like I was.

Christine grabbed my arm and told me to walk with her and tell her what happened. "Besides, I don't think you should be driving anywhere in the state you're in."

I started by telling Christine that I had gone into the hospital last night to collect Tina's belongings, and I explained about the missing puzzle book and how that was where Tina would write and leave notes for me. Then I told her about the cassette tape that I had made for her and how it was missing, and finally, I told her how the blue velour robe wasn't there but that they had included a pink hospital gown, and I assume it was what Tina was wearing when her lungs haemorrhaged.

"Why would you say that?" she asked.

"Oh, just because it is covered in blood."

A look of shock and horror came over her face.

A car stopped behind us, and I heard the window roll down. "Where is the visitor parking?" a familiar voice asked. It was my mom and dad and brother.

I quickly introduced Christine to my parents and brother and then pointed to visitor parking. As they pulled away, Christine asked if I was going to be all right. I told her yes and thanked her for listening. She told me when I got a chance to write down what items were missing, and she would go to the hospital later on and try to locate the missing items. I gave her a hug and thanked her.

Having my parents and brother arrive did little to ease my pain. I had to keep retelling the previous two days events and the story of the nightgown. If I wasn't filling them in, I could hear them talking on the phone to other family members retelling what had happened over the last couple of days. I just felt tired and cold all the time now. If only I could sleep, but every time I tried and closed my eyes, all I could see and think about was Tina, Tina, Tina, Tina.

Word had spread around work, and everyone was aware that Tina had passed away. I struggled to do what had to be done and made calls to the friends and family members who I wanted to be pall bearers. Someone, I think probably my mom, forwarded the information to Will at the funeral home.

I guess the Adavan must have kicked in, and I finally fell asleep for a short time. I awoke and someone had gone and got chicken. I wasn't hungry and couldn't understand how people could eat. I guess having my family come was a help after all; they had arranged for a handibus to transport my mother-in-law on the day of the funeral and had also booked several rooms for me and the kids and my sisters-in-law and mother-in-law. It was all being arranged somehow now. Things were just on autopilot. I felt like I was in a suspended state: I was conscious but not in my body, just drifting off in whatever direction a noise came from, and I would stare at who was speaking but nothing was being retained any longer. I just nodded and agreed.

We gathered Tina's items that Will had requested to prepare her for the funeral and some other necessities and left for Sackville shortly after 1:00 p.m. Saturday. My brother drove my van, and my parents took their rented car. Brad and I reminisced about the fun times we had only a few months earlier when he and his son and my dad had come down to visit us and to go to my grandparents 60th wedding anniversary. Tina could hardly wait to get home from work. My dad and brother would be awake, and we would have a few drinks of rum and play cards with them. Brad stopped at the funeral home first, and I gave Will the clothes and other items that I wanted Tina to be buried with. He commented about jewellery, and I told him to leave it on her.

"Are your sure you wouldn't like her wedding ring…maybe to pass on to her daughter?" he suggested.

After a brief reflection, I realised he was right. Odelia might like to have her mother's wedding ring and her diamond bracelet as well. When it was done, I agreed with Will to just leave on the costume jewellery, and the other items that contained precious stones he would remove just prior to sealing the casket. From the funeral home, we didn't have far to go to the motel, and my dad had already gotten the keys for our rooms and checked us in. My parents and brother headed to my grandparent's house for supper. I told them I would come over in a bit and that I had a few things to take care of first. I called my sister-in-law Dawn, and she told me they would be flying in early Monday morning, which concerned her because it was so cold and had been snowing, and if any bad weather delayed them, they would miss the funeral.

"Well, you just gotta do your best," was my reply.

Dawn was still upset with me and wanted to know how they were to get from the airport to the funeral. There was going to be six of them coming in together from Toronto. Dawn was driving her mom to Toronto to meet up with the kids and with her sister Beverly who was flying in from Florida. From there, they were all travelling to Halifax on the same flight.

"Don't worry," I told her. "Someone will pick you up at the airport."

I felt like a caged animal sitting in the motel room and decided to go to my grandparents. I passed the turnoff to their street and continued on, heading to Midgic to the cemetery. I wanted to make sure they had dug the grave as I had requested. As I pulled up and stopped, I saw a small amount of smoke coming from under a large piece of sheet metal. They were still in the process of burning coal and straw to thaw the ground so they could dig the grave. I got back in my van and drove further towards my grandparent's old farm that they had sold years earlier. As I looked up the long lane, I couldn't help but think of how sad I was that they sold this place. While we still lived in Sackville, almost every Sunday, our family, as well as my other two uncles and aunts and all my cousins, would arrive at Gram's and Pa's for Sunday dinner. Nineteen of us in total, and it wasn't uncommon for a few great uncles and aunts to show up as well. My grandmother was from a family of 17, and Pa had seven siblings as well. That was what family was all about and those were my happiest childhood memories. Once we moved out west things were never the same again.

I think that was what I liked about visiting Tina's family in Rochester, it seemed like whenever we were visiting Sunday was drop in day. Hyacinth and Dawn and Tina would pitch in and help as well, and they would start on Saturday evening preparing for Sundays big dinner, and by early Sunday afternoon, the house would be full of people. Not all family, but still it gave me a sense of community and safety and love; it always took me back to Sundays at Gram and Pa's. I dried my eyes, which were full with tears, and turned around and headed back to Middle Sackville and my grandparent's home. They were just sitting down to eat when I arrived. It would have been nice—Mom, Dad, my brother, and me here with Gram and Pa—f it weren't for the sad occasion that brought us all together.

I told everyone that Tina's family would be arriving the morning of the funeral. My mom volunteered to travel with the handibus to the airport to pick them up. I didn't know how I felt about that. She always tried to do the right thing and always had good intentions, but with the wrong word or a small incident, she became irrational and violent. I was so happy as I had gotten older that I was able to defend myself, and no longer had to suffer from her violent behaviour and the beatings I endured until I was about 13 and could fight back. But then it turned into emotional blackmail, and my brother and I were terrified that she would have an episode while our friends where at our home. We tried to mostly go to our friend's houses instead. It seemed like when we were younger, Mom had a little more control over herself, but lately, it didn't matter where she was or who was around when she was ready to erupt she erupted, public place or not, it didn't matter. I figured that, for Tina's sake, she would keep her composure and act appropriately. I mean, I really needed my mom to be my mom now more than ever. That was all I wanted my whole life: to have a mom like everyone else had. Once again, I let my guard down and placed faith in her. If my mom's bipolar illness could have only been diagnosed 30 years earlier, who knows how it could have changed our childhoods and our lives. My brother and I knew something was wrong and did nothing about it, but for my dad to ignore it for so long, why?

After eating dinner, a few hands of cards were played. I tried to get involved to take my mind off things, but it was no use. I excused myself and said I was going back to the motel for some rest. I had the two visitations to face at the funeral home tomorrow and wasn't looking forward to that. This was all so new to me. I think I had only been to three or four funerals before and didn't realize all that it entailed. Mom came back with me to the motel, and we reminisced for hours about things Tina and I, or her and Tina, had done, and after taking a double dose of the Adavan I fell asleep until around 2:00 a.m.

The cold Tantammar marsh wind was blowing hard, and the room felt cold. The motel was located just off the edge of the marsh. I looked over to the spare bed, and my mom was gone. She must have gone to her room, I guessed. I looked out the frost-covered window and saw my dad's rental car was parked outside. I hit the remote starter button on my key chain so my van could warm up a bit. I figured I'd go for a drive since I was awake and knew I wouldn't be able to get back to sleep right away. I only waited about ten minutes before going out. The wind was damp and cold and instantly chilled me to the bone. I said a small prayer and asked for nicer weather for the day of the funeral.

I slowly drove through town. It was all closed up for the night: nothing was open, and nobody was about. I drove up through Middle Sackville and continued on to the cemetery in Midgic. I was curious how the grave was coming and whether it had or was going to be dug. It wasn't dug, but I could see they had added quite a bit more coal and straw. The van was just now starting to throw out some warm heat, so I slowly drove back to town and the motel, enjoying the dry, hot air hurling from the dual heaters in the van.

I couldn't sleep and couldn't follow anything showing on the television but left it on for the company and read the two-day-old newspaper that was in my room. I was actually feeling hungry for the first time in a few days and could hardly wait for the motel restaurant to open up. I checked my watch and had another hour and a half before it was open. I decided to shave and shower and put on some clean clothes to help pass the time. The hunger I was feeling was all I could think about.

I called my home number to check my messages when the machine answered it startled me. It was Tina's voice that had recorded the message on the machine. There were a lot of hang-ups on the machine and a few messages of sympathy. The last message was from Tina's sister Dawn. They had managed to change and get an earlier flight and were going to arrive in Halifax around noon on Sunday. That gave me some relief. I was worried that something might have delayed them on Monday, and I wouldn't have known what to do.

I heard a knock at the door and hung up the phone to see who was at there. It was my mom. She hustled in through the door and quickly closed it behind her.

"Oh my God, it is so cold," she exclaimed. "I thought I heard you moving around over here. I've been awake for a couple of hours myself."

"Why?" I asked. "What's wrong?"

"Oh, just couldn't sleep…thinking about Tina," she replied.

"Speaking of Tina," I said, "her family is coming in today at noon instead of tomorrow. Are you still willing to pick them up or should I ask Brad?"

"Can we still get the handibus today?" Mom asked.

"I don't know" I replied. "Just take my van. You can all fit."

"What about Hyacinth's wheelchair?"

"Put it in the back of the van, between Dawn and Beverly and the boys. I'm sure you will have no problem getting her in the van."

"Just check on the handibus, if you don't mind," my mom said. "I'd feel more comfortable with that."

"Mom can you call Cindy? She is the one who arranged it; maybe she can arrange it again."

"It's too early to call right now but maybe after breakfast."

"Are you hungry?" I asked.

"You know me," mom replied. "I'm always hungry."

We bundled up and scurried across the parking lot to the restaurant like a couple of frozen chipmunks. The restaurant was nice and warm, unlike our rooms. We had almost finished breakfast when my dad and brother came in. They sat down with us and ordered. Mom was done and said she was going back to the room to check on the bus.

"Thanks" I replied.

My dad asked what the problem was with the bus.

"Nothing." I then explained that Tina's family was coming in today instead of tomorrow and asked Brad if he would go and pick them up.

"I'd rather not," he replied. "I don't know any of them and would be a bit uncomfortable, and I'm sure they would be, too. I think it's better if someone they know meets them. I'll drive you if you want, and you can pick them up."

"I can't go. I won't be back in time for the two o'clock viewing."

Truth being told, I wasn't eager to have to face them. My mind couldn't seem to rest. Why didn't I go to the hospital after work that night? So what if the nurse said they wouldn't have let me in? I should have made them. I partly blamed Paris…if only he hadn't asked me for a ride home. I felt that once the funeral was over, maybe my mind and stomach would finally settle down. My mom came back in and said she talked to my cousin about the bus, and it didn't matter if they were coming today or tomorrow, the bus couldn't pick them up.

"What do you mean?" I asked.

"The bus can't travel out of the province. The senior's home thought they were picking them up in Moncton at the airport there, not Halifax."

"What about the day of the funeral?" I asked.

"That's still not a problem," Mom replied. "Listen, you have enough to worry about, so I will go and pick them up for you. Just take me for a short drive in the van so I can get used to it, and I'll be fine."

"Thanks, Mom."

As the three of them continued with their conversation, my thoughts went to my mom's visit back in November. My mom had travelled with her mom to her mother's sister's funeral. When Gram stayed with her other sisters to visit, Mom came to Halifax to visit with me and Tina. Things had been pretty good when we picked them up and took them up to Sackville for my great aunt's funeral, but the time my mom had spent up there without us had allowed her to get into one of her moods. By the time she came to our place, she only lasted two days. When she erupted, both Tina and I were ashamed to poke our heads out our own front door from the language and screaming and slamming doors that she did. It finally got so bad I had to ask her to get her suitcase and leave our apartment. This was the last straw, as far as I was concerned. I wanted nothing to do with her again. It wasn't long and the phone rang, and it was my dad asking what the hell was going on. He said he got a call from my mother, and she was crying and said I kicked her out of the apartment. I tried to explain to my dad what happened, but as usual, he turned a deaf ear to her outrageous behaviour. He ended up telling us where she was staying, and Tina begged me to call her and work it out. I let it be and went to work. When we got home, mom had been back long enough to leave a letter telling me what a rotten person I was, and she went on to attack Tina and her family. I was used to this now. It had been happening my whole life, and every time I tried to get tough and keep her out of my life, she always managed to slide back in somehow, and I would forgive her. She did try at times, and when she was in a good mental state, she could be so caring and loving, like now, when she was willing to drive the two hours to pick up Tina's family and the two hours back. She was doing that for me because she loved me.

I tuned back into the conversation, and it was all about how cold it was and even with the room thermostats turned up, it was still so cold. I think the four rooms we had booked were the only ones rented, given the time of year, they were grateful for the extra business. The restaurant was always busy, though.

Mom drove my brother and me to my grandparent's house and dad followed shortly after. She felt fine with the van and familiarized herself with the turn signals and wipers. Mom only had a short visit at my grandparent's and left a little after nine o'clock. She wanted to be sure she got to the airport in plenty of time. I thanked her for doing this for me and told her what a big help it was. She replied she was doing it for Tina as well. It was just a bit past twelve, and my stomach and nerves were having a race. The first viewing was at two o'clock, and I had to go at least an hour before that to the funeral home to see Tina myself and make sure everything was done as I had requested. My dad and brother finished the lunch that Gram had made, and we went back to the motel to put on our suits. I couldn't wait for them to finish getting ready and decided to walk to the funeral home. It wasn't that far. The cold was the farthest thing from my mind, and I actually felt better for the walk.

Will, the funeral home director, met me at the door and ushered me in. I was so cold, but it helped the constant sick to my stomach feeling I had since Tina had passed away. Will explained the process of the next few hours and what took place during the viewing. Tina's casket was set up in the main parlour. The Pooh Bear flower arrangement I had ordered was placed next to the casket. It was an incredible job; more than I had expected. I wanted the best for Tina, and Will had made it happen.

As Will began to close the parlour doors to give me privacy, he pointed to the wall, and there was a small button to ring if I needed anything. I thanked him again and expressed my gratitude for the Pooh Bear flower arrangement.

"I'll pass your appreciation on to the florist," he replied as he left.

I slowly walked up towards the casket and struggled to look into it. My eyes welled up with tears, and I tried to dry them with the tissues I had in my suit pockets. Several attempts, and I still couldn't touch Tina or stay at the side of the casket yet. Will magically appeared through a side door with a box of tissues and asked if there was anything else I needed.

"No, no, thank you," I told him. "Just give me some time."

I sat down in the front row of chairs and started talking to Tina. I told her how much I loved her and how I missed her so much already. I told her Mom had gone to pick up her family and laughed to myself as I knew Tina would be laughing at that as well. The more I continued to talk to her, the more at ease I felt. As I sat there, I made a promise to Tina that I would make sure I took her kids to Jamaica to see where she was born and raised. We had often talked about this, and it was one of the things she had always planned to do once she had the children back in her life. The other thing was that she always wanted them to get to go to Disney World or Disney Land. That made me think back to our last trip to Los Angeles before we moved to Halifax and how one more of her dreams came true. We went to Disney Land and she got pure pleasure out of that. Having her life shortened so soon made me glad that we had done so much in our short seven years of marriage. I felt like she had truly had a second chance to get a taste of life. It came at such a high price, her children, but they had their whole lives ahead of them, and I was determined not to let their mom be forgotten.

I pulled myself together and approached the casket. Tina looked old to me now. She had never looked anything close to her 40 years of age before, but now, she looked every day of it. I wanted it to be me, and I wished it had been me. It felt eerie as I touched her lifeless body. With all my strength, I managed to kiss her on the forehead and tell her goodbye, then had to go sit down again. I felt as though I was letting her down, but I just couldn't look at her lifeless body—it made it all seem to real.

Will knocked and entered through the side door and told me some people were arriving. My dad and brother entered behind him, and they both went over to the casket. I followed Will through the side door, and he showed me a small family room where I could go to and from during the viewing. I was relieved to see my grandparents arrived, and my grandmother gave me strength. She sat with me and told me who some of the people were that I didn't even recognize—a lot of great uncles and aunts and distant cousins that I hadn't seen in years. Over the two hours, probably 25 to 30 people stopped by. My grandmother informed me that the evening viewing was generally much larger. Gram and Pa were going home, but Gram said they would be back for the evening viewing. I asked them for a lift back to the motel.

It was time to face Tina's family. I was sure they had to be back from Halifax by then. I saw my van parked out front and knew everyone must have arrived. I looked over towards the restaurant, and through the window, I could see that it looked like everyone was in there eating. I turned to go to my room. As I approached my door, the door next to it opened, and I heard a familiar voice call to me.

"Young man, come here." It was Tina's mother, she was quick to get me to come inside and close the door. We cried together almost instantly. "Why, why, why?" she kept saying over and over.

I kept saying, "I don't know, I just don't know."

It wasn't too long and Hyacinth was back in form complaining about the long trip to get here and that it was so cold and on and on. I knew she was going to be all right. Odelia came through the door to check on her grandma. She was startled to see me, but then she started in with the questions. She wanted to know what happened to her mom and why this and why that. Of the three kids, she was the one of action. She had a bit of trouble accepting that it was true and was eager to go to the funeral home to see her mother. The rest of the kids and my two sisters- in-law and my mom arrived over at Hyacinth's room. After a short debate, my mom, Dawn, and Beverly were going to go to see Tina, and I was going to follow with the kids once someone came back to stay with Tina's mom. She was too exhausted and cold to venture out again until tomorrow she said.

My dad was the first to arrive back. My brother had gone with a couple of cousins for something and dad came over to Hyacinth's room with a deck of cards. He had met her on one of her visits to Calgary, and she had always talked about what nice father and mother I had and how welcome she felt at their home when they had her over for cards one evening. With Hyacinth in the capable hands of my father, I took the kids in my van to the funeral home. Will took most of the pressure off me and answered a lot of the kid's questions about death and the whole process. Odelia was actually making me feel sick to my stomach with her morbid curiosity. I gave each of the kids an opportunity to be alone with their mother after they had viewed her as a group. I was so proud of them. They looked and dressed smart and presented themselves in a manner that would have made their mother proud. They had each done well seeing their mother alone.

Odelia, however, had disturbed me. She had removed her mother's clothing around her neck to expose the scar from her tracheotomy. Will quickly fixed it before the second viewing began. After the viewing and on the way back to the rooms, Odelia said she had heard her mother had a tube in her neck, and she wanted to see it. They were so confused. Hell, I was confused, let alone a young girl two days shy of her 18th birthday, and then her two brothers, only 15 and 13. I hadn't thought about what they must be going through. We drove past the motel and headed to the McDonald's restaurant just off the highway at the far side of town. I got the kids what they wanted, and Odelia suggested getting something for her grandma as well. From the McDonald's, I drove the kids north towards the cemetery in Midgic and pointed out my grandparent's home and my aunt and uncle's large farmhouse on the hill that overlooked the lake. The kids had me stop at the cemetery and went over to look at where the grave was now dug.

After answering a few questions about the grave and graveyard, I continued to show them around Midgic and my grandparent's old homestead and then continued down the Old Goose Lake Road that went through the marsh. Odelia was concerned that we were going to get stuck. I reassured her and pressed on, as I wanted to show them the last covered bridge in the area. I was trying to give them a sense of the area and why their mother loved it here so much. The boys were more eager to get back to the motel and were wondering if they had cable or not. The drive had been in the dark, after all, so I couldn't blame them for losing interest. Odelia took the food into her grandma and Dawn and Beverly asked where theirs was. I hadn't thought about them. They had two good legs to get around with, and if truth be told, Hyacinth would still be hungry if not for Odelia.

The kids settled into the room with their grandma while Beverly and Dawn took the room next to it. My mom offered to take them up to McDonald's and my dad and brother had me over to their room for a couple drinks of rum. I then knew what the mission was that my cousins took my brother on. When my mom arrived back, she told me Dawn and Beverly were looking to talk to me. I took a bottle of rum and some ice and mix back to my room and then called their room and invited them over. Things went okay. They commented how Mom and taken them by Gram's and Pa's house and how nice my grandparents were, and they could see why Tina was so comfortable with them. We had a few drinks, and before long, I was feeling pretty drunk and my two sisters- in-law were feeling pretty good as well. By the time they went back to their own room, I think we had pretty much dealt with some hurt feelings, and they realized I was doing the best I could given the circumstances. As I lay in bed, feeling the effects of the rum, I just wanted the funeral to be over, and I wanted to be home in my own bed and for everyone to be gone so I could grieve by myself. I found myself spending so much time now worrying that everything would be perfect.

I had a bit more sleep than usual, thanks to the rum. I lay awake and watched television until I heard movement next door. I called over and asked the kids if they were hungry and wanted to go for breakfast. They paused and said not right away. Tina's mom didn't want to venture out into the cold and asked if I could get her a cup of tea and some toast or something. I got up and showered and dressed and went to the café to get Hyacinth something to eat and drink. Kofi was dressed and ready to go, but Odelia and Ekow were still lounging.

We decided to make a run to McDonald's for breakfast, and Kofi came with me. He called his aunts and got their food orders, and I checked with my folks. Kofi filled me in on what life had been like lately. He said he was getting along pretty good with his dad but that his brother and his dad were always fighting. He said Ekow kept telling his dad when he was 16 next year, he was moving out on his own. Kofi caught me off guard when he asked me how was I doing and that it must be hard for me with Tina gone. For a 13-year-old boy, he never stopped amazing me. I always had a special feeling with Kofi. Maybe because he was the youngest at the time, and he seemed more accepting, but I think part of it was he had most of his mother's traits and reminded me nothing of his father. I wished now that he was the son Tina and I had never had together.

It was like a major production coordinating everyone. Hyacinth wanted to go the funeral home early, as she had yet to see her daughter, and her other daughters were worried about how well she would hold up, given the circumstances. The time passed quickly at the funeral home, and finally, it was time. I was a useless clump by now. I kept leaving the front row and making my way to the family room at the side trying to keep myself from crying. I made my way down the hall and thanked the pallbearers, who had their own special room. Will was soon giving them their instructions.

I struggled to try not to cry and give support to the kids and Tina's mom and sisters but found I had to keep my eyes to the floor to avoid coming apart. I briefly exited the room twice, once just after my brother delivered the eulogy. I took deep breaths realizing it would soon be over. The kids and I rode in the limousine to the graveyard. Tina's sisters rode in the handibus with their mother.

The weather had not cooperated, and it was bitterly cold. The reverend that had come from Halifax that afternoon went as quick as he could with the interring. Each family member placed a rose on the coffin, and finally, the Pooh Bear flower arrangement was placed on top of the casket just before it was lowered into the ground. Ekow surprised me first. Without anyone saying a word, he grabbed a handful of the freshly thawed ground and tossed it over his mom's casket. Odelia and Kofi followed his lead. The crowd slowly dissipated back into the warmth of their cars. The boys, Odelia, and I stood our ground as the cemetery workers began to fill the grave. Ekow took a shovel and helped them, his brother and him alternating until the cold finally drove them into the warmth of the waiting limousine. They asked me if we could stay until the grave was completely covered, and I did as they wished. After the last shovel full of earth was placed over the grave, Ekow got out of the car and from inside his coat he withdrew a single red rose and knelt down and placed it on his mother's grave, then kissed the spot and placed his hand down to the earth.

Rest in peace, Pooh Bear. Rest in peace.

CPSIA information can be obtained at www.ICGtesting.com
Printed in the USA
BVOW04s1002011014

369081BV00001B/52/P

9 781413 745962